SUMMON UP THE BLOOD

First in a brand-new historical mystery series featuring decidedly unconventional turn of the century sleuth, Detective Inspector Silas Quinn.

London, 1914. A killer is at liberty in the dark alleys of the city. The cadavers of his victims all have one thing in common: there is no blood in their bodies. As the killer's reign of terror continues, Scotland Yard's Detective Inspector Silas Quinn finds his suspicions focusing on the members of an exclusive gentleman's club ... Atmospheric and macabre, *Summon Up the Blood* takes the reader on a disturbing yet fascinating journey through London's aristocratic watering holes, seedy brothels and shadowy underworld in the turbulent months leading up to World War I.

SUMMON UP
THE BLOOD

A Silas Quinn Mystery

R. N. Morris

Severn House Large Print
London & New York

This first large print edition published 2013
in Great Britain and the USA by
SEVERN HOUSE PUBLISHERS LTD of
19 Cedar Road, Sutton, Surrey, England, SM2 5DA.
First world regular print edition published 2012 by
Severn House Publishers Ltd., London and New York.

British Library Cataloguing in Publication Data

Morris, Roger, 1960- author.
  Summon up the blood. -- Large print edition. -- (A Silas
  Quinn mystery ; 1)
  1. Police--England--London--Fiction. 2. London
  (England)--History--1800-1950--Fiction. 3. Detective and
  mystery stories. 4. Large type books.
  I. Title II. Series
  823.9'2-dc23

ISBN-13: 9780727896421

Severn House Publishers support the Forest Stewardship Council™
[FSC™], the leading international forest certification organisation. All
our titles that are printed on FSC certified paper carry the FSC logo.

Printed and bound in Great Britain by
T J International, Padstow, Cornwall.

For Rachel

Acknowledgements

I'd like to thank my editor, Kate Lyall Grant, for letting me write the book I wanted, the way I wanted; Sara Porter, for her skilled and sympathetic copy-editing; William Ryan, for his part in making all this happen; Rupert Morgan, for commissioning the original Silas Quinn story, *The Exsanguinist*, out of which this novel grew; and my agent, Christopher Sinclair-Stevenson, for his constant support.

LONDON
MARCH, 1914

Beneath Eros

It was all in the eyes. The whole business was transacted there. Minute signals sent and reciprocated. Jimmy was sensitive to many things but above all he was sensitive to eyes.

He knew what to look for: the old conflict of desire and fear; a flicker, too, of shame in there. Eyes that simultaneously sought him out and shied away from him.

It was approaching midnight. The glaring streetlights turned night to day, while the illuminated signs on the far side of Piccadilly Circus pulsated with tremulous excitement. To Jimmy, the brilliant studs of light were a million tiny eyes, winking at him over Eros's head.

BOVRIL
PROSET
BOTTLED BY SCHWEPPES

The dazzling words set up a rhythm in his head. Soon the letters lost all meaning – not that they had much to begin with. They became a mirage, a vague incitement, strangely in keeping with his mood.

Charged by their promise, he returned his gaze to street level. A boisterous crowd streamed around the statue, dodging between the faltering traffic; mostly taxis at this hour, touting for the after-theatre crowd.

Jimmy's glance was a question thrown out into the night. And he was quick and skilled in dispatching it.

The eyes that floated towards him were glazed with intoxication; quick to dismiss him, if they saw him at all. He always caught the sneer that accompanied such a dismissal. Jimmy knew full well what he looked like, and what an impression he must make. It was a calculated impression.

He was dressed for business.

A fellow had to know how to present himself to succeed at this game. It was a careful balance. If he went too far in a certain direction, he would attract the wrong kind of attention. He didn't, for example, hold with those boys who powdered their faces. That was inviting trouble. They had no one to blame but themselves if they were run in by the Old Bill.

But a touch of lavender in a necktie. A delicate lightness of shade to the tailoring. A fresh buttonhole, perhaps, if funds ran to it. A clean-shaven face; most of the gentlemen he aimed to interest preferred their boys fresh-faced. Shirt collar and cuffs impeccably turned out. The grey billycock hat set at just the right angle, somewhere between insolence and invitation. And a revealing tightness in the trousers.

These were the signs he relied on to sell his wares.

But the eyes, it always came back to the eyes. He was looking for eyes that held his for less than a moment. Then dipped to take in what he

12

offered.

On the dip of the gaze, he knew he had them. Without it, he wouldn't dare make the approach.

You see, your agent provocateur, your plain-clothes copper, in Jimmy's experience, you generally never got the little appraising dip with one of them. And even though they held your gaze, there was always something vindictive about the way they did it. No fear, neither. Unless – which was always possible – they were a bit that way inclined themselves.

They were the worst. Their hatred was the fiercest, because it was directed against themselves. It was themselves they were policing, themselves they were afraid of. They were always the ones you had to watch out for.

The pavements glistened from the heavy rainfall that had dowsed the capital for most of March. For the moment, Londoners were enjoying a respite, though a dour chill clenched the air, holding the threat of more rain to come. It had been unrelenting, in fact, the rain. Of biblical proportions, and indeed the papers had been full of the floods in other parts of the country.

For a man such as Jimmy, the wet weather was a setback. He needed to be out and about. It was a question of economic necessity. This was where he made his living, on the streets, in the parks and the public places. Admittedly, he could always loiter in an arcade – the Burlington was a favourite. And there were the public lavatories, of course. But when the weather forced men of his type off the streets, they tended to congregate in the same few locations. Too much

13

competition was bad enough. But these little gatherings clustered in doorways only made it easier for the Old Bill.

Jimmy had already spent a month sewing mail sacks under the 1898 amendment. For a second offence he was looking at six months inside, plus a whipping, if luck was against him. He had to be careful.

Besides, there were times when the last thing he wanted was the company of men of his type. He had come just now from the Criterion bar. More accurately, he had fled the place. Too many familiar faces. He had a horror of familiar faces. Admittedly, there was a certain party he had clocked whom he wished to avoid; the small matter of an outstanding debt. These trivial details had a habit of flaring into unpleasantness, especially when the party in question was involved. Better to slip away quietly.

Jimmy had come to the realization young that he was alone in the universe. Strangely it did not sadden him. He was not demoralized by his isolation; he exulted in it. He felt it to be the source of his strength. And if ever it was breached, if ever he let anyone in, he felt it would be the end of him.

Perhaps that was another reason he placed such store by his clothes. Like the cocksure swagger he affected, they were a barrier between himself and the world.

From time to time in the practice of his chosen profession, he was required to remove those clothes. But the disrobing was never complete, he made sure of that. He always contrived to retain some article of apparel, ideally his hat, something of a trademark with Jimmy. At the very least, his socks. Strangely, no one had ever insisted on his removing his socks.

And when it came to it, when it came to that moment of being naked with a stranger – that was the moment he would withdraw his gaze. He would allow men to do all manner of things to him, but he would not allow them to look into his eyes when he was naked.

Yes, the break in the weather was welcome. He felt a sense of release, able at last to be out on the street. He also felt a share in the common surge of appetite and desire that this brief intimation of spring provoked. Perhaps his step was more urgent than that of others in the throng, his appetite closer to hunger. He knew that the rain could come back at any moment, closing down his opportunities with each dark spot it threw down upon his fawn jacket.

His gaze was more desperate too. This was dangerous. He was taking risks. Abandoning caution. This was how mistakes were made. If you weren't careful, in your eagerness to ensnare your prey, you ended up getting trapped yourself.

All it took was for you to look, for a moment, into the wrong eyes.

Jimmy could tell the man was a toff. There was the top hat and evening suit, and the open over-coat slung loosely from his shoulders. But anyone could put on a suit of clothes, as Jimmy knew. This one had the bearing of one born to make rules rather than obey them. That should

15

have warned him; even so he held the man's gaze. The *question* had been answered.

The man showed no sign of fear. That, too, should have warned Jimmy. He always looked for fear. These days he preferred to earn his crust by blackmail than buggery. But he was forgetting his own rules. And it was not just down to carelessness or greed, brought on by the man's evident wealth. Something about those eyes compelled him, as if he knew the danger they contained, but went towards it anyhow.

The man was watching him from afar, the only figure not moving in the tide of humanity, as stationary as the statue he stood beneath. He was waiting for Jimmy.

Another bad sign. Jimmy preferred the punter to make the first move. It was safer that way. And it established his control of the situation. Whatever happened, he could always say they brought it on themselves.

But it was another of his rules that he chose to ignore and he could not say why. The only answer to that question lay in the other man's eyes. He had to get a closer look at those eyes.

'Are you lost?' But it was Jimmy who was lost, even as he asked the question.

There was a certain weakness to the toff's mouth. Physically, it seemed lacking. But the mouth was not the thing about his face that mattered. What mattered were those eyes. And what mattered about them was not the colour, but their strange, empty coldness.

If Jimmy had felt himself alone in the universe before, he was even more alone now, gazing into those eyes. Anyone else, perhaps, would have been repelled by such a quality. Anyone else would have run from them. But Jimmy was fascinated.

The mouth curled into a grin and looked up. 'Lost? Here? Beneath Eros? I would have to be a special kind of fool if that were the case.'

It was Jimmy who felt the fool. The heat rushed into his face. 'I only meant...'

'I know what you meant.' Indeed, it was as if the man knew all there was to know about Jimmy. He seemed already to have lost interest in him, and this Jimmy found extremely galling.

'Why were you looking at me?' demanded Jimmy.

'Was I?'

'Yes.'

'Why shouldn't I look at you? You're quite a sight.'

'Do you like what you see?'

A thin tongue licked out to moisten barely existent lips. 'Don't flatter yourself.'

'You're wasting my time,' said Jimmy, though he felt a pang of regret as he said it. Had he gone too far?

But it seemed he had judged it right. He felt a softening of the other man's demeanour. At the same time, he felt himself regarded with re-newed interest – respect, perhaps.

'My dear boy, I fear we have got off on the wrong foot. And the fault is all mine, I'm sure.' The toff flashed a silver cigarette case towards Jimmy. It sprung open, revealing two neat rows of fat yellow cigarettes. There was a moment as

17

they absorbed themselves in the business of lighting up, a moment of solemnity and thrill, of hands brushing and gazes exchanged. Something was confirmed in the transaction of fire and smoke. The tips of their lighted cigarettes bobbed and sparkled excitedly. 'Perhaps you will allow me to buy you a drink? We are but a few steps from the Criterion, which I believe is not unwelcoming to gentlemen of your class.'

'What do you mean by that?'

'Merely that I have seen low renters in there before.'

'Do you mean to insult me?'

'Do you mean to blackmail me?' The man held Jimmy with his empty gaze for a long moment. Then his slit of a mouth opened and a burst of savage laughter broke out in swirls of outraged smoke.

'You're quite a wit,' said Jimmy. All at once he felt the man's grip on his upper arm, tightening quickly into a band of pain.

The man pulled him towards him and whispered, 'Whatever I ask you to do, you will do. Yes?'

'Yes.'

'And do you know why?'

'No.'

'Because you are a low renter.'

The man released his grip and hailed a taxi.

'I thought we were going to the Criterion,' said Jimmy forlornly.

'I've changed my mind,' said the other. He threw his cigarette down and ground it with the heel of a shoe that was as black and glistening as a beetle.

A taxi stopped in front of them, and the man opened the door for Jimmy. Jimmy hesitated for a moment, casting a look of boundless nostalgia back towards the bright lights of the Criterion.

He thought of all the old familiar faces in there, and even of the certain party he had wished to avoid. For some reason he couldn't explain, he had the feeling that if he got into the back of that taxi, he would never see them again. Equally hard to explain was the swell of heartache that he experienced at the thought.

Special Crimes

In a room in New Scotland Yard, Silas Quinn sat and waited.

A female secretary busied herself rather self-consciously – it seemed to Quinn – in the operation of a typewriting machine. But he knew that her whole being was focused on ignoring his presence.

He searched her face for clues as to why he had been summoned, a fruitless exercise. Besides, he presumed it was the usual business; time for one of those periodic dressing-downs over methods. His last case had once again ended with the death of the main suspect. But Quinn knew that no matter what his superiors might say about his methods, there were no complaints when it came to his results. He was confident that there would be no formal reprimand.

The secretary wore a mask of impassivity. She may have been young, but she was not flighty. Prim, was the word. He could see why Sir Edward Henry, the Commissioner of the Metropolitan Police, had chosen her as the custodian of his threshold.

Stuck-up cow, Quinn decided.

Well, two could play at that game. He turned his head away from her with what he hoped would be taken as a contemptuous sigh. Of course, he couldn't resist a sly glance back to see how that had gone down.

You are a weak man, Silas Quinn, he said to himself.

The little kink of a smile on her lips, a momentary quiver before the mask descended again – what was he to make of that? He really couldn't fathom out the female species. Unless it was a question of female criminals, that is.

It had come as a shock to him when he had started out on the force. But it could not be denied: there were such creatures as women criminals. In his experience, a woman certainly had the potential to be as vile and vicious as any man. One could safely grant them equality in that.

'Do you think Sir Edward will be long?' He had no particular interest in the answer to the question. He simply wanted her to acknowledge him. Once she had done that, he would let her be.

'I really don't know.' She did not look at him as she spoke. Instead, she gave a little shake of her head, an unconcealed gesture of impatience.

'You're very quick,' said Quinn, surprising himself with the remark.

She looked up. 'Beg your pardon?'

Quinn held up both hands and wiggled his fingers in a mime of typewriting.

The secretary smiled, though for herself rather than him, he thought. Evidently, she took pride in her speed.

Quinn thought he was on to something. 'Do you play the piano too?'

'No.' Her private smile became an open smirk. She did something quick and oscillating with her eyes that fascinated Quinn. He wanted to ask her to do it again but found he had lost all confidence.

It was always the same. He could hunt down a ruthless killer without fear, but when it came to making small talk with a young, and quite possibly pretty – yes, he had no doubt, she could be considered pretty, although was *pretty* really the word? – woman ... when it came to that he found his courage failed him.

He reminded himself that he had no interest in her in *that way*; that it was merely a question of getting her to acknowledge him. But why was he so concerned that she should acknowledge him? What was she to him, after all?

'Lucinda Bracewell,' he heard himself say.

'I *beg* your pardon?'

'Lucinda Bracewell. One of the first cases we investigated in Special Crimes. Sir Edward will

21

remember it. Seven men, she murdered. That we know of. Her tenants, they were. Killed them one after the other. Poisoned them. Arsenic. Chopped their bodies up. Very small. And boiled the bones. Remarkable patience that woman had. It must have taken her a good while to cut them up into such small pieces. Speaks well of her strength too. She'd have to heft the bodies about, you see. I expect you're wondering why she came under the remit of Special Crimes.'

'I–'

'That was on account of the penises, you see.'

'The–?'

'Yes. She severed the penises and sent them to various Members of Parliament. That counts as a special crime, you see.'

'Why are you telling me this?'

But the door to Sir Edward's office opened at that moment, saving Quinn from having to explain himself.

The man who came out was unknown to Quinn. He was tall, clean-shaven, and dressed in the frock coat of a gentleman. Greying at the temples, he carried himself with a patrician air, spine straight, shoulders back, head angled up slightly: the perfect posture for looking down on lesser mortals like Quinn, in whose direction he did not, however, direct his gaze.

He was undoubtedly a very important person indeed. Even Sir Edward's secretary seemed cowed by him. It gave Quinn momentary satisfaction to realize that this imperious being was unaware of her presence; effortlessly so, in contrast to her own determined efforts to ignore

Quinn. But then, remembering his own discomfiture of a moment ago, he felt immediately sorry for her.

A grimace of pain showed on Sir Edward Henry's silver-whiskered features. At first sight, it seemed that his pain was caused by Quinn's entrance, with which it coincided. But Quinn knew better.

'The old wound troubling you, sir?'

'It's the weather, Quinn. It always plays up in the damp.'

Instinctively, Quinn glanced towards the window of Sir Edward's office. The unrelenting rain lashed against the panes. It was more than a week ago now since there had been a brief let-up, after which the deluge had returned with renewed force.

'It must take you back, sir,' said Quinn.

'What? Eh?'

Quinn nodded towards a framed photograph of Sir Edward, wearing a linen-swaddled pith helmet. He looked out from beneath the canopy on the back of an elephant, his expression one of imperious bewilderment. 'To India. In the monsoon season.'

'Have you ever been to India, Quinn?'

'No, sir.'

'Thought not.' Sir Edward left it at that. Distracted by another spasm of pain, he clenched his right hand into a tight fist. With his other hand he gestured for Quinn to sit down.

'May I ask you a question, Sir Edward?'

'Eh?'

'Why did you speak in his defence? Albert

23

Bowes.' Quinn was alluding to the assassination attempt that had been made upon Sir Edward two years earlier. Sir Edward had opened his front door to a deranged man with a grudge against him. Quinn couldn't remember the details, but it was over something ridiculously trivial, he felt sure. At any rate, the man was armed with a revolver. He discharged several shots, one of which struck Sir Edward in the abdomen. It was typical of Sir Edward that he spoke in his assailant's defence at the trial, which no doubt went some way to reducing his sentence.

'Alfred, Quinn. His name is Alfred. I didn't call you here to discuss that.'

'No. I'm sorry, forgive me. I had no right...'

'Judge not according to the appearance. That's all I'll say. John, seven, twenty-four.'

'But the man tried to kill you.'

'A troubled soul, Quinn. Sick at heart. I do not believe he was of sound mind at the time of the incident.'

'Nevertheless...'

'I know it is not your way, Quinn.'

'What do you mean, sir?'

'Come now, Quinn. You know what I'm talking about. How many is it now?'

'How many what, sir?'

'How many *what*, the man says! Good grief, Quinn. How many suspects have died – have *you* killed,' Sir Edward corrected himself, 'in the course of your investigations?'

'You must know, Sir Edward, the people I am forced to confront are desperate, dangerous, *ruthless* individuals. They will do anything to evade capture. In all these cases, it has been a question of self-defence. Of kill or be killed.'

'And in all too many of these cases, there has been no independent witness to corroborate your version of events.'

'What are you suggesting? With respect, sir, I have a right to ask that question.'

'It looks bad.'

'But what about John, seven, twenty-four?'

'What? Eh? Doesn't apply to coppers. You know that, Quinn. Especially in the Met.'

'Is this an official reprimand, sir?'

'There's no need to take that tone, Quinn. It's a warning, that's what it is. You cannot set yourself up as judge, jury and executioner.'

'I don't.'

'So what is it then? Carelessness?'

'These decisions, to shoot or not to shoot ... One cannot afford to think about it for too long. It's a split-second decision. You know yourself, from your experience with Bowes, how quickly a situation can turn nasty. My primary concern, always, is to minimize the danger to the public. Invariably, that requires me to close down the criminal's opportunity for violence.'

'By killing him?'

'You knew, Sir Edward, when you set up the department and put me at its head, the nature of the work I would be involved in. I think it's fair to say, also, that you were not deceived as to the approach I would take.'

'You had form, if that's what you're saying.'

'If you wish to put it like that.'

25

'Please get down off your high horse. I have always supported you, and I continue to support you. However, the Special Crimes Department works best when it is noticed least.'

Quinn felt himself the object of Sir Edward's sympathetic compassion, which, he realized, put him on a level with the would-be assassin Bowes.

'Regrettably, your department has come to the attention of certain ... how can I put it? Influential parties.'

'Is this to do with the gentleman I saw leaving your office?'

'Don't be impertinent, Quinn. I'm not one of your suspects, whom you can interrogate at your will.'

'Forgive me, Sir Edward.'

'But, yes. That gentleman is Sir Michael Esslyn.'

The name meant nothing to Quinn.

'The Permanent Secretary to the Home Office. He has the ear of the Home Secretary.'

Quinn's rather literal imagination supplied the image of a severed ear in a velvet-lined box.

'And in many ways, he is more powerful than the Home Secretary, because he is more permanent. He tells me that it is the Home Secretary's view – or very soon will be – that the Special Crimes Department has outlived its usefulness. The Home Secretary is minded to close you down, to revoke the special warrant that established your department. Of course, the Home Secretary doesn't yet realize he is so minded.'

Quinn felt the surge of a familiar emotion. It

was so comforting and so at home in him that he no longer recognized it for what it was: rage.

He rose from his seat, unsure what he would do or say next. 'I am grateful to you for informing me of the Home Secretary's decision. Do you wish me to communicate the news to the men? I think it would be better coming from me, as their immediate commander.'

'Sit down, Quinn. It hasn't come to that yet. No *decision* has been made. Sir Michael made it clear that the Home Secretary is also aware, and appreciative, of the spectacular successes you have achieved. You are an extraordinarily gifted detective, Quinn. No one doubts that.'

'It is simply a question of application, sir. I do believe in applying myself.'

'It is more than that, Quinn. It is almost as if there is something personal between you and the criminal. You hound them out.'

'As I say, sir, application. I do not like to think of them getting away with it.'

'Your good work has not gone unnoticed. But then again, neither, regrettably, have these unfortunate accidents. The newspapers are beginning to make something of it. Our masters don't like it when the newspapers get hold of things. It's generally taken as a sign that we're losing our grip.'

'I don't concern myself with what the newspapers print.'

'The *Daily Clarion* has dubbed you "Quickfire Quinn". Did you know that?'

'I did not.'

'I don't like that look, Quinn. It's a dangerous

27

look. It's the look of a man whose vanity is flattered.'

'No, sir. With respect, I wasn't thinking of myself. I was thinking of the department. I was merely wondering, is it necessarily a bad thing? For me to have such a reputation, I mean. Will it not tend to have a deterring effect?'

'It is *vanity*, Quinn, however you may wish to justify it to yourself. No. Obscurity. That's what we want from you. Stay in the shadows, keep your head down. Same goes for your men. Stop getting yourself written about.'

'I'm not sure that's within my power to achieve, sir. I cannot control what the newspapers print.'

'Just try not to kill anyone!' cried Sir Edward with sudden force. Realizing, perhaps, the impossibility of what he was asking, he relented and added: 'For a while.'

Sir Edward gave another flinch of pain, which he attempted to cover with an energetic nod. Quinn took it for a gesture of dismissal.

'No, no. There is one more thing: a case, on which your help is required. The Whitechapel Division have sent word up. A body has been discovered in the London Docks. You are to report to Shadwell Police Station. The body itself is being held at Poplar Mortuary, pending the coroner's inquest.'

'A body found in the East End? May I ask, in what way does that constitute a special crime, sir?'

'I take a special interest in the area, Quinn. I was born there, you know.'

28

'In Shadwell?'

'That's right.'

'I did not know.'

'Leaving that aside, it is a...' Sir Edward cast about for the appropriate word. 'Volatile area. Criminality is a way of life for many, of course. There are foreign influences to consider. The Lascars, Chinks and Yids. And the dockworkers are a militant bunch. There is a delicate balance at play. If it were to be upset in any way, it could be catastrophic given the importance of the Thames for the life of the capital, the country and even the Empire.'

'With all respect, Sir Edward: even so, I am not convinced that it warrants our involvement.'

'The body, Quinn, was drained of blood. Every last drop. *Utterly exsanguinated*, was how the Whitechapel police surgeon put it.'

'I see.'

'There are other aspects to the case that make it sensitive. We have so far managed to keep the details out of the papers, in order not to alarm the general public. I mentioned the coroner's inquest ... that will take place *in camera*, without a jury.'

'*In camera*? Isn't that reserved for cases in which there are issues of national security?'

Sir Edward nodded in confirmation. 'These are dangerous times internationally. Go to Shadwell Police Station. The case file is there. You can read the details for yourself.'

'I shall leave immediately.'

'Good man. Oh, and be careful, Quinn. Look upon this as a test, for you and your department.

The Home Secretary's eyes will be on you.'

A second excessively literal image forced itself upon Quinn. He fled the room, as if he believed it contained the eyes in question, having perhaps been delivered in another velvet-lined box by the Home Office mandarin he had seen earlier.

East

The Special Crimes Department had been set up as something of a pet project by Sir Edward. He was very much the man for pet projects. There were times when Quinn almost believed the department had come into being purely as a way of accommodating his own peculiar talents within the Met.

To begin with, Quinn was assigned a permanent staff of two, Detective Sergeants Inchball and Macadam. There was the promise of more men in the future. Enough years had gone by for Quinn to accept that it was a promise that would never be fulfilled.

When the need arose, he had licence to call upon additional officers from whatever police division he was assisting. However, the call was not always answered, at least not with alacrity or enthusiasm.

There was invariably a degree of horse trading for which Quinn had little taste and less aptitude.

He never could understand why the station sergeants did not share his sense of urgency. How could an overturned collier's wagon compare with the flight of a vicious multiple murderer, even if one or two passers-by were engaging in a spot of opportunistic looting?

What made it even more galling was that the division inspectors often took the sergeants' side. But Quinn knew he had the backing of the commissioner. If he had to go right to the top, he would. Most superintendents knew this. So Quinn usually got the men he needed before it was necessary to trouble Sir Edward.

But it was all such a terrible waste of energy and time.

It was only natural that he allowed these frustrations to fuel his rage. His mission – and yes, he had a sense of mission – required him at these moments to be in a state of heightened, and wholly righteous, aggression. He had to turn himself into a human weapon, directed by society's need for justice.

He had to keep in mind the defiled virgins, the butchered widows, and the woeful lethargy of his colleagues in the Metropolitan Police Force. And he had to allow the rage to take him over. Sometimes he could feel it flooding through his veins. He would wait until he had a sense of it filling his hands, up to the fingertips, before unleashing himself.

Against all this, it must be said that Special Crimes had been granted an extraordinary privilege. They had been allocated the use of a motor car.

The black 1912 Ford Model T was Sergeant Macadam's pride and joy, emotions in which Quinn consciously took no part. He preferred to see the vehicle as no more or less than they were entitled to. After all, they were called upon to cover an area that stretched from Dagenham in the East to Uxbridge in the West, and from Potters Bar in the North to Epsom in the South.

Yes, there were railways, but when responsiveness and speed were of the essence, at all hours of the day and night, the railways could not necessarily be relied upon. Bicycles had been suggested. But Sir Edward must have caught something in Quinn's eye that discouraged him from pressing forward with that particular plan.

Macadam had taught himself to drive on the job, largely through a process of trial and error. There had been one or two accidents, especially in the early days, but only one fatality.

Fortunately, that incident had not dented Macadam's enthusiasm for motoring, and had gone some way towards inspiring Quinn with respect, if not reverence, for the vehicle. It was not just a convenient mode of transport, he realized. In the right hands, it was a lethal weapon.

Quinn stood in the drizzle on the Victoria Embankment, waiting for Macadam to bring the Ford round. He was grateful for his herringbone Ulster coat and black bowler hat. The two items of clothing formed a protective layer around him, keeping at bay more than just the moisture in the air. He felt that he would be lost without them, his bowler in particular. It was like the carapace of a tortoise: part of him, but also a shield against everything in the world that threatened to overwhelm him. Even when he was not wearing it, he felt its clinging ghost in place; he was never at one, never fully himself, until he had restored it.

He watched clumps of sodden debris float away on the surface of the turbid river, carried east by the tide. The river's depths were impenetrable to his gaze. His peculiar imagination filled the blank with dark and sinister forms.

The day presented such a despondent face that it seemed almost malign. It was the face of a beggar. It would take everything from him, if he let it.

He stood with Big Ben and the Palace of Westminster at his back, feeling the presence of his lords and masters looming over him, watching his every move. Earlier he had caught a glimpse of one of them, the Home Office mandarin, who by now would be safely ensconced in his room in Whitehall; or more likely, in his club, his work for the day done.

But however much men like that believed they were in control, however much they believed they had their hands on the tiller of state, there would always be some ungovernable little thug somewhere undoing their work. Rendering them powerless.

Because when a man picked up a length of sharpened steel and plunged it into another man's heart, at that moment he, the killer, was in charge. All the power of the world flowed through him.

This was something Quinn understood. It was the source of his vigilance. And the root of his darkest fears.

The silver-templed civil servants were powerless against such individuals. To keep them in check, they needed men like Quinn. That was why he knew that ultimately there was no danger of them revoking the special warrant, the paper talisman from which Quinn drew his own power.

All he had to do was show them how much they needed him.

A familiar, almost cheery sound drew his attention: the throb and rattle of the Ford's engine. Macadam, inscrutable in his driving helmet and goggles, gave a redundant hoot of the horn as he pulled up.

Quinn stepped on to the running board and let himself into the rear passenger seat. The car was fitted with a canopy, but was open to the elements at the sides. Macadam had the double windscreen folded over to stop the moisture obscuring his vision. The glass discs of his goggles, however, were already covered with droplets, despite the fact that he had only driven a few hundred yards.

'Where to?' said Macadam.

'East.'

Macadam wrenched the gear lever into position. Metal snarled in protest. The Model T lurched forward and Quinn was thrown back into the coach seat.

They followed the course of the river, first north past Charing Cross and Cleopatra's Needle, then banking east at Waterloo Bridge.

The motor car ripped past the slow-moving barges and lighters on the water, an upstart in the society of vehicles, pert and frisky in comparison to their ponderous solemnity.

Quinn remembered what Sir Edward had said about the importance of the Thames to the Empire. No doubt he had been thinking of the trade that flowed in through the estuary: food and raw materials from every corner of the globe.

Could one corpse found in the London Docks really jeopardize all that? No matter how savagely and strangely it had been killed?

The stench off the river was tangy and ripe. Not altogether an unpleasant smell, though there was a strand to it that both fascinated and repelled. It was the whiff of something that you wanted to get to the bottom of. But the more you nosed it out, the more you realized that its source was something rotten.

Already, even before he had begun, Quinn had the sense that there was more to this case than met the eye. First there was the presence of the Whitehall mandarin in Sir Edward's office. Then there was Sir Edward's warning. Why had it come now?

He wondered if he were not being set up for a fall. But why? In whose interest was it for him to fail?

There could only ever be one answer to that question.

They reached Blackfriars, where the road parted company with the river. Quinn thought he detected a look of startled resentment on the face of one lighterman who glared after them as they drew away. Perhaps there was also a hint of envy in his gaze, for their freedom as well as their speed. The river was his life, his destiny. He was trapped on it.

Their easterly progress was signified by the dingy state of the houses on Upper Thames Street, once great mansions fallen into dilapidation. It was hard to believe that these overcrowded slum dwellings had formerly been the homes of a privileged few.

The street was caked with filth. Children played listlessly, shoeless and ragged. They looked up at the din of the car, cowed by its implausible gleam. With their grime-blackened faces, they reminded Quinn of photographs he had seen of native children in Africa.

Only minutes before, he had left the stately glory of the Victoria Embankment, with its imperial monuments and edifices of Portland stone. Was it really possible for such scenes to coexist in the same city?

Quinn had never seen the attraction of 'slumming', the fashionable pastime among certain members of the upper classes. It was like a grotesque inversion of the Grand Tour. Instead of the cultural pinnacles of Europe, these tourists visited the impoverished hives of the East End. But then he was not of their class, not quite. He was not buffered from the deprivation they witnessed by the same layers of wealth and privilege. Unlike them, Quinn was but one degree away from destitution. His job was all that kept it at bay. If he lost that, he would lose everything; all the trappings of respectability he currently enjoyed would be in tatters. He had nothing else to fall back on.

Quinn's father had been a doctor. Indeed, Quinn himself had studied medicine, or at least begun his studies, at Middlesex Hospital. But it was not to be.

His father's suicide was one reason he gave for his breakdown. There were others. Quinn did not care to dwell on them.

At the time, Quinn had been unable to accept that his father had killed himself. A more genial, robust and hearty fellow it was impossible to imagine. He was far from the archetypal Victorian paterfamilias. Quinn remembered him as a warm and indulgent parent. A man of standing in the community, yet approachable. He was respected by all, loved by many.

It was simply inconceivable that he would take his own life. Not because of the old cliché: *he had so much to live for*. There was more to it than that. His father had *believed* in life. He had committed himself wholeheartedly to it. Not just by his choice of profession, and by the fact that he spent every working day preserving life in others. But he engaged in his own life – the life he had created for himself through his family and friends – with a consuming energy. The glow of his father's presence lit up Quinn's boyhood.

In retrospect, such energy struck Quinn as nothing short of heroic. Certainly, he could not come close to emulating it.

How could such a man kill himself?

As a young medical student, Quinn had been convinced that there must have been foul play behind it. And so his father's death was the first mystery he set himself to solve.

Someone else must have administered the diacetylmorphine overdose that killed him. But at that age, Quinn lacked the skills and the resources to investigate the matter thoroughly. He had fallen ill; his mind and spirit had given way, overwhelmed by his sense of having failed his father.

What he refused to countenance was that his father had failed him.

They came out at Tower Hill. The old fortress was suddenly there in front of them, almost shocking in its antiquity, its determination to endure. The newfangled vehicle seemed flimsy in comparison, and their assumed modernity in driving it, a passing fad.

As a policeman, Quinn was naturally interested in the building's history as a place of imprisonment, torture and execution. Something about its grim, grey walls impressed him deeply. He felt a resonance in the oldest part of his soul.

They left the Tower of London behind them. Skirting St Katharine Docks, they entered a warren of narrow sun-starved streets, criss-crossed by the footbridges that linked the high commercial buildings of the docklands.

They sped past a beggar on the corner of the street. He held out a tin cup hopelessly towards them, as if he expected Quinn to toss coins from the back of the automobile.

There was something incongruous about the

man. For one thing, he seemed to be smiling, and what could such a destitute wretch have to smile about? Perhaps he was momentarily uplifted by the sight of the car. More likely, he was the kind of witless imbecile who smiled at everything. The passing clerks gave him a wide berth, as if his madness was common knowledge.

And yet, filthy as it was, the man's face projected an intelligence that was more than the brute cunning of a slum-dweller. Well-educated, Quinn would have said. Possibly even the scion of a noble family, fallen on hard times. But something about the mouth hinted at the degeneracy that must have lain behind his downfall.

If Quinn hadn't known better, he would have said the fellow was laughing at him.

Perhaps the man's story was not so far from Quinn's own. Even before the funeral, details of his father's debts began to emerge. It soon became clear that he had left his widow and son with nothing – with less than nothing, in fact. Quinn's mother was to face a future of penury.

What was less clear was how this had come about. The household expenses could easily be met by his father's income as a general practitioner. It was evident that there was some other drain on funds known only to his father. People began to talk about a secret vice.

The possibility that his father had a secret life in which the word 'vice' played a part may have contributed more to Quinn's emotional and psychological collapse than the simple fact of his death.

It was hard for him to deal with his mother's

bitterness too. Undoubtedly, she had been left in a difficult position, for which her husband was solely to blame. (It came to light that he had even squandered the money that had come to him through his wife.) The depth of bitter feeling, which at times was indistinguishable from hatred, had shocked Quinn. He suspected it unhinged her reason, as it led her to acts of irrational and self-destructive spite. There was the time she made a bonfire of his father's library. Judging from their bindings, some of the volumes must have been exceedingly valuable.

They pulled up in a street of tenement houses. The usual ragged children clustered. They were not playing. It was as if the concept of play was alien to them. They seemed bewildered and lost, as if they were waiting for something to happen.

Quinn looked up. A gigantic sign advertising DEWAR whisky towered over the rooftops. At night, it would be illuminated, revealing the enormous kilted Scotsman in all his glory, a new constellation offering comfort to the shivering poor of the East End. Perhaps that was what they were waiting for. The moment the sign lit up the sky.

Atypical Features

Shadwell Police Station was a square, two-storey building at the corner of Juniper Street and King David Lane. Imposingly constructed with projecting masonry details, it was significantly more solid and better-preserved than the houses that occupied the rest of the street.

The street urchins descended on them as soon as the engine had shuddered into silence. 'Oi, mistah! Watchya mo'or for yer?'

'Here's sixpence to bugger off,' said Macadam, throwing a handful of farthings away from the car. The children ran screaming after the coins. 'Think I'll stay with the motor, sir, if that's all right with you. They'll strip her clean. Like locusts.'

The desk sergeant was a type Quinn was familiar with: all bulging eyes and bristling whiskers. Quinn sensed the man straighten as he entered, almost jumping to attention. The air of respectability that Quinn presented must have been unusual in those parts.

'Good day. I am Detective Inspector Quinn of the Special Crimes Department. I have been told to report here.'

'Ah yes, sir. I-spector Langdon is i-specting you, sir. *Hif* you will come this way.'

The sergeant led Quinn up a flight of stairs. 'A nasty business, would you not say, sir?'

'I am not in a position to make any comment, as yet, sergeant. Not having been apprised of the facts of the case.'

The sergeant seemed to find this remiss on Quinn's part. His eyes bulged a little more than usual, with a special significance.

He knocked on a door at the top of the stairs, opening it without waiting for a reply. 'The detective is here, sir. About the body.'

'Thank you, Salt. That will be all.' The uniformed inspector rose almost reluctantly. He was tall, a clear three inches taller than Quinn. It was as if he liked to keep his height in reserve, like a secret weapon. 'You must be Quinn?'

Quinn noted that Langdon did not offer his hand to be shaken.

'What do you know?' asked Langdon, resuming his seat.

'Practically nothing. I am relying on you for the facts.'

Langdon frowned, as if he received even this with suspicion. 'A body was found. Male. Age, approximately eighteen to twenty years. As yet, unidentified. There were no letters or papers of any kind on him. No one has come forward reporting any missing persons fitting his description. He is not a local villain known to us.'

'Where was he found?'

'On the dockside. You know the Dewar sign?'

'I've seen it.'

'He was found underneath that.'

'By whom?'

'A dockworker by the name of Thomas Man-ningham.'

'You took a statement?'

'Of course. It's in the file. Do you want to read it now?'

'I'll read it later. Please continue.'

'Have you been told about the ... uh ... peculiar circumstance?'

'You mean the blood? Or rather, lack of it.'

'Yes. He had been drained. Like...'

'A slaughtered pig.'

There was a moment while the two men considered the image Quinn had supplied. Langdon frowned distastefully. 'Have you ever come across a case like this before?' he asked.

Quinn shrugged. It was not his habit to say what he had or had not encountered in the past. 'Were there any other unusual details about the body?'

'The lack of blood is not unusual enough for you?'

'Oh, it is spectacularly unusual. I might say rather distractingly so. It may be designed to draw our attention away from some more subtle, less noticeable detail.'

Langdon gave a small but noticeable smirk. 'Quite the Sherlock Holmes, aren't you?'

'Has the police surgeon offered an opinion as to cause of death?'

'His throat was slit?' The questioning tone was sarcastic, as if to say, *Is that cause of death enough for you?*

'I see.'

Langdon sighed, bored with the conversation.

'Perhaps it is best if you read the medical report yourself. You know what you're looking for, I dare say.'

'But I am interested to know your opinion. That is to say, if you have reached any.'

Langdon pulled a face that just stopped short of a sneer. 'Oh, don't expect me to do your job for you. I've enough on my plate already. There's the file. We'll find a room for you to use. I'll even have Salt bring you up a cup of tea if you wish.'

'Much obliged, I'm sure. If it's not too much trouble, might he also take one out to Sergeant Macadam, who is waiting for me outside in the motor car?'

Langdon hiked up his brow in surprise. He seemed on the verge of expressing his wonder at the idea of Quinn's possessing a motor car, but just stopped himself in time. *I won't give him the satisfaction*, or something like it, was no doubt going through his mind.

The room that Langdon provided was hardly bigger than a broom cupboard. There was a small deal table and a chair with unequal legs. A hatstand took Quinn's damp Ulster and bowler.

The file was marked UNIDENTIFIED SODO-MITE.

Quinn opened it up and spread out the photographs. *Yes, it was entirely possible*, thought Quinn, as he studied the young man's face. He was what you might call a pretty boy. Girlish looks, accentuated by long curling locks. Judging by the tone of grey in the monochrome images, his hair was blond. He would find out for sure when he saw the body later.

The dark bruises around the anus, shown in a close-up photograph, explained the file's title.

The wound at the throat was neat. One wide, sweeping slash from something very sharp indeed, a razor most likely. The blood must have gushed out from there with tremendous, instant force.

And so it was striking to see not a drop of blood, anywhere, in any of the photographs.

The victim's clothes and body were immaculate.

Photographs of the young man's penis were included in the file. It appeared to be of prodigious length. It was hard to reconcile his delicate, girlish features with this coarse appendage. Quinn presumed these particular photographs had been taken because they provided evidence of a distinguishing feature that might aid identification.

It was possible that the victim was a male prostitute. If so, the combination of physical beauty and an oversized member might be a considerable professional advantage. At least Quinn supposed so.

He returned the photographs to the file for now, and turned his attention to the dockworker's statement.

I was on my way to work. I was working the early shift. It is a six o'clock start. I was not the only one wot seen him. No one else would come forward. Your dockworker is not a great lover of the Ole Bill, pardon me for saying, not since the trouble there was with the strikes an all. Still, I

45

says, someone has to report it. He was lying face down at the bottom of that big sign. Some of the blokes had a good ole larf at that. Him being beneath the Dewar sign an all that. Drunk as they supposed. But I thought there was something fishy about him. He dint look right, if you know what I mean. So I went over to him. Alright, mate? I says. Nothin. I gave him a little shake. Stiff as a board, he was. I thought maybe he was frozen from sleepin out all night. Come on mate, I says. Then I rolled him over so as I cud get a look at his boat race. That was when I saw it. His throat. Cut from ear to ear. Someone had better fetch the Ole Bill, I says. Some of me mates refused even to draw straws for it. That is how much they hate the Ole Bill round here. So I came straight here and fetched the constable. I have no love for the Ole Bill myself. But I seen that someone had better fetch them. I hope you will tell the company where I have been.

The deposition, written in one hand and signed in another, had presumably been taken down by the desk sergeant; the poor literacy was consistent with the man's spoken solecisms and typical of the ignorance and mental confusion of desk sergeants in general. It was dated Wednesday, March the eighteenth, five days earlier. The medical examination would have been conducted in the intervening time.

The police surgeon's report was written in the usual technical language, as neutral in tone as Dr Bugsby – the physician in question – could manage, given the extraordinary condition of the body. But Quinn had seen enough of these documents to read between the lines. The frequent use of the word 'atypical' he recognized as a coded way of saying, *I have never seen anything like this before in my life!*

The complete absence of external hypostases was the most immediately apparent atypical feature. Hypostases were the dark, livid marks which appeared on the skin on the underside of a cadaver, caused by the blood settling in the capillaries as a result of gravity.

Hypostases begin to form within eight to twelve hours of death. The time between the discovery of the body and its examination alone was longer than eight hours, so it would have been reasonable to expect to see some external hypostases present. In addition, rigor mortis was well established, and had been at the time of the corpse's discovery, according to the dockworker's description. For rigor mortis to be so established, the victim must have been dead at least as long as the time required for external hypostases to occur.

The absence of this feature clearly struck Dr Bugsby as highly significant. He went so far as to quote from Casper:

'[Hypostases] are formed after every kind of death, even after death from haemorrhage.' (Casper, Vol. I.)

Bugsby had added his own commentary on the relevant passage:

Casper is emphatic that external hypostases are a universal characteristic of cadavers, and are indeed one of the fundamental signs of the presence of death. He forcefully refutes Dever-

gie's contrary opinion, showing the one case Devergie cites in support of his argument to be unscientific and anyway inconclusive. We may note that in the example Devergie gives, of a cadaver supposedly without external hypostases, death resulted from the throat being cut by a razor. Casper seems to imply that the only conceivable explanation for the non-formation of external hypostases would be if the body had been drained entirely of blood. This is clearly a circumstance so far beyond his personal experience, and even comprehension, that he does not deem it worthy of further discussion.

Dr Bugsby then went on to consider internal hypostases, which *were* present in the body, but again 'atypical'. Internal hypostases were generally looked for in the brain, lungs, kidneys, intestines and spinal cord. As gravity did its work, the blood would congest in the area of those organs closest to the ground, usually the rear, as most corpses lie on their backs.

However, the victim had been found face down, so it would not have been surprising if the blood had gathered at the front of each organ. This was not the case. Internal hypostases were in fact located at the tops of the organs, apparently in defiance of gravity.

However, Bugsby's external examination had already noted abrasions around the ankles, which were consistent with rope tearing the skin.

A picture was emerging. It seemed the victim had been strung up by the ankles while the blood was allowed to drain from the wound in his neck. The absence of blood on his clothes indicated that he was naked when he was killed, whereas the absence of blood on his body suggested that he had been washed after his death.

The skin was bruised as well as torn at the ankle. His wrists bore similar marks. Quinn believed this meant the victim had been alive when he was bound. Whether he had also been alive when he was strung up was another question.

One thing was beyond question: his circulatory system was devoid of blood. Upon opening, the pulmonary artery and the vena cava were found to be entirely empty, as was every vein to which the persistent doctor took his scalpel. The heart too. The instances of internal hypostasis were the only evidence of blood remaining inside the body.

According to the report, the wholesale exsanguination of the corpse made it more difficult to ascertain an accurate time of death. In Dr Bugsby's opinion, the absence of blood would delay the process of putrefaction, making the body seem better preserved than it would otherwise be. All he could say with any certainty was that the victim had been dead long enough to be drained of all his blood.

Dr Bugsby also addressed the issue of the victim's anus, which he described as smooth, enlarged and 'destitute of *rugae*'. Such an appearance, he declared, was consistent with an addiction to unnatural practices. Seminal discharge inside the rectum, as well as fresh lacerations of the rectal wall, indicated that the victim had recently indulged in his addiction.

The file shed no light on the identity of the victim. It seemed to Quinn that so far no serious attempts had been made in that direction. Judging from the collated police reports, only the most perfunctory local enquiries had been made, a handful of arbitrary interviews. The wording on the cover of the file was a judgement more than a description, and one that seemed designed to discourage too much zeal in the prosecution of the case, the implication being that he was no great loss. Good riddance, in other words.

A list of the victim's effects contained only one item: a silver cigarette case.

The Missing Clue

Following Sergeant Salt's example, Quinn knocked on Inspector Langdon's door and opened it without waiting for a reply.

'Solved it?'

Quinn ignored Langdon's facetious greeting. 'The file mentioned a cigarette case. Found on the body. I would like to see it.'

'I shall see that Sergeant Salt brings it to you.'

'I will need to take it away with me.'

'Provided you sign for it, I can see no objection.'

'Yes, of course.'

'Small items like that have a habit of going missing.'

Quinn gave Langdon a steady stare. The man seemed to be impugning his honesty. 'I hope it has not gone missing already.'

A minuscule spasm of amusement quivered on Langdon's lips. Evidently he enjoyed these games far more than Quinn did. 'Will there be anything else?'

'Whatever crimes he may be guilty of, he did not deserve to die like that.'

Langdon's expression was ambivalent. He made no comment.

'I will be taking the file away too. Our priority is to identify the body.' Quinn remembered Sir Edward's wish to keep the details of the case out of the newspapers, and yet the press could be a useful tool in gathering information. Quinn inadvertently voiced his thoughts. 'It would help if we were able to release a photograph of the dead man to the newspapers.'

Langdon smirked. 'Which one would you use?'

'One of his face, naturally. Inspector Langdon, does this case amuse you?'

'Gallows humour, my friend. Have you never heard of it?'

'I have heard of it but I don't appreciate it.'

'No. I imagine not.'

'I think we owe it to the deceased – to all deceased – to treat them with respect and seriousness.'

'Do you, now?'

'Yes.'

'So. You have sympathy for his type, do you?' Langdon's tone was unmistakable.

'For the dead, you mean?'

'You know what I mean. Queers.'

'We cannot say for certain...'

'Oh, come now. You saw the photographs, I'm sure. You read the doctor's report. He was addicted to unnatural practices. Does that not disgust you?'

'I have to set aside such feelings. Besides, the law does not punish his crimes by death, let alone by such a death as he suffered. Indeed, the severest penalty under law is the birch.'

'What is your point?'

'My point being that the law recognizes that the crimes perpetrated against him – which may include kidnap, indecent assault, torture, as well as murder – are far more heinous than any offences he may have committed. Which, as far as we can tell, are limited to allowing his own person to be used unnaturally by other men for their sexual gratification. It is a crime against himself, if it is against anyone. Therefore, even once we have put his offences into the balance, the scale of transgression is still weighted heavily towards his murderer. We are duty-bound to investigate his death.'

'Well,' said Langdon, after considering Quinn for a long time. 'I can see they have found the right man for this job.'

Quinn resisted the temptation to respond to Langdon's innuendo. 'Please don't trouble yourself about the cigarette case. I shall speak to Sergeant Salt myself.' He did not miss the flicker of panic across Langdon's face.

'A cigarette case, you say?' Sergeant Salt's eyebrows descended into a dark, perplexed V.

'Yes,' said Quinn. 'It is mentioned in the file. The victim's sole effect.'

The sergeant gripped the edge of his mahogany desk, as if this new information threatened to overturn the fabric of his universe. 'In that case, it will be in the evidence room.'

'I need to see it. Be so good as to fetch it for me.'

Salt hesitated to let go of the desk. 'What does it look like?'

'I have no idea. Other than I presume it shares certain features in common with most every other cigarette case. However, I haven't seen it. Surely you have some record of it? An evidential log book? It should be a simple matter to locate it.'

'Oh, yes. I should be able to put my hand on it.' At last Salt lifted a hand away from the desk, only to place it down again, flat on the surface.

'Then please do.'

This seemed a surprising suggestion to Salt, though eventually he began to move away from the desk. He kept Quinn fixed for as long as possible with a sidelong glance.

Quinn read the public notices as he waited for Salt to return. There was nothing he had not read before, in countless other police stations across the capital. Rewards offered, information requested, missing persons sought. Greying and dog-eared, they signified a world of mundane crime: forlorn, lacklustre, pathetically unimaginative. They spoke of lives lived on the edge of misery.

And yet, somehow, they absorbed him.

By the time he had read every last one of them, he realized that Salt had been gone an ominously long time.

The door to the street opened and a stunted bundle of a woman shuffled in. Her clothes were dusty and old, but otherwise respectable. She could have been aged anywhere between sixty and eighty. She walked with a rolling, arthritic limp. Bad hips, Quinn speculated. A powerful unwashed smell came off her.

She did not look at Quinn but walked straight up to the desk and pushed down the bell. She then sank on to a seat at the edge of the room with a sigh of relief.

Now he had her face to read, and it was equally absorbing as the public notices. It was covered by the same grey patina of melancholy.

He wondered what her story was; what succession of moments had made up her life and led her to this police station.

He suddenly found it unutterably sad to think that someone might have committed a crime against her, however trivial.

'Bad news, sir.' It was Salt, back at last. 'The *h-item* you requested cannot be found at present.'

'How can that be?'

'It is not where it ought to be. I am at a loss to explain it. However, I might add, I have not yet given up 'ope.'

'It is a piece of material evidence. Its loss is a

severe setback in the investigation. It does not reflect well on this station.'

'I'm sure it will turn up, sir. It's probably just misplaced. Someone 'as no doubt taken it, believing it to be...'

'Believing it to be what, exactly?'

'Superfluous. It's just a cigarette case, after all. All it proves is that the fellow smoked.'

'There might have been an inscription in it.'

'Good heavens, sir! I believe there was! How did you know?'

'Did you make a note of this inscription?'

'Myself, sir, no.'

'Did anyone?'

'I do not believe it was thought necessary. No one here could make head nor tail of it. And I suppose the i-scription was there for anyone to read on the cigarette case itself, if they had so wanted to.'

'But the cigarette case has now gone missing.'

'Gone missing, yes. That's a very good way of putting it.'

At that point, Inspector Langdon emerged from the inner door to join Salt behind the counter. Quinn could not miss the flash of silver in his hand. 'Is this what you are looking for?'

'Good heavens, sir!' cried Sergeant Salt, his amazement rather overdone, or so it seemed to Quinn. 'You've found it!' To Quinn, he added: 'What did I tell you, sir? I knew it would turn up.'

Quinn took the cigarette case from Langdon. 'Remarkable.'

'I cannot understand how you failed to find it,

Salt,' said Langdon. He was watching Quinn closely as he spoke. 'It was exactly where it was supposed to be.'

'I must have been looking in the wrong place, sir.'

'Yes, that must be it. That or we will have to get your eyes examined by an ophthalmologist.'

'There's nothing wrong with my eyes, sir.'

Quinn felt compelled to cut short the music hall act. 'I see that it is empty. Can you confirm that it was empty when it was found?'

'Of course. What are you suggesting?'

'I merely wondered if whoever took the case may not also have smoked the cigarettes.' Quinn held Langdon's gaze.

'No one took the case,' insisted Langdon. 'It was where it should be all the time.'

Quinn gave an exaggerated nod. 'I think you had better attend to this lady now, Sergeant. She has been waiting rather a long time.'

'Ole Janet? Don't you worry about Ole Janet, sir! She comes in every day. Mostlys just to get out of the rain.'

'She rang the bell. She must have something she wishes to talk to you about.'

'Yes, an' I heard it a thousand times already. I i-spect she just wants to tell us about her cat. Her cat went missing, you see, sir. And she comes in every day to tell us it's still missing. I'm afraid we've got too much on our plate to go looking for missing moggies.'

'When did she first report the cat missing?'

'You're going to solve that mystery too, are you?' said Langford.

'Not much point looking into that, sir,' advised Sergeant Salt. 'The beast is dead, if you ask me. I tole her so but she wasn't having any of it. It was all she had in the world, you see, sir. Very sad, I don't doubt, but what can you do about it? It's the Jews what done it, I reckon. It's the Jews what had them all.'

'What are you talking about, Sergeant Salt?' demanded Quinn.

'The Jews what came over from Russia. The local cats started going missing after that. We found a lot of them dead. Very nasty business. I reckon it's a Jew what's killed your queer, sir. Either that or a Chinky. You should see the knives some of them Chinkies have. I saw a Chinky cook chase after a fellow with a meat cleaver once.'

Quinn nodded in distracted agreement. In truth, he was scarcely attending to what Salt was saying. He had released the fastener on the cigarette case.

Quinn felt a dark, furtive excitement. He had glanced inside the cigarette case and read the inscription.

He closed the lid on it quickly, reluctant to bring it up with Langdon and Salt. It was too important. Indeed, his instinct was to get the cigarette case out of there as quickly as possible. They did not deserve to share in its secrets. The fools had had it in their possession and failed to appreciate it for what it was.

No one here could make head nor tail of it, Salt had said.

There was no doubt in Quinn's mind that it had

come from the murderer.

More than that, he had the sense that through it the murderer was communicating directly with him. Directly and personally. Quinn was convinced that he alone was capable of understanding the words inscribed inside the lid, in the sense that the murderer meant them.

To handle the object was to communicate with hands that had bound and slaughtered another human being. Quinn discovered that his heart beat with a more savage, a fiercer throb at the cold touch of the metal. As a detective, he was aware of all the modern developments in crime detection, of which Sir Edward was an enthusiastic proponent. He knew how important it was to handle any piece of evidence as little as possible, in order not to contaminate any fingerprints that might be found on it. But the strange magnetism of the cigarette case was too powerful for his fingers to resist.

Quinn affected an air of indifference. 'I believe I have everything I need for now. I see no necessity to take up any more of your time. Good day, gentlemen.'

His eagerness to be gone did not go unnoticed by Inspector Langdon. It seemed the man set himself to oppose Quinn in everything. 'One moment, Inspector Quinn. You are forgetting the necessaries.'

For one startling moment, Quinn thought Langdon was soliciting a bribe. But he made an entry in a ledger book and pushed it across the counter for Quinn to sign. 'A formality, you understand. But I must insist on it. I saw the way you were looking at that cigarette case. If we don't watch out, you'll have it for your private collection, I'm sure.' The tone was one of forced jocularity, tinged with resentment. Quinn was left in little doubt that Langdon had entertained similar plans for the object, now thwarted.

Quinn looked up at a sky of unbroken grey. The earlier drizzle had gathered itself into hurtling streaks of rain. The street urchins were nowhere to be seen.

He dashed over to the Model T, his body stooped over the file protectively. The rain drummed the taut round crown of his bowler. Macadam was evidently dozing in the chauffeur's seat. The slam of the door and the jolt of the car as Quinn got in woke him.

'All done, sir?'

'Not quite, Macadam. I need you to drive me over to Poplar.'

Macadam peered out dubiously at the downpour, from which the car's open-sided canopy provided little protection. 'Very well, sir.' He waited a moment for the rain to ease but, as it showed no sign of abating, leapt out anyway. Quinn saw him bend down in front of the car to give the crank half a turn. The Ford juddered into noisy, shaking life, the rattle of the engine drowning out the muted patter of the rain.

'Such a reliable starter!' said Macadam cheerfully, as he settled back behind the wheel. A clear droplet hung from the tip of his nose. 'Say what you like about the Model T, but she cannot be beaten for starting.'

'A boon on days like this,' observed Quinn.

Macadam eased the car away skilfully. He nodded vigorously, shaking the raindrops loose.

Quinn moved into the middle of the back seat, the furthest point from the rain splashing in from both sides. 'It's a shame the old mortuary at Saint George in the East is no longer in operation, Macadam. I could have walked round there.'

Macadam snorted dismissively. 'That was nothing but a primitive shed. I hear the new mortuary at Poplar is equipped with electrical refrigeration units.'

'Is that so?'

'Perhaps I might come in with you to see them, sir?'

Quinn's first instinct was to deny Macadam's request. He wanted to be alone when he confronted the body. 'Wouldn't you prefer to stay with the car?'

Macadam must have sensed his resistance. He didn't push it. 'What do we have then, sir? An interesting case?'

'Certainly the case does appear to have some unusual features. The body was drained entirely of blood.'

Macadam gave a whistle. 'Who's the victim?'

'Identity unknown, as yet.'

'Anything to go on?'

'He appears to have engaged in unnatural practices with other men.'

'Ah. One of those. In that case, he may have a criminal record, sir. Gross indecency, vagrancy, soliciting. That sort of thing. There could be a mugshot in the Rogues' Gallery. I take it you

60

have a photograph of the corpse, sir? We might be able to match them up.'

'Good thinking, Macadam. Given his youthfulness, we need not go back too far.'

'We'll go back as far as it takes, sir.'

Macadam accelerated to overtake a horse-drawn collier's van as they pulled out on to Commercial Road. In keeping with the street's name, the road was interspersed with business premises on both sides, but there was a rundown air to most of them. The traffic was sparse. Clusters of men sheltered beneath shop awnings, their faces an array of skin shades from Nordic to African. The same expression of sullen boredom was engrained on them all, beneath incongruously English flat caps. Sailors without a ship, they could offer little in the way of custom to the local shops. A group of them huddled in the entrance of a beer shop, presumably without the funds to go inside. They scowled across at a ship-breaking concern, as if they held it responsible for their misfortune.

Through the arch of a railway viaduct, Quinn had a glimpse of the merchant ships in Regent's Canal Lock. The masts and rigging were stripped, the funnels denuded of smoke, the engines idle: a dejected, sodden vignette. For the briefest of moments he entertained a fantasy of escape, imagining himself borne away on one of these long, low vessels, away from the unrelenting dampness of the English spring to a far-flung, sun-blasted outpost of the Empire. Away, too, from the sickening nastiness of his new case and from the necessity to go where he was now going. The grim photographs of the victim had formed a monochrome area of unease at the centre of his mind, a premonition of impending difficulty and pain.

But the promise of escape was gone the moment it was glimpsed. The image of the boats now felt like a dream he couldn't quite recall. There was to be no other end to his journey today than the mortuary.

Despite his reputation, Quinn had no appetite for the grisly side of the job. He had a horror of cadavers. He had felt it as a medical student, and perhaps it had contributed to his precipitous abandonment of that career. The nightmares he had experienced in the immediate aftermath of his breakdown were peopled with the dead.

His father was among their number, of course; in these dreams he had been both dead and not dead. The great healer had used his talents to bring himself back to life. He had also been able to reanimate anonymous corpses based on the cadavers Quinn had seen in the dissecting room. In some cases, the reanimation was extremely limited, the twitch of a hand, the swivel of eyes, the upheaval of swallowing in the throat. One or two raised themselves to sitting position. At which point, Quinn's father would turn to him, the glare of defiant pride in his eyes.

The dreams did not end there. How could they? They were born out of mental illness and collapse. And so he was denied the usual relief of waking at the worst point of the nightmare.

Quinn turned his gaze to the other side of the street, as if he were looking away from the morbid images of his old dreams. The Lime-house Liberal and Radical Association presented an innocuous, even respectable, facade. It brought to mind the agitation of the living rather than of the dead, the complex, compromised struggles of political aspiration.

They passed Limehouse Town Hall and turned right into Three Colt Street, Macadam gratuit-ously sounding the horn as he made the manoeu-vre. The sound disrupted Quinn's thoughts. He was about to rebuke Macadam but relented. Perhaps his thoughts needed disrupting. They had been drifting away from the case.

He kept his gaze fixed on the looming, soot-blackened tower of St Anne's church, as if its sinister, almost fantastical presence held the key to the mystery he was investigating. What strange rite had been performed in the sacrifice and bleeding of that unknown young man? The sergeant at Shadwell had pointed the finger at the Jews. No doubt the man was an imbecile, but Quinn had an idea that the method of slaughter insisted upon under Jewish law placed emphasis on the removal of blood.

Dangerous, dangerous, thought Quinn, as he watched the church recede. He remembered Sir Edward's vague warning about foreign influen-ces and precarious balances in the East End. He would have to tread carefully, there was no doubt.

Before long they had turned into Limehouse Causeway. Quinn noticed the increase in Chinese names on the shop fronts. The mysterious strokes and dashes of the alien language fascinated him. He mistrusted the innocuous English translations that appeared alongside: Grocer's, Laundry, General Stores. *So where were the signs for the opium dens and gambling houses?* he wondered.

Like the sailors he had noticed earlier, the Chinamen he saw were dressed in the uniform of the English labouring poor. There were no long ponytails, no silk tunics or straw coolie hats; just black serge and cloth caps.

Chinatown continued across the West India Dock Road into Penny Fields. It ended as abruptly as it had begun as that road turned into Poplar High Street.

The Poplar Coroner's Court was a recently constructed red-brick building with stone-mullioned windows, a compromise between the nostalgic romanticism of the architect and the parsimony of the local borough council. The front entrance on Poplar High Street was a somewhat grandiose affair, studded doors in a vaguely medieval style set into an arched doorway.

The mortuary was a separate building at the rear, connected by a covered way. The styling was more functional: most of those who entered by the rear were beyond being impressed by architectural gestures.

Macadam parked in the alley that ran along the side of the building, close to the entrance to the yard.

Quinn passed the file over to him. 'I suggest you familiarize yourself with the details of the case while you wait for me.'

Unlike some of the crude sheds and improvised dead-houses Quinn had visited, the Poplar mortuary was planned and built along rational lines, in keeping with the latest scientific thinking. The sanitation and drainage facilities were exemplary. And as Macadam had said, it was fitted with the latest electrical refrigeration equipment. There were two mortuary rooms, the one furthest from the coroner's court being reserved for victims of infectious diseases. The post-mortem room was at the rear of that, with a laboratory and stores adjoining. The mortuary complex had been completed just three years earlier, and so it still had about it an air of newness that its daily contact with the dead had not yet eradicated.

Quinn's energetic knocking belied his reluctance to enter. *The only way to overcome your fears is to throw yourself into them*, he decided. Besides, he wanted to get out of the rain.

Quinn kept up the hammering until the door was opened by a caretaker in a leather apron and black bowler hat. With his grey, sunken face, he reminded Quinn of the animated dead of his dreams. As the door was opened, another man with his jacket lapels pulled up around his face slipped out from behind the caretaker and ran across the yard to the exit.

Quinn gave his head a quick shake of distracted surprise. 'I am Inspector Quinn of the Special Crimes Department. I have come to examine the body found at London Docks.'

The caretaker's face cracked open. His grin revealed gums endowed with isolated teeth of monumental length. It was in the gaps between the teeth that the secret of his sunken cheeks lay revealed. 'Ah, yes. A fine specimen. Doctor Bugsby says he ain't never seen one so big.'

Quinn pushed his way past the man. 'I'm not interested in that.'

'No?' The caretaker seemed disappointed. 'A prodigy of nature, is what Doctor Bugsby called it. Like a comet or a *ee*-clipse. Such a thing might only come round once in a man's life. While you're here you may as well look upon it. You may regret it if you don't.'

Quinn was struck by a sudden suspicion. 'My man, I had better not discover that you have been charging members of the public money in order to view this corpse.'

'No, no,' said the caretaker emphatically, but not wholly convincingly. He hurried ahead of Quinn down the corridor. 'This way then, sir. He's in the first mortuary room.'

Quinn paced after him. 'Who was that individual whom you let out as I came?'

'Him? Oh, that was ... William. William helps me out now and then.'

'Is Doctor Bugsby here?'

'Not today, sir. He is at his surgery today.'

'Does Doctor Bugsby know about your arrangement with this William?'

'He knows there's always much to do,' said the caretaker vaguely.

Quinn felt the chill of the mortuary room at the root of every hair on his body. Every follicle seemed to clench in a repulsive reaction. He was aware of a strange resonance, to which the atoms of his being were compelled to respond, re-arranging themselves in a fatal alignment. He felt it as a low thrumming in the air. He cocked his head to locate the source.

'What's that sound?' Quinn's voice was hushed, fearful.

'That's the refrigerator. We have a refrigerator, you see. The doctor likes to keep the bodies cold.'

'Yes, of course. I forgot. I had heard that the mortuary rooms here were equipped with refrigeration units.'

Now wearing protective leather gloves, the caretaker crossed to one of the small enamelled doors that filled one wall. Quinn felt his heart throb in time to the room's vibration as the man grasped the gleaming handle of the door. 'He's in here.'

As the door opened, the temperature of the room dropped perceptibly. A fine haze of frozen particles swam around the aperture. The long drawer on which the body lay was pulled out on well-oiled runners. The dead man emerged briskly, head first.

'That's far enough,' said Quinn. The body was out as far as the chest.

It was the unnatural pallor of the flesh that repulsed him most. It was the pallor that he wanted to push back into the freezing compartment and hide away forever. The skin was roughly stitched together along the sweeping incisions made at the post-mortem examination, like a patchwork of fine, translucent gauze lying over frail bones. The musculature was slight, wasted away, as if the young man was under-nourished. He had lived on his nerves, by the looks of him. His head almost seemed out of proportion, or perhaps it was just that it was so physically riveting – even in death, even with the colour drained from his flesh by a savage wound – that the rest of him could not compete.

And the wound, it was almost a relief to look away from the unbearable pallor of the flesh into the dark edges of that strangely neat, strangely deliberate parting at his throat.

'Do you not want to see...' the caretaker paused facetiously '...the other wounds? The marks on his wrists and ankles?'

Quinn nodded. The drawer slid out further. The arms lay at the side of the body, touchingly delicate at the wrists where the damage had been inflicted. The photographs had not done justice to the sharp intensity of the bruises. Quinn believed he could make out the imprint of the rope that had bound him.

And of course, now, he could not avoid confronting the man's penis.

'There, see, I told you,' said the caretaker. 'A monster, ain't it?'

'Turn the arm over for me,' said Quinn brusquely. 'I want to look at the underside.'

'Do you not want to do it yourself? They say it's good luck to touch 'em.'

Quinn frowned away the comment. But perhaps there was something in what the caretaker said.

Is this why I do it? he wondered. *For this moment?*

68

Quinn reached out and touched the frozen shock of dead flesh. He turned the arm over quickly. The fleshier underside was deeply indented, the skin broken. He withdrew his hand hurriedly and shook it, as if that would be enough to rid it of any contamination.

The Wall

The Special Crimes Department occupied an attic room in the northernmost building of New Scotland Yard. It had a sharply sloped ceiling, interrupted by a dormer window. Quinn himself was just short of six feet tall. He was only able to stand up straight at the highest part of the room. He frequently forgot this, especially when rising from his desk.

More or less the same height as their chief, Sergeants Inchball and Macadam also brought a great deal of physical bulk to the department. It was a cramped space for three big policemen.

The photographs that Quinn had tacked to the one full-length wall seemed to reduce the space even more. It was not a wall any decent person would want to go anywhere near. It turned one corner of a perfectly respectable red-brick and granite building into a cubicle of Hell.

Only Quinn showed any willingness to approach the wall. For the briefing, Inchball and

Macadam were forced to huddle, bowed, beneath the incline of the roof. It seemed an appropriate posture in which to face the savagery depicted.

Quinn had had one other photograph made, an enlargement of the inside of the cigarette case, showing the inscription:

To be entirely free
D.P.

Inchball frowned. His brows flowed together in a slow, viscous ripple. Macadam scratched his scalp, visible through the sparse stubble of his razor cut. Both men exchanged perplexed glances: it seemed the chief had finally lost it.

Quinn knew that he was overexcited, or that that was how it would seem to his men. He knew that they would look at the neat calligraphic script blown up large and wonder what all the fuss was about.

'Who of us can say that he is truly free? From the moment of our birth, we are bound to others. As children, we are subject to the rule of our parents. As adults, we are constrained by the conventions and expectations of society. By the necessity to earn a crust. By the obligations placed on us by our fellows. The ties that bind us are the claims of our common humanity. It is only by renouncing those claims, by severing those bonds, that we are able to break free. Every transgression, every act of rebellion, is a moment of freedom. The schoolboy who steals an apple from an orchard.' Quinn glanced at the photograph of the unidentified victim's anus. 'The young man who rents out his arse to strangers. The depraved monster who pays for that accommodation and slits the throat and drains the blood of the one providing it. The greater the crime, the greater the freedom. Freedom is rooted in power. He who is powerful is free. And there is no more power-filled act than the taking of a life. *To be entirely free,* gentlemen. *To be entirely free!* That is why one kills. And that is why I am in no doubt that this cigarette case is a gift from the murderer. A gift for us.'

'Away with the fairies,' muttered Inchball, who had a habit of saying whatever was on his mind. It was largely on account of this habit that Quinn had wanted him on his team.

'What was that, Inchball?'

'Nothing, sir.'

'I distinctly heard you say something.'

Inchball did not need much prompting. 'Begging your pardon, sir, with respect and all that, but I have known some murderers in my life. Some of them have been what I would call, sir, pathetic individuals. Would not say boo to a goose to look at them, that is, sir.'

'Very good, Inchball. As ever, I value your contribution. Your point is well made. But it does not contradict what I was saying. One may be powerless and downtrodden in every other aspect of one's life, defeated and depressed by countless frustrations. But to the extent that one is capable of depriving another of life –'

'Of murder, sir? It's murder what you are talking about?'

'Yes, Inchball.'

'Then I would be obliged to you, sir, if you

71

would use the word. Let's call a spade a spade, I say, sir. All this talk of depriving individuals of life. *Murder*, sir. That's what it is.'

'Thank you, Inchball. Where was I? Yes. To the extent that one is capable of *murder* – and especially in the moment of committing it – one is all powerful. Before that point, the frustrations accumulate. The destructive emotion – we might call it rage – intensifies, until at last it cannot be denied. It must be sated. The power must be allowed to flow. Blood must be shed.'

'Well, sir,' said Inchball. 'You certainly sound like you know what you are talking about. But if I may say, sir, where does it get us?'

'It gets us closer to the murderer. Mark my words, this cigarette case will take us to him.'

'We've had it dusted for prints, sir,' said Macadam in a discouraging tone. Macadam was a great one for the scientific approach to policing. He frequently attended lectures, subscribed to a number of incomprehensible journals, and was forever suggesting to Quinn that the department employ the services of this or that expert to help them in their investigations. He had been Sir Edward's choice, but Quinn valued him all the same, because his approach was so different to his own.

Quinn hesitated a beat before asking, 'And?'

'Nothing, sir. Well, nothing once they had discarded certain extraneous prints. If you don't mind me saying, sir, if you could remember to don the cotton gloves when handling items of material evidence, it really would make the forensic boys' lives a lot easier. Mind you,

72

you're not the only one. Apparently, the inspector at Shadwell had left his prints all over it too.'

'I find the gloves ... get in the way.' Quinn avoided Macadam's disapproving glower.

'Well, it's something to aim for, isn't it, sir? A target, we might say.' Macadam gave a small mime of flexing and releasing the string on an archer's bow. Because of the stoop imposed by the sloping ceiling, the imaginary arrow was aimed at Quinn's foot.

'Did the *forensic boys* find anything at all that might enlighten us?' Quinn hoped that by using Macadam's term he might appease him.

The sergeant reached across to his desk to retrieve a slip of paper which he handed to Quinn. 'Their report, sir.'

Quinn scanned the document, ignoring the complaints about contamination. At last his eye was caught by the very detail he was looking for. 'Excellent!'

'Is that the tobacco flake, sir?'

'Yes, Macadam. This may be just the breakthrough we need.'

'A single tobacco flake, sir. It's not much to go on. But I was chatting to Charlie Cale. He's my friend in the lab, sir. A very clever young man, if I may say so. Well, Charlie Cale has made a bit of a study of tobacco, sir. Got the idea from Sherlock Holmes, I don't doubt. He's a great one for reading detective stories.'

'That's all we need,' said Inchball.

'Yes. But that needn't concern us. He reckons the tobacco found in that cigarette case, sir, came from an Egyptian cigarette. The tobacco is actually Turkish. But it is a type of Turkish tobacco used by Egyptian cigarette manufacturers.'

'Can he identify the exact brand?'

'What he can say, sir, is that the tobacco had been soaked in opium.'

'And so, we are looking for a killer who smokes opium-soaked Egyptian cigarettes!'

'With respect and all that, sir, we cannot say that for certain,' objected Inchball. 'We may only be able to say that this cigarette case once contained such cigarettes.'

'Your caution is commendable, Inchball. But what of the letters D.P.? Are we at least able to say that we are looking for a murderer whose initials are D.P.?'

'Again, sir, I do not know that we are permitted to draw that conclusion. In the first place, why would the killer put his initials on an object which is bound to come into the police's possession?'

'To tantalize us? I believe we are dealing with an arrogant individual. It is always the arrogant ones who play these games.'

'Now there I agree with you, sir...'

'Really, Inchball? I am flattered. And I agree with you. On consideration, I believe they are unlikely to be his initials. Perhaps he means us to assume they are. He is trying to mislead us. But if they are not his initials, what do the letters stand for? I feel they must mean something.'

'Differential Pressure,' said Macadam quickly. 'D.P. – Differential Pressure...? No?' Sensing the scepticism of his colleagues, he had another stab: 'Or it might be Dramatis Personae. In plays, you know, sir. Then there's Deceased Person. Oh, and Dreadnought Programme.'

'It also stands for Detective Prick,' said Inchball bluntly.

The three men were startled by the ringing of the telephone, a recent addition to the department. Sir Edward had insisted on its installation.

They had all been trained in its use, although Macadam, as the most technologically inclined, viewed it as his preserve. He leapt to answer it now. 'Special Crimes.'

He listened breathlessly for a moment, before handing the device to Quinn.

'The answer's no, Quinn.' The tiny voice sounded like a wasp trapped inside a snare drum. A more absolute buzzing filled the earpiece as the line went dead. Quinn gave the telephone back to Macadam.

'Bad news, sir?'

'It was Sir Edward. I put in a request to release the photograph to the newspapers, or rather an artist's rendition of it, without the wound. He has vetoed it.'

'So we must find out the queer's identity the hard way?' said Inchball.

'I've been through the Rogues' Gallery, sir, as we discussed.' Macadam's voice was again discouraging. 'Nothing, I'm afraid. I've made a start going back through relevant case files now. There may be photographs in there that haven't found their way into the Rogues' Gallery, for some reason. You never know. Many a slip twixt cup and lip and all that.'

75

'Your thoroughness is commendable, Macadam. Now, where were we? Ah yes, the inscription. Let us go back to the first part. *To be entirely free.* Does it not strike you as the kind of thing someone might get out of a book? A quotation, in other words. Couldn't D.P. refer to the title of the book in question? Or the author?'

Macadam and Inchball regarded the enlargement of the inscription thoughtfully.

'That makes sense,' said Inchball.

'Where do we begin, though, sir? There have been so many books written,' said Macadam forlornly.

'We must think about the kind of books that would appeal to a decadent individual such as is capable of doing this.' Quinn gestured vaguely at the wall.

'I know a couple of bookshops in Soho that stock the kind of literature you have in mind,' said Inchball.

'Perfect. However, we must find a way to elicit their cooperation without intimidating them. In my experience, such establishments tend to be wary of the police. Perhaps it would be best to conduct our inquiries there discreetly. One of us could pose as a gentleman interested in material of that nature.'

Macadam and Inchball looked at one another uneasily. 'With respect and all that, sir,' began Inchball, 'I think you might be the best man for that job.'

The chief's reaction seemed to surprise the two sergeants. 'I have no objections to that. Indeed, I think it is an excellent suggestion. It will allow me to get deeper into the mind of the individual we are looking for. To understand the man, explore the milieu. So I will go to these bookshops, and to other places where these types are found. Despite the fact that the body was found in Shadwell, I do not think that was within his usual orbit. He may have come from the East End originally, we cannot know. But if he made his living as a renter, as the state of his anus suggests, then I believe his occupation will have drawn him closer to the West. Piccadilly. Tottenham Court Road. Hyde Park. And yes, Soho. He must have had friends, associates. These are the places where we will find them.'

'And you mean to go undercover, sir?' Macadam was uneasy.

'Yes.'

'Posing as a sodomite?' wondered Inchball.

'I wouldn't put it quite like that. My objective will be to draw as little attention to myself as possible. So I will not be posing as anything. However, I shall endeavour to blend in. I expect I will play it by ear.'

'Dangerous,' was Inchball's judgement.

'It need not be. I shall simply be asking a few questions. I shall have to think of a plausible cover story, of course.'

'Very dangerous.'

'What are you worried about, Inchball?'

'For one thing, that we might find you with your throat slit and your arse full of spunk.'

'I will be careful, of course.'

'It doesn't matter how careful you are. If you go in like this, you've got no protection. Anything could happen to you, sir. With respect and all that.'

'I shall simply be trying to get the lie of the land. I shall not even have with me a photograph of the dead man to show.'

'I am glad to hear that, sir. Because that would be very dangerous.'

'No, I shall stick with my plan to create an artist's rendition of the dead man. Instead of releasing it to the newspapers, I shall use it in my enquiries. I shall speak to one of the police artists – Petter would be the man. I'll have Petter draw a living portrait from the post-mortem photograph. I shall have it framed. My cover story will be that I am looking for a friend...'

'A friend whose name you don't know?' objected Inchball.

'A friend whom I believe gave me a false name.'

'Not much of a friend then?'

'We met at ... Victoria Station. In the public bar.'

'Public bar or public convenience?'

'Public bar. I do not want to appear too overtly deviant. We met while waiting for our respective trains – or so I thought.'

'Yes, good,' said Macadam. 'You should appear rather innocent, sir. Perhaps even naive. You didn't realize that he was there to pick men up. If that could come as a shock to you, sir, that would strike the right note, I think.'

'I shall endeavour. At any rate, we struck up a friendship. He seemed a troubled young man. Reminded me of myself when younger.'

'Really, sir. In what way?'

'He seemed lost. I wanted to help him. But he ran off before I could.'

'How did you get the portrait?' demanded Inchball.

'I – he gave it to me.'

'Indeed. And why would he do that?'

'He seemed to have a premonition that something bad was about to happen to him. He had had this portrait done by a street artist. He wanted someone to remember him as he was now.'

'Why you?'

'I don't know. I can't explain it. It is one of those things that cannot be explained. He was drawn to me for some reason. I asked the same question. But he ran off, without giving an answer.'

'Very, very dangerous,' decided Inchball.

'What name did he give you?' wondered Macadam.

Quinn hesitated. It was a good question. Suddenly he had the answer. 'Daniel.'

'Why Daniel?' asked Macadam.

'I don't know. That was just the name...' Instead of saying *that came to me*, Quinn said, '...he gave me.' It was as if he was already beginning to believe in the details of his lie.

'I don't like it,' said Inchball. 'I don't like it one bit.'

'It's not a bad name,' said Macadam.

'I don't mean the bleeding name. I mean the whole thing. I don't hold with all this subterfuge and pretence. We should go in as who we are. Straight up. Coppers. Making enquiries about a

79

dead renter. Round them all up and throw them in the cells, if necessary. If they don't like it, tough. One of them will squeal eventually.'

'That is one approach,' said Quinn. 'And I do not rule it out entirely. However, before we resort to such measures, I feel it would be useful for me to familiarize myself with the world of our victim.'

'What do you want *us* to do, sir?' asked Macadam. 'Stay on your back?'

'Steady!' said Inchball.

'No. We simply do not have the resources for all three of us to be engaged in the same operation. Finish reviewing the files to see if our victim shows up as having any form. Then I want you to talk to tobacconists. Which ones stock opium-soaked Egyptian cigarettes? Who are their customers? Do they recognize the cigarette case? Also, try silversmiths and jewellers. It must have come from somewhere. And someone must have made that inscription.'

'Perhaps the murderer is skilled in engraving?' suggested Macadam. 'It may seem unlikely, but I myself once took an evening class in metal engraving. It's not that difficult, if you have a reasonable dexterity and are used to working with tools.'

'Blimey!' interjected Inchball. 'Is there anything you haven't taken an evening class in?'

'It became quite a passion of mine, at the time. I thought it would be a good way of earning a few extra bob. Still have the burin at home somewhere.'

'The *what*?' snapped Inchball.

'The burin. It's what you call the tool. The graver. Haven't used it for years. I could bring it in if you'd like to see it?'

Quinn found Macadam's boyish assumption that others would share his enthusiasms touching. He did not have it in him to be discouraging. 'As you wish, Sergeant.'

Inchball evidently felt no such compunction. 'I'll show you what you can do with your bloomin' burin.'

'Macadam's theory is plausible,' cut in Quinn. 'The killer would naturally wish to limit the number of people he involved in his activities. A man may teach himself all manner of skills.'

As he made the observation, Quinn drew himself up self-consciously. He imagined himself at the centre of a crowd of strangers, all of whom had their gaze fixed upon him. The image was a premonition. He would go amongst a group of men whose lives he had often wondered about but never experienced. He would go amongst them to investigate them. And yet – the image seemed to be saying to him – he would find himself the object of their scrutiny.

And somewhere in that crowd of phantoms, one man closed his hand around a cutthroat razor.

Before he left for the evening, Quinn wrestled the telephone from Macadam one more time to make a call.

'Am I speaking to Doctor Bugsby?'

'You are. To whom am I speaking?'

'You are speaking to Detective Inspector Quinn of the Special Crimes Department.'

'Good evening to you, Inspector Quinn. How may I help you?'

'You recently conducted a post-mortem examination of a body found at the London Docks in Shadwell.'

'Ah, yes. The exsanguinated corpse. A very nasty business.'

'May I ask you, did you make any test for opium poisoning?'

'Why would I do that? It was obvious how the victim died. Massive haemorrhaging caused by a deep wound at the neck, which severed the external carotid artery.'

'I was merely wondering whether the victim might have been drugged before he was bound and cut. And whether he was conscious or unconscious when he met his fate?'

'It doesn't make a difference to the cause of death.'

'No. However, it may have made a difference to his sufferings. I have another reason for asking, however. We found a cigarette case, in which there were traces of opium-soaked tobacco. I wonder whether it is possible to tell if the victim may have smoked opium-soaked cigarettes.'

'Impossible to say. All I can say for certain is that I saw no obvious signs of opium poisoning. However, given the extraordinary state of the cadaver, that is perhaps not surprising. And anyhow, the post-mortem changes in cases of opium poisoning are not marked. We might look for some turgidity in the cerebral vessels. But in this case, the almost entire lack of blood in any

vessel would have confounded any such observation. Occasionally we see some subarachnoid
effusion of serum at the base of the brain or
around the spinal cord. There was none. You
should know that there is no direct chemical test
for the presence of opium and the only indirect
test we have is highly unreliable. Certainly, the
amount of the drug absorbed from smoking a
cigarette would be too small to be conclusively
detectable. Neither would it have been enough to
render the victim unconscious, though it may
have altered his perception of the experience.'

'I see. Thank you, Doctor.'

'Was there anything else, Inspector?'

'When I examined the body, I was struck by
the depth of the indentations left by the rope.'

'Yes. He was tightly bound.'

'I wondered if you recovered any material
from those wounds.'

'Material?'

'Fibres, for example, such as might help us to
identify the type of rope used to bind the victim.'

The line crackled emptily. Either the doctor's
answer had been swallowed up by the inter-
ference, or he had said nothing.

'Doctor?'

'That would be useful to you, would it?'

'It may prove to be. One cannot be sure.'

'Very well, I shall go back and look again at
those wounds. I confess that the focus of my
previous examination was on the numerous
atypical features that the corpse exhibited. Perhaps I allowed myself to be distracted by them.'

'If you discover anything, please be so kind as

to send it to the forensics laboratory here at New Scotland Yard.'

'Of course.'

'Doctor, have you ever seen a case like this before? I mean, the blood. The draining of the blood.'

'No. I have not.'

'Do you have any expertise in criminal psychology, doctor?'

'I know enough to say that you are dealing with a madman.'

'My feeling, Doctor, is that one victim will not be enough for him.'

'That is my feeling too, Inspector.' There was another long crackle of static. At the end of it, Quinn heard: '...luck, Inspector.' The line went dead.

A Domestic Interlude

Silas Quinn lived in a four-storey lodging house just off the Brompton Road. It was a respectable house in a pleasant location, close to Hyde Park and Exhibition Road. Quinn saw enough unpleasantness in his professional life; he wanted his home to be somewhere good, clean and wholesome.

On Saturday afternoons, if his duties allowed, he would sometimes visit one or other of the museums. His favourite was the Natural History. In truth, these days his duties rarely did allow. He vaguely had it in his head that it was months since he had last browsed the mineral galleries, or craned his neck at the giant fossils. It was, in fact, years.

From time to time, he wondered if it was strictly the call of duty that kept him away. Or rather, if his willingness to answer that call came from the fact that he simply found his work more absorbing than his leisure. A pastime, after all, is ultimately an empty activity. It lacks the point of a task, and falls far short of the purpose of a mission.

No doubt it is pleasant if one has the company of a friend, particularly a young and pretty friend of the female sex. But Quinn lacked such a resource. His visits to the museum were always solitary. He invariably left there more alone than when he went in, even if he had managed to consume an afternoon, and treated himself to tea and cakes in the tea room. The public scale of the buildings had a desolating effect.

Aware of his tendency to solitude, and wishing to guard against it, Quinn made heroic efforts at the house to forge relations with his fellow lodgers.

What was the point, he said to himself, *of clearing the streets of killers and criminals, if he could not hold down a polite conversation with ordinary, decent people?*

He made sure that those ordinary, decent people knew nothing about the nature of his work. To his fellow lodgers, he was simply Mr

Quinn. He did not know if they speculated about what he did for a living. None of them had ever taken enough interest in him to ask.

It rather amused him that they might imagine him to be a clerk or a shopkeeper, or possibly a commercial traveller, given his irregular hours and occasional absences.

His landlady was a Mrs Ibbott. She had a daughter, Mary, who occupied his thoughts from time to time, in a manner of which he was not all together proud. It was a dangerous situation, very similar to one that had got him into trouble as a young man, about the time of his father's suicide.

Perhaps that was why he had chosen this particular lodging in the first place. Not for its proximity to Exhibition Road, or its generously proportioned rooms, but because it reminded him of the most humiliating and miserable time of his life. It was the emotional equivalent of a dog returning to its vomit.

Of course, Mrs Ibbott and her daughter knew nothing of the episode in question, and he was determined that they never would. Was he taking a risk in living under their roof, or was he proving to himself, daily, that all that was in the past?

He opened the door to a familiar homely smell. The walls had soaked up the vapours of count-less meaty reductions. So that now the aroma of food was permanent. For once, he was back in time for dinner. Usually, the lingering ghost of it was all that was left to him.

The hinges creaked – as they did every night –

as he closed the door. Mrs Ibbott herself peeped out from the kitchen to see who it was. 'Mr Quinn! I wondered if it was you.'

'Good evening, Mrs Ibbott.' Quinn defensively clutched the furled newspaper he had bought from a vendor on the way home, as if he were intending to beat his landlady away with it. He held his bowler in the other hand, out in front of him like a shield.

'And will you be joining us for dinner?'

'Thank you. I will eat in my room tonight, I think. I have some important work to prepare for.'

He saw the honest disappointment in her face, the measure of her goodness. 'But we see so little of you, Mr Quinn. We're all worried that you are working too hard. Miss Dillard mentioned it only yesterday. She said the strain was evident in your eyes.'

'Miss Dillard said that?' The name provoked a wave of sadness in Quinn. He relaxed his grip on the newspaper. Now the wrong side of forty, and by some margin, Miss Dillard had once supported herself by working as a children's governess. But that was many years ago. These days she was entirely reliant on the small income left to her upon the death of her parents. It barely covered the rent for her room, the smallest in Mrs Ibbott's house.

As the years slipped away from her, and her hopes with them, Miss Dillard had fortified herself against disappointment by occasional recourse to spirituous liquor, her favoured tipple being gin. Her private income could not meet the combined expense of both alcohol and food. Being human, she naturally prioritized the former. Some months, if she ate at all, it was entirely due to the charity of Mrs Ibbott. From time to time, she drank herself into a tearful, stinking state, from which she was rescued by the appearance of her three married sisters (all younger than her) who would cram themselves into her tiny room for several days, nursing her back to health.

There had once been a suitor, or so the gossip went. The affair itself had been conducted so discreetly that it was practically invisible. The gentleman had been one of the other lodgers. A Mr Newlove, appropriately enough. In fact, Quinn rather believed that it was his name more than anything that poor Miss Dillard had fallen for. But it was not to be. One day, Mr Newlove disappeared, taking himself out of her life without a word of explanation.

That had precipitated the first of her alcoholic crises.

After she had recovered, she began to look at Quinn with something approaching sympathy. He was terribly afraid that she saw in him a kindred spirit; even more afraid that she might be looking to him as a replacement for Mr Newlove.

He found the possibility terrified him more than the prospect of confronting any murderer.

He also found that he had never quite believed in Mr Newlove, his name least of all. He had known from the outset that it would end badly. If people would only refrain from trying to forge these hopeless bonds of affection, they would spare themselves a deal of pain.

But tonight, somehow, he found himself strangely touched by Miss Dillard's concern. *How nice of her to notice*, he thought. He also told himself that the period in which she had entertained romantic hopes on his account had long since passed. By now she must have realized that there was no reciprocal interest.

'On second thoughts, Mrs Ibbott, I think I will come down to the dining room. It will do me good to have some company this evening.'

Quinn heard a voice in his head, Inchball's: *Dangerous.*

'Miss Dillard *will* be pleased.'

Very dangerous.

'I wonder if you could have Betsy bring some hot water up to my room. I would like to shave before dinner.'

'Of course, Mr Quinn. She'll bring it right away.'

It was a high, narrow house, lives piled up one on top of the other. Quinn's room was on the first storey. On the stairs, he passed Mr Timberley, one of the two young gentlemen who shared the other room on his landing. Both were employed in some capacity or other at the Natural History Museum, but they were far from being the studious scientific types that Quinn might have imagined. They were, in fact, a pair of droll wags, who took pleasure in baiting the other lodgers. Quinn himself had more than once been on the receiving end of their wit. But what irritated him more than anything about them was their habit of conversing with each other in Latin in front of everyone else.

They were just a couple of overgrown schoolboys, Quinn had decided.

He noticed that tonight, uncharacteristically, Mr Timberley's eyes were red and moist.

Timberley brushed past Quinn without returning his greeting. He bounded down the stairs and dashed out of the house, slamming the front door.

Quinn closed the door to his room and looked around as if he was not sure what to expect. *Is this really where I live?*

The recent rain had abated and the early evening sun now streamed in through the large bay window, silhouetting the dark furniture.

I suppose I have to live somewhere. And here is as good a place as any.

The thought went some way to reconciling him to the room, which he had never fully succeeded in making his own. His efforts in that direction – purchasing prints to be framed and mounted on the wall, selecting books to fill the shelves, browsing the markets for knick-knacks – he had never found entirely convincing.

The room was comfortable enough. It met his needs.

Quinn sat in the armchair and turned the pages of his newspaper. It did not seem as though the press had got hold of the story yet, which was just as well.

An article on one of the inside pages caught his eye:

It was announced today that the flamboyant Hungarian aristocrat and distinguished amateur ethnologist, Count Lázár Erdélyi, whose arrival in London was noted by this correspondent last week, is to deliver a lecture this evening at the Royal Ethnological Society. The talk is to promote the publication of the Count's latest book, entitled Killing the Dead: The Folk Beliefs and Rituals of Transylvania. *Copies of the book will be available for purchase at the Royal Ethnological Society. Count Erdélyi, whose name means 'Transylvanian' in Hungarian, is recognized as an expert on that class of super-natural creatures which inspired the author Bram Stoker to pen his gothic romance,* Dracula. *When questioned as to the existence of vampires, the Count had this to say: 'I have spoken to many people who claim to have seen such creatures. I have recorded their accounts. I have been present when the hearts of those believed to be vampires were excised and burnt. I have studied and analysed the variations and similarities of these cases. Certainly, belief in their existence is extremely powerful. It is as if we need them to exist.' Pressed further on the matter, the Count revealed that he has settled the question once and for all in his book, which he would urge anyone interested in knowing the answer to purchase.*

There was a knock at the door. The maid, Betsy, came in with the hot water.

'Thank you, Betsy. On the table is fine.'

Betsy stood with her hands on her hips, regarding Quinn with a narrow, sceptical gaze. 'What are you up to?' she demanded.

'What am I up to?'

'That's what I said.'

Quinn had an idea that he knew what this was about. 'I ... simply thought that I would take dinner in the dining room.'

'I've got only one word to say to you. Be careful.'

'I don't know what you mean. And that's two words.'

'Miss Dillard. That's what I mean. I hope you're not intending to play fast and loose with her affections.'

'Betsy!'

'She feels things deeply, does Miss Dillard.'

'I know that. I mean, I imagine you are right.'

'So, you should not get her hopes up in this way...'

'Get her hopes up!'

'By encouraging her like this. Unless you're serious?'

'Serious? No! I mean, I'm not encouraging her. I simply said that I would join the others for dinner.'

Betsy shook her head, unconvinced.

'What do you mean to say? That I am no longer allowed to eat my dinner in the dining room?'

'I'm not saying that, no. You're allowed to eat your dinner where you like. Of course you are. But the thing is, you always eats your dinner in your room, if you eats it anywhere. But tonight, you're going to eat it in the dining room. Funny that, ain't it?'

'Is it?'

'Oh, and it's got nothing to do with Mrs Ibbott saying Miss Dillard had been asking after you?'

'No, I ... well, if you think it's for the best, I'll eat up here, after all.'

'Oh! Men! Give me strength!'

'What?'

'That would just break her heart, that would! After Mrs Ibbott has told her that you're going to be dining with the rest of them.'

'Mrs Ibbott did what?'

'Mrs Ibbott is very excited about it all. She's helping her fix her hair. I don't know what you said to her.'

'I didn't say anything.'

'You must have said something.'

'Only that I would join the others for dinner.' Quinn felt the enormity of the situation crash down upon him. 'No, this is dreadful. Quite dreadful. I can't do it. I won't do it. I shall eat out. You must make my excuses to Mrs Ibbott.'

'It's not Mrs Ibbott you should worry about.'

'She will explain it to Miss Dillard. Something has come up. I have to go out.' Quinn glanced down at the newspaper hanging limply in his hand. 'I have to attend an important lecture. It is to do with a case.'

'A case?'

'My work, I mean. You will make my excuses, please.'

'Well, I have never heard of anything so *cowardly*!'

'Cowardly?'

'Yes! Cowardly. You're running away. You haven't got the courage to face Miss Dillard and explain yourself.'

'I ... think it would be better coming from Mrs Ibbott.'

'Cowardly!'

'That's unfair, Betsy.'

'What are you afraid of, Mr Quinn? What *are* you running away from?'

'This situation is not of my making.'

'Could it be, after all, that you're running away from your feelings? The feelings you do in fact harbour for Miss Dillard?'

'Betsy, I don't know where you got that idea from. Nothing could be further from the truth.'

'Why do you say that? How do you know?'

'How do I know? It's my feelings we are talking about, I think.'

'You would be the last to know.'

'Is that really so?'

'Yes. You men are hopeless.'

'But Miss Dillard!' protested Quinn.

'What's wrong with Miss Dillard?'

'I think I am a little younger than her, am I not?'

'She has not borne the years well, I'll grant you, but that is because she has had a lot to contend with.'

'I really *must* attend this lecture.'

'She is a person, all the same. A person with feelings.'

'It can't be helped. I ... I ... I'm not hungry any more!' Quinn cried, as if he believed this would

94

put the matter beyond dispute.

At last, with much shaking of the head, and muttering of the word *cowardly*, Betsy left him to his shaving.

Killing the Dead

Quinn left the house in such a hurry that he failed to make a note of any of the details of the lecture, such as the address or the starting time. However, he had a memory of seeing a plaque for the Royal Ethnological Society during his strolls along Exhibition Road. It had piqued his curiosity, for some reason.

The evening was bright, the rain in abatement: spring flexing its muscles prior to taking hold. And so he went out without his Ulster. If he was unable to find the place, it wouldn't be too much of a hardship to wander the streets until it was safe to go back to the house.

However, Quinn's topographical instincts didn't let him down. Almost without conscious thought, he found himself standing in front of the polished plaque he had remembered. The Society's headquarters were a rather modest building of red brick and stone, tucked between two grander institutes.

The entrance hall had a dusty museum smell. Tribal artefacts hung on the walls: shields made of stretched animal hides, spears, ritual masks and totems. A glass-fronted cabinet displayed some rather dull-looking fragments of pottery.

A small crowd was gathering. Quinn glanced slyly at their faces. It was not a comfortable experience to get the measure of the company he was keeping: a rather eccentric lot, by all appearances. The men, in general, wore their hair a little longer than was necessary and seemed to favour untidy beards. Instead of Quinn's sober black bowler, which he doffed as he entered, there was a preference for colourfully embroidered oriental headgear, such as fezes and tarbooshes, which they made no move to take off.

Among the women, he noticed a fashion for loosely fitting robes of strong colours. Bosoms were large and amorphous. Men and women alike raised their voices excitedly and gave the impression of being incapable of acting with restraint. Their eyes stared intently.

He had wandered into a gathering of Blavatsky-ites and freethinkers, he concluded.

The cost of admission was threepence, refundable upon purchase of a book. Copies were piled high on a table. *Very well*, thought Quinn. But he would wait to see what the Count had to say for himself before splashing out on one.

Inside the lecture room, Quinn was relieved to see that the audience already seated appeared distinctly more respectable. Predominately male, perhaps reflecting the Society's membership, they waited quietly for the beginning of the lecture.

And they had removed their hats, Quinn was gratified to see. Mostly homburgs, he noticed, which they rested on their laps, pointing towards the platform expectantly. Quinn had been considering switching to the homburg for a number of years now. He wondered if its preponderance among members of this learned society meant that the time had finally come. Or perhaps it signified that he had missed the boat?

Suddenly, all thought of hats went from his head. He had caught sight of someone he recognized: the civil service mandarin he had observed leaving Sir Edward's office.

He took a seat a few rows back, just to the side, enabling him to keep the man in view, without being seen himself.

It was not inconceivable that such a person, who was no doubt Oxford-educated, should be a member of the Royal Ethnological Society. *Knowledge is power*, Quinn reminded himself. Ethnology categorized the primitive peoples of the world and therefore subjugated them. The *subject* of study, as the word indicated, is always inferior to the eye, and mind, of the one studying.

Yes, he could see the attraction for such a man.

At the same time, the coincidence nagged at him.

Quinn examined his own motives for coming to the lecture. Leaving aside his wish to avoid Miss Dillard – there were any number of ways he could have achieved that – he realized that he was there because of the case. It was surely not unreasonable to speculate that the person who had committed the crime he was investigating had at least a passing interest in creatures reputed to feed off the blood of others.

An eruption of applause drew Quinn's attention to the stage. The man's name came back to him. *Sir Michael Esslyn.* He would try to remember that.

An elderly gentleman stood at the podium, waiting for silence. With his great white beard and bald head, he had something of the appearance of Charles Darwin in his later years. Quinn doubted this was the Hungarian Count.

No, Count Lázár Erdélyi, author of *Killing the Dead: The Folk Beliefs and Rituals of Transylvania*, was far more likely to be the man in the swallow-tailed evening suit and white gloves seated to one side. As a sign of his noted flamboyance perhaps, he wore a blood-red carnation as a buttonhole. His face presented a strangely symmetrical appearance: hair and moustache were centrally parted and held precisely in place with pomade and wax.

Aged about thirty, Count Erdélyi was younger than Quinn had imagined. His complexion was extremely pale. Quinn suspected this was due to the use of face powder. He had a small, budlike mouth, which he held puckered as if he were in permanent expectation of being kissed.

The applause subsided. The elderly gentleman began by making some announcements that could only have been of interest to members of the Society, and possibly not even to them. Once 'the housekeeping' was out of the way, he acknowledged the presence of the guest speaker, whom he described as distinguished. Count Erdélyi received the compliment ironically by contracting the pucker of his lips even further.

The sounds of appreciation as the Count took the podium were extraordinarily warm. Possibly it was the audience's excitement at the subject he was about to address. But it was also true to say that Count Erdélyi cut a charismatic figure, especially next to the old gentleman who had introduced him. There was unmistakably something sharp and compelling about his presence. He possessed the space he occupied more intensely than other men. Whether you would describe his person as attractive or not is difficult to say. Nevertheless, you had the impression that here was a man who invariably got his way through the force of his personality.

It was a shock when he started speaking: his voice bore not the trace of an accent and was equally without affectation. It was obvious that the Count had been educated in England, and had spent much of his life here. If it wasn't for his name, he could have passed for an Englishman.

He spoke without notes, and with barely any hesitation. 'Thank you. Thank you very much.' Count Erdélyi nodded to the white-bearded gentleman who had now taken his seat. 'When Professor Lewis introduced me, he very generously used the word *distinguished*. I do rather blush to hear myself described thus by a man who genuinely warrants the epithet.' Count Erdélyi nodded in approval at the flurry of applause for the professor. 'I don't doubt there are some of you here who would have chosen a different adjective for *me*! Notorious, perhaps?' He paused again, this time to allow the embarrassed laughter to gather confidence. He added with perfect timing: 'I've heard worse, let me tell you. Notorious, yes. Usually closely followed by the word *charlatan*. I confess, why I'm thought to be a charlatan, I don't quite know. I make no claims. I do not pretend to have mystical powers. I consider myself to be a scientist. An *amateur*, yes.' His impeccable pronunciation of the French word revealed his foreign origin. 'But a scientist, nonetheless. I go to places. I make observations. And I write them up. I have never claimed that vampires, as they are popularly imagined, exist. My book, *Killing the Dead*, is a book about folk beliefs and rituals in a part of the world that I know quite well. It is not a book about supernatural monsters. I dare say that civilized people like you – like me even! – I hope I can claim to be civilized – can put it all down to ignorance and superstition, if we wish. By our standards, there is a lot of ignorance and superstition among the peasants of Roumania. But I put it to you, ladies and gentlemen, that that is rather too easy – too lazy – a position to take. Anyone who has a serious interest in the science of ethnology – and that is the only claim I make for myself – has a duty to try to understand these things. The ignorance may turn out to be our own.'

Quinn settled back. There was something disarming about the Count's style of delivery; he made it all seem perfectly reasonable.

Quinn's glance took in the side of Sir Michael Esslyn's face. His expression was serious, but neutral. It was impossible to tell what he made of it all.

'Have I ever seen a vampire?' continued Count Erdélyi. 'That is the question I am most often asked.'

The Count paused for effect. A man from the audience filled the space with a jocular shout: 'Well, have you?' Quinn thought he recognized the voice. He turned in his seat and saw Mr Timberley. He was interested to note that the young man seemed to have regained his composure.

Count Erdélyi smiled. 'I'll tell you what I have seen. With my own eyes. In the village of Racinari, which is one of two villages in the Rainari commune, in the county of Sibiu in Transylvania. In the churchyard there, I saw a body exhumed – a recently buried body – that was found to have fresh blood around its mouth. Blood that was not there when it was interred.'

There was a gasp from the audience.

'The dead man was a farmer called Petre Petrescu, an inhabitant of Prislop, the other village in Racinari commune. His body was dug up by his son-in-law, Ion Lupescu and a number of his relatives. I saw one of these men hold a stake against the dead man's chest while Ion Lupescu drove it through Petre Petrescu's heart with a mallet. And I heard a sound – I can only describe it as a groan – emerge from the dead man's mouth. So was it a vampire that I saw? Ion Lupescu certainly believed so, as did all the other villagers who went with him to perform this ritual. And that's the point. That's the point of interest to an ethnologist. Not whether I believe it. Or whether you believe it. But the *fact* that they believed it.'

'How do you explain it, if it was not a vampire?' The shout came again from Mr Timberley.

'I do not. I cannot.' After a beat, the Count added: 'I am not required to.'

After the lecture, Count Erdélyi was mobbed by a cluster of admirers. Quinn noticed that Sir Michael Esslyn was among them. He was evidently on friendly terms with the Hungarian, whose hand he shook warmly. Quinn overheard Sir Michael invite Count Erdélyi to join him for dinner at his club. It seemed that a number of other men were to be of the party.

One of them was a slightly corpulent man in a pale lilac suit. His hair was blond and curly. With his bloated face, he had something of the appearance of a baby wearing a monocle. Quinn would have described him as even more overtly 'flamboyant' than Count Erdélyi. His voice was piercing, his complexion flushed with colour, as he declared excitedly: 'Of course, you know what the word *vampire* really means? It's the argot term for the species of renter who likes to blackmail any poor fellow who is unwise enough to fall for his wiles. I myself have been the victim of more than one vampire.'

'Really, Pinky, you are too much!' cried Count Erdélyi indulgently.

Sir Michael Esslyn's tone was more forbidding, almost chillingly so. 'Yes, Pinky. This is not the time or place for such indiscretions.' Quinn sensed the man's demeanour relax a degree. He could not see his face, but he would have said that he was smiling now, though he imagined it to be a curiously cold-blooded smile. 'You must at least wait until we get back to the club. You may be permitted to speak with more licence there, provided you don't do anything to let the side down on the way.'

'Pinky will always let the side down.' The comment was made wearily by a man about forty years of age. Quinn had the vague, unnerving sense that he had seen the man before, though he could not say where. Something about the man reminded Quinn of his father, though it was certainly not any physical resemblance. No, for some reason, his mind was insisting on a hidden association that he could not fathom.

The man was still handsome; possibly he had once been thought strikingly so. Now, however, there was something undeniably flawed about his face.

He possessed a full head of dark brown hair. He kept the fringe long and appeared to be in constant battle with it, flicking the troublesome lock out of his eyes repeatedly. Aside from this slight preoccupation with his hair, the man appeared the most robustly masculine of the group.

Even Sir Michael had a certain epicene quality about him, although the effect in him was of a being devoid of sex, or of any sexual interest at all. The mandarin seemed to have placed himself outside and above all such sordid considerations.

'Mr Quinn!'

Quinn turned sharply at his name. 'Ah, Mr Timberley. I thought I spotted you earlier. Indeed, I could hardly have missed you. You seemed to take a lively interest in the subject.'

'Oh, I only came out of boredom. I thought it might be amusing. What about you? Why are you here? I would not have taken you for someone who's interested in this sort of thing.'

The question caught Quinn off his guard. 'Oh, I ... don't know. I saw a notice about it, and came on a whim.'

'Running away from Miss Dillard?'

'I'm sure I don't know what you mean.'

'She's rather set her cap at you, I'm afraid, Mr Quinn. That's what everyone's saying, anyhow.'

'Everyone is saying that?'

'I'm afraid so.'

'I see. And is Mr Appleby not with you?'

'Why should he be?'

'I meant only that you are friends.'

'We're not inseparable, you know. We simply work together and share a room, on grounds of domestic economy. Which, before you say it, *is* a tautology, I know. I'm well aware that the word economy is derived from the Greek *oikos*. Which means the same as the Latin word *domus*. That is to say, house. At any rate, I am not Mr Appleby's keeper.'

The raw pink that Quinn had noticed in Timberley's eyes earlier had faded a little. He had recovered his customary liveliness, though there was a spike to it that was noticeably more brittle than usual. 'I trust there has not been any irreparable rift between you two gentlemen?'

104

'Why do you say that?'

'Only that you seemed upset when I saw you earlier.'

'How very observant of you, Mr Quinn. Yes, I was upset. I'd had some bad news. But it was nothing to do with Appleby.'

'I'm sorry to hear about your bad news.'

'Thank you. I mustn't feel sorry for myself, whatever happens. So I would appreciate it if you would say nothing of this to anyone. Least of all to Appleby.'

Quinn nodded with appropriate solemnity.

'I can't tell you what it's about. That wouldn't be fair on you.'

'Of course.'

'It is something I must bear alone.'

'I understand.' Quinn looked away in embarrassment. He saw that Count Erdélyi's group was getting ready to leave.

Timberley followed Quinn's gaze. 'Do you think there's anything in it? Beings who live on after death by drinking the blood of others? Is that possible, do you think?'

'You're the scientist, Mr Timberley.'

'I suppose so. In which case, I would have to say that it is all poppycock.'

'But?'

'But I am not *just* a scientist, am I? Any more than you are *just* a policeman.'

Quinn was too amazed to deny it. 'How did you know I'm a policeman?'

'Oh, everyone knows you're a policeman, Mr Quinn. It is rather obvious, you know.'

'I had no idea. No one had ever asked me.'

'Because there isn't really a need to. Shall we go back to the house now? It should be safe, I think. Miss Dillard will be back in her room, drowning her sorrows in private.'

'I do wish you hadn't said that. It doesn't make me feel any better.'

On the way out, Quinn stopped at the table of books. Timberley assumed a sardonic expression, as if he would think Quinn a fool if he bought a copy. Nevertheless, Quinn handed in his admission ticket and the price of the book minus threepence. 'I find him an interesting individual,' he explained, as his book was wrapped.

Developments

'An excellent job,' said Quinn, angling the pen and ink sketch so that it caught the light from the dormer window. 'I congratulate you, Mr Petter. You have not only captured his likeness, you have brought him to life.'

Petter gave a half-smirk and avoided Quinn's eye. He was an unlikely-looking artist. His clothes were a little shabby, but otherwise respectable; sober, even. He looked more like a clerk in a booking office than any kind of Bohemian type. It was perhaps just as well given the environment in which he worked. It seemed he kept the artistic side of his nature locked away and under close guard.

If Petter had any awareness of his own talent, he never betrayed it. He held himself slightly bent over, with his face perpetually averted, and often spoke in a mumble that Quinn had to strain to catch. In his response to Quinn's compliment, it was possible that the word 'pleasure' featured.

If only he had more confidence, Quinn thought, he might have been an artist of some note.

'A very handsome subject.'

Quinn looked up in surprise. It was rare that Petter was able to express himself so distinctly. He even flashed a tentative glance towards Quinn, before sweeping it away almost immediately.

'I am very glad, Mr Petter, that I chose you to do the portrait.' Quinn gave an encouraging smile. 'You've done him justice.'

A further surprise: 'Who was he?'

'We don't know. That's why we need your help. It is my hope that this portrait will help us discover his identity.'

'It makes a change from my usual work.' Petter's hand moved in an involuntary mime of drawing. Quinn's meagre encouragements were producing remarkable results. 'Sketching suspects based on witness statements. Makes a change to have some proper reference in front of me. The photographs, I mean.'

'Yes.'

'Even if he is dead in them. Not quite the same. But ... I left out the wound. As you requested.'

'Yes, that would have rather spoilt the effect, I think.'

The artist reverted to barely audible mumbling for his next comment.

'What was that?' Quinn thought he had heard something that had set his heart thumping.

'I said I think I recognize him.'

'Are you sure?'

'I've seen him around. I don't know him. But I've seen him somewhere. A physiog like that. You remember it. Very pretty face, for a man. Even in the pictures of him dead, you can tell that. It's the bone structure. You have to look past the flesh to see the bone structure beneath.'

'Where?'

Petter touched his own face at the cheekbones.

'No. Where have you seen him?'

'Oh.' Petter's answer was incomprehensible.

'Again, please. More slowly. Louder, if you don't mind. My hearing is not what it should be.'

'I said I think it was at the British Museum. Sometimes I go to the British Museum. The Greek and Roman galleries. To sketch the statues. You get a lot of young men in there, Inspector.' Petter turned his face more sharply than ever from Quinn, but at the same time endeavoured to keep his eyes on him. 'But I remember this one. He used to go there quite a lot, you see. If I'm not mistaken.'

'Did you ever see him there in anyone's company?'

'Oh, yes! He was always with some friend or other. That is to say, he always left with someone.'

Quinn had a sudden insight into what Petter really kept locked away inside him. And what it was that made it hard for him to look policemen in the eye. 'And you never ... *you* never left with him yourself?'

Petter's reply was a smothered blather of mumbles.

'Mr Petter. I'm not quite clear. Did you ever leave with him?'

'No!' The force of Petter's denial seemed to startle even him. He took a moment to regain his composure, before bowing himself into an ever sharper stoop. In which posture, with his face resolutely turned away from Quinn, he left.

'Well, well,' said Inchball from his desk.

'What do you make of that?' asked Quinn.

'An interesting development.'

'A breakthrough?'

'Not quite, with respect and all that, sir. Hardly a breakthrough. It merely confirms what we already thought. That Sonny Jim was a renter. We can now include the British Museum among the places where he used to tout for business.'

'Yes, it seems that way.'

'Does this information alter your plan in any way, sir?' wondered Macadam. 'This is a definite sighting, after all.'

Quinn's answer was a polite command. 'Sergeant Macadam, would you be so kind as to run after Mr Petter and ask him to return to the department for me?'

Developments. There were always developments.

But the thing was, not to lose sight of the plan.

109

Further conversation with Petter produced little else that was salient to the case, except an indication of the best day and time to visit the Greek and Roman galleries of the British Museum. That is to say, the best day and time for observing gentlemen who went there for a purpose other than admiring classical antiquities.

It wasn't easy getting even this nugget out of him. Sensing the importance that the three policemen placed on his testimony, he clammed up entirely at first. His eyes widened in panic. His mouth – though it quivered occasionally – remained firmly shut. Quinn's assurances only seemed to add to his fear. 'It's all right, Mr Petter. You're not in any trouble. There's no question of any action being taken against you.'

A high-pitched whimper was all that this tack elicited.

Sergeant Inchball gave vent to his exasperation by repeatedly banging the table with his fists. It was not an interview technique particularly well-suited to the timid artist. Quinn sent him away to see if he could procure some tea for their guest.

'He's frustrated,' Quinn explained. 'It's not your fault. It's his temperament. He's prone to it, frustration. We all have our weaknesses, I suppose.' If Quinn meant anything by this, it was not what Petter took him to mean. He realized he had made a mistake when he saw the terror flash in the young man's eyes. 'Take me,' he added quickly. 'I have weaknesses too. Oh, yes. What I could tell you about my weaknesses!'

'What are they?'

Quinn looked over to Macadam, who shook his head warningly. The sergeant was probably right. To confess to an unfortunate habit of killing suspects would probably not help the situation. 'Legion. You wouldn't believe it. Sergeant Inchball's weakness is he's too easily frustrated. Sergeant Macadam? Well, he does like his motor car. It wouldn't be going too far to say he loves it. Harmless. Harmless weakness. Most of them are. Now then, Mr Petter, you like to draw, don't you? Not that that's a weakness. It's a great talent you have there, Mr Petter. Obviously you like to draw; you're an artist. That's your job. But you also do it in your own time. In your leisure time. You like to go to the Greek and Roman galleries of the British Museum to draw the statues. And I expect you're very good at it too. I would very much like to see some of your drawings of ancient sculptures.'

Petter mumbled what Quinn understood to be an offer to bring in examples of his work.

'No, no. That won't be necessary. What I propose is that we go there, you and I, together one day. And you show me how you do it. I like to visit museums myself, so I would very much enjoy it. And if, while we're there, sketching – I might even take a pad and stick of graphite along myself – if you happen to see anyone, any gentleman, whom you think you may previously have witnessed in the company of our unknown friend, I would like you to point him out to me. Discreetly, you understand. A nudge in the right direction. Do you think you could do that?'

The spasm that wracked Petter's head was possibly an agonized nod of assent.

'Now then, when do you think would be the best time to do this?'

'To draw the statues?'

'To draw the statues, yes. But also to see the gentlemen. The most likely time to see the gentlemen. That's what I'm especially interested in, you see. We can draw the statues any time. They don't come and go. They stay put.'

And so it was that just as Inchball was returning with the tea, Petter was finally able to divulge: 'Saturday afternoon. The last hour or two before closing. The galleries are especially popular then.'

'Bugger me,' said Inchball. 'I should go out of the room more often.'

The Lady Draper

After lunch, Quinn took a stroll north to Wardour Street. He preferred to walk rather than take the omnibus or have Macadam drive him there, because it gave him a chance to collect his thoughts. Besides, he needed Macadam to get on with his own enquiries.

His route took him along Whitehall, past the great offices of state: the India Office, Foreign Office, Treasury, Admiralty, and the War Office.

The imposing edifices loomed up around him, solid in their foundations, symbols of the unshakeable Empire. Of an enduring world, ordered and organized.

The day was fine. The pavements were drying out at last. Civil servants, errand boys, nannies pushing perambulators, ladies and gentlemen of leisure, tourists – all ventured forth with optimism and ease. Gone were the days of scurrying head-down between cloudbursts, it seemed.

He had placed the portrait Petter had drawn in a small gilt frame, which he felt weighing down the inside pocket of his jacket. His plan was to start his enquiries at one of the two bookshops Inchball had tipped him off about.

Inchball had spent some time 'in Vice'. That was how he put it, as if *Vice* were a place. If it was, it was a place you never really left. Quinn recognized that his time working 'in Vice' had given Inchball an expertise that would be useful in the case. However, as the episode with Petter had illustrated, it had left him with an unsympathetic approach that was bound to alienate men they needed on their side.

The city grew distinctly more disreputable as he left Trafalgar Square behind him. Crimes that were unimaginable in Whitehall began to seem inevitable in the grimy backstreets through which he now wove.

With its French name – *La librairie des amis de la littérature* – it was little wonder that the bookshop had aroused the suspicion of a man like Inchball.

It was next door to a draper's, into the window

of which Quinn now pretended to gaze in order to observe the comings and goings at the book-shop for a moment or two before entering. He had not given a thought to the nature of the shop he had chosen as a decoy. But now it struck him that it was possibly odd for a man to appear so intently interested in the contents of a draper's window.

Suddenly flustered, he looked beyond the bolts of cloth on display into the shop's interior. He was surprised to discover that he was not the only male to evince an interest in drapery. In fact, the shop's only customers were two men. They were standing very close to one another, so close that they appeared to be touching. They seemed to be engaged in feeling samples of cloth between thumb and forefinger. But some other business was being decided, he felt.

So, thought Quinn, *this is what goes on in drapers' shops.*

Their faces were turned away from him, but it was clear that one of the men was considerably older, and stouter, than the other.

Quinn glanced uncertainly towards the book-shop, torn between implementing his original plan and exploring the potential new lead pre-sented to him. Either of these men, the apparent renter and his likely client, might have been acquainted with the dead man.

He sensed an angry tension between them, despite the fact that their bodies were touching. Occasionally their gesticulations were angular and uncontrolled. It seemed increasingly likely that they were having an argument, albeit one conducted *sotto voce*; that what was being passed from mouth to ear in hot whispers was all recriminations, taunts and ultimatums.

He wanted to see their faces. His entrance, he thought, would precipitate a precautionary glance towards the door from them. It might also bring about their flight. If so, he would talk to the shopkeeper.

Somehow it did not surprise Quinn to discover, in the jangling of the shop door, that one of the two men – the older, stouter one – was the vociferous monocled baby he had seen at Count Erdélyi's lecture. Pinky, he remembered the man had been called by his friends.

As he had anticipated, the men drew apart. Pinky fled the shop entirely. Quinn noticed that he was in tears. His face, which had shown a tendency to colour the previous night, was a lurid pink. *That explains the soubriquet*, thought Quinn.

Pinky's young friend received his departure with a loud peal of laughter. He looked Quinn up and down before leaving at a languid dawdle, his laughter more brazen and loutish than ever.

Quinn found he had the shop to himself. There was a bell-push on the counter top. Its tart ping eventually produced an extraordinarily tall woman, somewhat overdressed for shopkeeping. She had long, glistening locks, which Quinn suspected of being a wig. She viewed Quinn haughtily through a lorgnette, but said nothing.

'Good afternoon. I wonder if you can help me.' Quinn paused, suddenly losing all confidence in the cover story he had concocted. It was

115

too late, however, to come up with anything else. 'I ... this is a little embarrassing ... it may sound strange. I hope you will forgive me, madam.'

The lady rippled her rather heavy brows indulgently.

'I'm looking for a friend. An acquaintance, really. A gentleman I met ... at the British Museum. I was in the Greek and Roman galleries.'

She nodded for him to go on.

'He told me his name was Daniel but ... I'm not sure he was telling the truth.' Quinn smiled affectionately at the memory of a moment that had never happened. 'We rather hit it off. But ... he had to go. He seemed in some distress. He took his leave of me as if ... Well, as if he was taking his leave of his oldest friend. Not of a stranger. For I was, really, a stranger to him. He said that I might look for him here. At your shop.' Quinn ventured a brave smile.

The lady draper contracted her brows quizzically.

'I confess I was curious. I wondered if there really was a draper's shop at this address, or whether it was a fabrication. I began to think I had dreamt the whole encounter. When I happened to find myself in the area and caught sight of your shop, well, I determined to call in and satisfy my curiosity. For some reason, I have not been able to get the thought of that strange young man out of my head.'

The woman nodded, as if this was only to be expected.

'And so, here I am!'

'Daniel, you say?' The voice was remarkably low, in a register more usual for a man than a woman.

Quinn hoped that he kept his surprise to himself. 'That's what he said.'

'I don't know no Daniels.'

'Oh ... I thought as much. We were standing in front of a frieze of lions. And when I asked him for his name, he hesitated. Then he caught sight of the frieze and grinned. "Daniel," he said, just like that. I thought it was a little strange at the time.'

The draper shrugged.

'I'm not surprised he lied to me. I had no right to ask for his name in the first place. But before he ran off, he gave me something.' Quinn produced the portrait.

The draper took it and glanced at it quickly. She then regarded Quinn with a slower, more suspicious gaze through her lorgnette.

'I had the impression that he was in trouble. That he believed that something terrible was about to happen to him. He said that he wanted someone to remember him as he was now. I don't know why he gave it to *me*. It doesn't make any sense, I know.'

'His name isn't Daniel.'

'You *do* know him!'

The draper thrust the portrait away, as if she wanted nothing more to do with it. She turned her head away from Quinn, though she kept her lorgnette pointed in his direction.

'Who are you, mister?'

It was disconcerting to be addressed by a

117

lorgnette. 'I ... my name is Sallis. Quentin Sallis.' It was the false name Quinn always used, an anagram of his own with the addition of the letters TEL. As Quinn's middle name was Terence, which is frequently shortened to Tel, he found the pseudonym both satisfying and memorable. 'I ... just want ... to know ... that he's all right. The young man. I felt I could have done more to help him. He ran off before I had a chance.'

'Why did you want to *help* him?'

'I don't know ... I was...'

The draper turned her head back towards Quinn, so that her eyes were on him again, enlarged by the lenses of the lorgnette.

Quinn looked down at the picture. 'I felt that we could have been friends.' He was surprised at the tug of wistful heartache in his voice. 'I know what you're thinking. If he didn't give me his real name, why should you? But he did tell me to look for him here. I think that he wanted me to find him. Perhaps it was a test. He didn't want to give ... his friendship to me too easily, perhaps. That's the only explanation I can think of.'

'But his *friendship* is something you truly desire?'

'Oh, yes. Truly.'

'Jimmy. His name's Jimmy.'

'Ah, Jimmy. Thank you. You don't happen to know...?'

The draper thrust her lorgnette forward, as if to parry further questioning.

'Where I might find Jimmy? Where he lives?'

118

She shook her head forbiddingly.

'Well, thank you, madam. I'm extremely grateful to you for your help. *Jimmy*. I can't express to you how much it means to me just to know his name. Jimmy...' Quinn returned the portrait to the inside of his jacket. 'You wouldn't know his surname too, would you?'

The draper shook her lorgnette in an agitated flurry.

Quinn bowed. 'I am indebted to you.'

'You could at least buy something! This is a draper's shop, after all. Not an information bureau.'

'Of course. I...' Quinn cast about him hopelessly.

'A gift for Jimmy, for when you renew your friendship.'

'What an excellent idea! Thank you. What do you recommend?'

'Some silk, perhaps?'

'I'm entirely in your hands, madam.'

Now she handled her lorgnette rather as a scientist might a microscope, to observe an interesting specimen trapped in a glass slide. A smile that could only be described as flirtatious skipped across her lips. The low pitch of her voice disturbed Quinn. But that smile terrified him.

He heard the resonating rasp of the pinking shears against the cutting table. The blades swept through a sea of shimmering colour. Quinn felt a pang of longing and loss at the richness and complexity of the fabric's hues.

The lorgnette spun on a chain around the

draper's neck, as if dizzied by the intoxicating vision. 'This'll be perfect,' growled the draper. 'Jimmy'll love you for it.'

La librairie des amis de la littérature

With the length of cloth enclosed in brown paper, as if its colours were too dazzling and rare to be revealed to public view, Quinn left the draper's and ventured next door to the bookshop.

The relief he felt at no longer being subjected to the lorgnette-refracted gaze of the draper gave way to a new confusion.

The interior of the bookshop seemed like any other, apart from the preponderance of yellow-jacketed books on the shelves. At first glance, even a bookshop serving the needs of libertines will appear respectable enough. Reading, after all, is an activity engaged in by the educated classes. And the few, exclusively male, customers he could see browsing the shelves certainly gave every appearance of being gentlemen.

What confused and disturbed Quinn was the fact that he blended in so easily with them. They accepted him as one of their number without demur.

And yet he knew that Inchball would not have sent him to this shop without reason. He sensed the presence of other customers, lurking out of sight, hidden behind the stacks. These would be the depraved monsters his imagination required.

Quinn scanned the spines of the books erratically, his concentration shot. His education at a minor public school had equipped him with a passable proficiency in reading French, though he was less confident in his ability to speak it. He knew the names of a number of French authors. As a boy, he had particularly enjoyed, though in translation, the works of Alexandre Dumas, whose name was the first to jump out at him from the shelves. He pulled down an edition of *Les Trois Mousquetaires*.

He turned the uncut pages distractedly. He had not come here to read Dumas. And yet there was something comforting and wholesome about the stirring tale of adventure, something he could not quite tear himself away from.

The book represented the lost innocence of his boyhood, a time when his father was still a hero to him, when the dream of being a doctor himself had not yet been poisoned. When the notion of love between a man and a woman could still be conceived of as a romantic ideal, rather than the frustrating clash of miscommunicated desires. Or, as Quinn had experienced it, a sickness.

To his mind, the world in which he was planning to immerse himself was the extreme antithesis of the novels of Dumas *père*. The dangers it held were far more threatening to him than any faced by d'Artagnan. This bookshop, stacked with innocuous-looking volumes, was part of that world.

Quinn replaced the Dumas and approached the counter. To his dismay, the bookseller did not rise to his feet. In fact, he steadfastly refused to glance up from his book.

Quinn squeezed the package he was carrying. The crisp crackle of fresh brown paper at last drew the bookseller's attention. A balding middle-aged man with a sour expression that only just fell short of a sneer, he looked at Quinn with obvious disdain. *'Oui?'*

'To be entirely free?' said Quinn.

'Pardonnez-moi?'

'To be entirely free. It's a quotation, I think. It came into my head. But I can't remember where I read it. I was hoping you might be able to help me.'

'I'm sorry, *monsieur*. We only stock French books in the *original*.' He spoke good English, but with a stubborn accent, giving certain words their French pronunciation. 'No English books. No *translations*.'

'Are there perhaps some other books that you have, that you keep in the back room possibly, or under the counter, shall we say? Books that you have not yet put out on display? Or indeed, that you are not intending to put out on display, because their contents are such as cannot be exposed to the common view? Not because there is anything wrong with their contents. But because they are too ... sophisticated for the average reader to understand.'

'Monsieur?'

'If a gentleman were bold enough to reveal to

you an interest in a certain kind of literature ... literature of a highly specialist taste. A refined taste. A particular taste. One might almost say, a peculiar taste. If such a gentleman were to be so bold, I trust you would greet his revelation with discretion and sympathy?'

'*Monsieur?*'

'Do you have any books that deal with the subject of ... the love ... that ... I believe the expression is ... the love that dare not...' Quinn trailed off, not daring to complete the phrase.

The bookseller made no attempt to come to his aid.

From somewhere behind Quinn came a snigger. It had something of the loutish quality that he had detected in the laughter of Pinky's friend. Not all the *amis des littérature* were such gentlemen as all that, it seemed.

Quinn glanced around. All eyes were on him. And they were so far emboldened that they did not shrink from his challenging glare. The young man whom he had seen in Pinky's company in the draper's was leering at him from around the corner of one of the book stacks.

'I have made a terrible mistake,' said Quinn to the bookseller. 'I beg your forgiveness. I was under a misapprehension regarding your premises. A friend of mine had told me that I might find such books here. Jimmy. Perhaps you know him?' Quinn took out the portrait and offered it to the bookseller.

'You are a friend of *Zhimé*'s?'

'Yes.'

'I 'ave never seen you with him.'

'Well, you know Jimmy. He has a lot of friends. One cannot hope to know them all.' Quinn did not hurry to return the portrait to his pocket. Instead, he brandished it rather ostentatiously.

'That is true.' The bookseller closed his book and placed it on the counter. 'You have a ... particular book in your mind, *monsieur*?'

'There was one that Jimmy mentioned. I can't remember the title though. I think it began with D. D-something, P-something, perhaps? I should have written it down.'

'I do not know of that book. But I know the kind of book that *Zhimé* likes. I think that also you will like it.'

The bookseller disappeared into the back room. Quinn gave another glance around the shop. The other customers appeared once again engrossed in their browsings. Pinky's young friend had disappeared.

A moment later, the bookseller returned with a second brown paper package for Quinn. 'Do not open it until you get home. Do not open it in front of your wife, if you have a wife. You will not be disappointed. I recommend it very much to you. It is *Zhimé*'s favourite. It could be the story of his life.'

Quinn hesitated before taking the parcel off the bookseller, as if he was afraid it would burst into flames in his hands. When he finally did accept it, he discovered it was disappointingly cool and neutral to his touch.

Quinn was aware of someone on his heels as he left the bookshop. He spun round on the pavement to see Pinky's companion from earlier. The young man pushed the pale brown bowler back on his head and grinned.

'What do you want from me?' asked Quinn.

'What do you want from *me*?' parroted the young man, weighting the emphasis with a challenge.

'What makes you think I want anything from you?'

'I've seen you looking at me.'

Quinn could think of no answer to that.

The young man took out a silver cigarette case. Quinn's heart began to pound like a steam hammer.

The cigarette case flashed open. A row of fat cigarettes lay in languid readiness. With the waft of tobacco came a sense of temptation and disrepute. The enlarged girth of the cigarettes and the faintly yellow papers suggested that they were Egyptian.

Quinn's companion took out a cigarette and snapped the case shut before whisking it out of sight.

'Where did you get that?' said Quinn.

'What?'

'The cigarette case. I would like to see it. I was looking for just such a case.'

'A friend gave it to me.' The young man spoke with the unlit cigarette bobbing on his lips. The effect was insolent. He made no move to take out the cigarette case and show it to Quinn.

'Was it the gentleman with whom I saw you in the draper's shop? Pinky?'

'You ask a lot of questions, doancha?'

'Perhaps I am interested in you.' Quinn couldn't look at the youth.

The other sensed his discomfiture and laughed. 'I thought you was a friend of Jimmy's?'

'Do you know him?'

'Ain't seen him around for a while.'

'Do you know where he lives?'

'Mebbe I do, mebbe I don't. Who wants to know?'

'My name is...' Quinn hesitated, consciously stopping himself from giving his real name. 'Quentin.'

'Quentin? You don't look like a Quentin.'

Quinn shrugged.

'Well, *Quentin* –' The young man gave the word a sceptical emphasis. He held his cigarette affectedly between his second and third fingers. 'Why are you so interested in finding Jimmy? As if I didn't know.'

'If you already know, then I don't suppose I am obliged to answer your question.'

'I seen all what Jimmy has to offer.' The young man raised his eyebrows. 'You got a light, Quentin?'

Quinn took out a box of England's Glory. His hand shook as he struck up the match and held it to the young man's face. He was shocked by the other's touch, hand enclosing hand to steady it. In fact, the touch was more than shocking; it disturbed him deeply.

He wanted to snatch his hand away, to clench his fist and punch him for his impertinence. And the unflinching challenge in the young man's steady gaze indicated that he knew full well what turmoil Quinn was suffering.

The young man held on to Quinn's hand long after the cigarette was lit. He blew out the match with a swirl of smoke just as it was about to burn Quinn's fingertips. When he finally did release his grip, which was all the more disturbing for its lightness, he twisted his index and middle fingers together. 'Me and Jimmy, we're like that.'

'So you do know where he lives?'

'Jimmy likes to move around. Like you said in there, he has a lot of friends. He likes to visit them all from time to time. He likes to put himself about, you might say.'

'He has no fixed abode?'

'Ooh. Harken to you. No fixed abode. What do you sound like?' The young man's face hardened. 'I'll tell you what you sound like, friend. You sound like a rozzer. Is that what you are? One of them lousy agent provokers?'

'No.'

The young man smoked his cigarette in silence as he considered Quinn's denial. 'What you got there?' he said finally, nodding at the parcels Quinn was holding.

'I bought a book.'

'So I heard. What's in the other one?'

'Some silk.'

The young man snorted.

'What's so funny?'

'My my, what an innocent you are, Quentin. You're so innocent, I really think you must be a copper after all.'

'Why do you say that?'

'Nobody goes in that shop to buy cloth, Quentin.'

'I see.'

'Were you looking for Jimmy in there too?'

Quinn nodded.

'And she sent you next door, did she? Cheeky bitch.'

'Where else should I look for Jimmy?'

'Forget Jimmy. Why don't you and me go somewhere private so we can look at that book of yours together in peace? It might give us some ideas, you know, of what to do with ourselves.'

'What's your name?'

'You can call me Tommy. If you like.'

'How did you come to this life, Tommy? What led you here?'

'Yer what?'

'Listen to me, Tommy. This, what you do, picking up men in the street ... you're putting yourself in grave danger. Mortal danger.'

Tommy gave a careless laugh. 'If it's my soul you're worried about...'

'No. Not your soul. Your soul is no concern of mine.'

'What then? My arse'ole!' Tommy was inordinately delighted with his joke.

'Don't you ever worry? Aren't you ever frightened? There must be some men you meet...'

'I ain't frightened a' nobody. You don't understand where I come from. What I've been through. I seen what it's like in the workhouse. In the Limehouse men's ward. Why should I get bummed by some dirty tramp for nothing when

128

I can get ten bob off a gentleman what's had a bath and smells of cologne?'

'Tommy, listen to me. Jimmy is dead. His throat was slit. Most likely by a gentleman smelling of cologne.'

'No!'

'When did you last see Jimmy?'

'I don't believe you! How do you know? Who are you?'

'You were right. I am a policeman. But, Tommy, listen. I'm not interested in anything you've done. Your crimes. I'm trying to find out who killed Jimmy. I'm going to need your help, Tommy. And the help of boys like you. But more than that, Tommy, I need you to take care. I implore you to be careful. The man you were arguing with in the draper's, Pinky ... Who is he?'

'Pinky wouldn't hurt no one. Pinky wouldn't hurt a fly.'

Quinn was not ready for the speed of Tommy's reaction, though he recognized what fuelled it: rage. He didn't see the fist coming. The fist that whipped up into his nose. In truth, he did not believe it was a heavy punch. But it was perfectly timed and fast. It was enough to knock him off his balance.

As he staggered back he threw out his arms, dropping both his packages.

'That's for wasting my time, you lousy agent provoker!' screamed Tommy, as he snatched up one of the parcels and ran off.

Quinn put a hand to his face and felt a profuse dampness streaming from his nose. When he looked at his hand it was red with blood.

The Cigarette Tin

Macadam was replacing the earpiece of the telephone just as Quinn came into the department. 'Blimey, sir! What happened to you?'

Inchball looked up from the report over which he was labouring, like an overgrown schoolboy at his prep. His eyes widened in alarm.

'A minor injury sustained in the course of my investigations. Nothing to worry about.'

'We can't allow this, sir – with respect and all that. Police inspectors assaulted while going about their duties...'

'I appreciate your concern, Inchball, but I wasn't assaulted. It was an accident. A door swinging open caught me in the face. It's fine. Nothing broken. Just a bloody nose.' Quinn couldn't explain to himself why he chose to lie to his men.

Inchball's next remark provided justification enough: 'Just so long as it warn't one of them queers what done it.'

Quinn cleared his throat. 'How have you two men been getting along? Have you uncovered anything of interest?'

'I have made some progress in the identification of the cigarette case,' said Macadam. 'But

first, sir, may I offer you an arnica tablet?'
Macadam opened a drawer in his desk and took
out a large brown bottle. 'I have found it very
efficacious over the years, sir, in minimizing the
manifest effects of the injuries I have sustained
in the execution of my duty. It was a tip passed
on to me by a pal of mine who used to box.'

'Gawd, what next?' muttered Inchball.

Quinn studied the bottle sceptically. 'It doesn't
really hurt, I tell you.'

'It's not an analgesic, sir. It stops the bruising.'

'Very well,' said Quinn, slipping one of the
small white tablets on to his tongue. A shining
bruise in the centre of his face was the last thing
he wanted. It would only draw attention to him
as he continued his investigations. 'Please continue what you were saying about the cigarette
case.' He made to hand the bottle back to Macadam.

'No, sir. Hang on to it for a day or so. You'll
need to keep taking them every few hours.'

Quinn gave a frown of annoyance, but pocketed the pill bottle all the same. 'Really, Macadam,
you're making too much fuss. Now, the cigarette
case.'

'It's a widely available item manufactured
from electroplated nickel silver by a firm in Bir-
mingham. A relatively cheap product, retailing
for between one shilling and one shilling and
sixpence.' Macadam produced a silver cigarette
case from his jacket. 'I took the liberty of purchasing a sample. I trust you will approve the
expense, sir?'

Quinn took the case and opened it. It was

empty, of course, and the inside of the lid was blank. This was only to be expected, and yet the object felt incomplete somehow.

'Virtually every jeweller and silversmith I visited – and I visited quite a few, let me tell you – either stock it or have stocked it at some time. However, I was unable to trace the source of the actual case in question, sir. No one recognized the inscription. Of course, if the killer did the inscribing himself ... All he'd need is one of these.' Macadam produced a small tool with a mushroom-shaped handle and a fine shaft. 'My burin. I brought it in like you asked me to.'

Inchball rolled his eyes.

Quinn took the burin and examined the finely bevelled tip. He held it over the blank surface of the inside of the cigarette case and mimed the act of engraving. He was enacting Macadam's theory; and if Macadam was right, it was another way of imagining himself inside the mind of the killer. 'Had any of the shops noticed any unusual patterns of purchasing? The same individual ordering a high volume of these cases, for example? There's a possibility he likes to give a similar gift to all the young men he befriends.'

'If you will give me a chance, sir, I was coming to that.' Macadam closed his eyes lightly in an expression of superhuman patience. 'No.'

'No?'

'Nothing unusual along those lines, sir. I'm afraid the cigarette case takes us nowhere.'

Quinn handed the burin back to Macadam. 'And what about the records? Any sign of our victim amongst convicted sexual offenders?'

Macadam shook his head disconsolately. 'It didn't help that the files were in such a parlous state, sir. Very shoddy.'

'Very well. Any better luck with the tobacco, Inchball?'

'According to Sergeant Macadam's chum, the cigarettes have less than one per cent opium in their contents. Which means they are not covered under Schedule One of the 1909 amendment of the Pharmacy Act, sir. That is to say, their open sale is permitted. In other words, we are not obliged to look for a licensed source or an illegal source, sir. Or to put it another way, they could have come from any Tom, Dick or 'Arry.'

'I see. So your investigations have been equally fruitless?'

'I dint say that now, did I, sir? With respect and all that. Thinking back to my time in Vice, I recalled that your opium-soaked cigarette is something of a speciality taste. Your normal healthy smoker prefers a normal healthy cigarette, sir. One that hasn't been tainted by the fiendish Yellow Man's drug. This particular type of cigarette, sir, is favoured particularly, if memory serves me right, by individuals of an aesthetic bent. I seem to recall that that feller Wilde was always puffing away on one. The type of person you or I would call a degenerate deviant, sir, though I believe the scientific term is an invert. Macadam will correct me if I'm wrong.'

Macadam nodded to signal that he acquiesced in Inchball's terminology.

'And so, sir, I decided to begin my enquiries with those tobacconists I knew to be favoured by the brotherhood of the bum.'

'That's not a scientific term, I take it?'

'Correct, sir. It's a term used by the officers in Vice. I knew of one such tobacconist, sir – Featherly's, in the Burlington Arcade. A known haunt of the kind of deviants we are dealing with here, sir.'

'I see. And so you visited this shop – Featherly's?'

'I did.'

'I hope you were tactful in your approach, Inchball. No banging of fists on the counter.'

'I was as good as gold, sir. Like an angel, I was. I discovered that Featherly's do indeed stock a brand of Egyptian cigarettes which, as the label is obliged to indicate, have been infiltrated with opium. The Set brand. I took the liberty of purchasing a tin.' Inchball held up a slim, crudely printed cigarette tin. The design on the lid depicted an Egyptian-style illustration of a human figure with a strange animalistic head. 'I too trust you will sign off the expense form, sir.'

Quinn took the tin and studied the figure in the illustration. The head was that of no animal he recognized. Printed solid black, it had a curved bird-like beak and two long ears that stood up straight and were strangely square at the end. The lettering, in a typeface designed to suggest Egyptian hieroglyphics, announced the brand name, and other particulars: SET. THE EGYPTIAN CIGARETTE COMPANY. CAIRO (EGYPT). IMPORTERS AND MANUFACTURERS OF TURKISH TOBACCO. EXPORTERS OF TOBACCO AND CIGARETTES. EST.

Quinn sprang open the lid, releasing the corrupting waft of tobacco. The fat cigarettes rolled in pale yellow papers were identical to the ones he had seen in Tommy's case. 'What else did you discover?' Quinn knew by Inchball's eager stance that he had something significant to reveal.

'I was able to extract certain disclosures from the tobacconist concerning his clientele, which he was at first reluctant to divulge.'

Quinn winced. He was grateful he hadn't been there to witness the methods Inchball had employed.

'Most of the Set brand cigarettes he sells go to what he describes as passing trade. However, the majority of these customers, I would say, are regulars, many of whom are known to him by name. I managed to persuade him to provide me with a list.' Inchball retrieved his notebook from his desk, thumbing the pages. 'Here, sir.' He handed the notebook to Quinn, open at a long list of names: some Christian names, some surnames; the latter given with a respectful 'Mr' added. Quinn scanned the list and noticed a 'Tommy' but no 'Jimmy'.

'Now it's your turn to go back to the records, Inchball. Cross-check these names against the files. See if any of them come up in connection with previous investigations.'

'It's a safe bet they will, sir.'

'What we are looking for in particular is any history of violent criminality. There is sometimes a progression of violence. The man who

135

kills today may have grievously assaulted in the past. Of course, it's perfectly possible that our man has kept a lid on this aspect of his nature until now, which may explain why it has manifested itself so ferociously and spectacularly.'

Inchball took the notebook back from Quinn and turned the page. 'And then there was this, sir. A list of customers who have placed regular orders for Set brand cigarettes at Featherly's.'

'Let me see that.'

'A mixture of fashionable restaurants, public houses and well-established gentlemen's clubs, sir. All apparently above board.'

Quinn scanned the list. Two names were marked out: one with an asterisk, the other by underlining. 'Why have you indicated these places?'

Inchball took back the notepad. 'Ah, yes. That one, sir – the Criterion – that was known to me from my time in Vice. It was popular with a certain class of men, if you take my meaning, sir. Not to put too fine a point on it – queers.'

'Yes, and the other place? The Panther Club?'

'That's his biggest customer, sir. For Set brand cigarettes, I mean.'

'I see. What is it? Do we know?'

'Some kind of toffs' club, sir.'

'Did you ever hear of it in connection with anything?'

Inchball shook his head. 'No, sir. It's not known to me. However, I have made some enquiries, sir. It's located on Pall Mall. Along with all them other toffs' clubs.'

Quinn nodded his head thoughtfully. 'Well done, Inchball. This is good work.'

'How did you get on, sir?' asked Macadam. 'Apart from sustaining a bloody nose?'

'I was able to make one important discovery. Our victim now has a name. Jimmy.'

'Jimmy?' Inchball was unimpressed.

'Yes.'

'With respect and all that, sir, it ain't much to go on. A surname would be more use to us.'

'It's more than we had before, Inchball. Naturally, I intend to continue my investigations tonight. The night is the natural element of these men. Paradoxical as it may seem, I have a feeling I shall discover more under cover of darkness.'

'Very good, sir,' said Macadam.

'Brown-noser,' was clearly audible from Inchball.

'One other thing,' said Quinn. 'In the course of my investigations today, I made contact with an individual by the name of Tommy –'

'Tommy?'

'Yes, Tommy.'

Inchball rolled his eyes. 'Tommy ... Jimmy ... Who next? Bobby?'

'This individual was of interest to me for a number of reasons. First, he claimed to know Jimmy. He also had in his possession a cigarette case similar to the one found on Jimmy. Not only that, he smokes cigarettes that look remarkably like these ones here. And just now I happened to notice that there is a "Tommy" listed among the names comprising Featherly's passing trade.'

'Why didn't you bring him in, sir?' demanded Inchball.

'One reason was because not all of this information was known to me at the time. But more importantly, I felt that I would get more from him by winning his trust.'

'And did you, sir? Win his trust?' asked Macadam.

Quinn's hand involuntarily flicked up to his nose.

'I'll take it that is a no,' said Inchball in a heavily resigned tone.

'I visited the bookshops you had indicated, Inchball. I discovered that Jimmy was known at the first of these, the French bookshop in Wardour Street. It was outside this shop that I had my encounter with Tommy. Oh, and I bought this there.' Quinn held up the brown paper parcel.

'What is it?'

'A book. Which book precisely, I don't yet know. The bookseller wrapped it in secret and urged me not to open it until I had it home. And even then, not in front of my wife.'

A curl of disgust twisted on to Inchball's mouth as he looked at the package.

'He assured me that it was Jimmy's favourite book. He described it as practically the story of his life.'

'Don't expect me to read it,' said Inchball. 'I wouldn't touch it with a bargepole. That kind of filth is sickening.'

'To be fair, we don't know what kind of filth it is yet, Inchball. Or indeed, if it is any kind of filth at all.' Quinn placed the book on his desk and sat down. He opened a drawer and took out

138

a pair of scissors.

Inchball stood up sharply, cracking his head against the sloping ceiling. After an oath worthy of a man who had spent part of his career investigating prostitutes, pimps and pornographers, he said: 'If it's all the same to you, I'd rather not be in the room when you open that. I'm likely to vomit.'

'Good grief, Inchball. How on earth did you manage to stay in Vice for all those years?' Quinn snipped the tensioned string, which sprang apart with an eager pop. He pulled away the brown paper to reveal a cheaply produced volume in dog-eared paper binding. The mustard yellow cover bore the title of the work, *The Profession of Shame*, together with a subtitle, *Being the confessions of an unrepentant renter*. The author was given as *Anonymous*, and the book was published by the Erotika Biblion Society of London.

Quinn experienced an irrational disappointment at the book's title. He realized that he had been hoping, absurdly, for the solution to the mystery of the letters D.P. on the cigarette case.

Inchball had not yet fulfilled his threat to leave the office. Quinn felt his presence at his shoulder. The sergeant's breathing was laboured. 'I don't want to worry you, but that's not a new copy. Hands other than yours have touched it. Hands that are filthy in ways you cannot imagine.'

Quinn thought back to Tommy's hand on his as he had lit his cigarette. *What would Inchball have said to that?* he wondered.

He gave a small shudder as he opened the book at random:

cock in both his hands and began gently frigging me. His lordship then placed the swollen bulb at the end of my cock into his mouth, continuing the action of pumping the shaft while sucking hard on the tip. He gradually increased the speed of his frigging.

'Oh, my Lord!' I cried. 'I fear that if you continue in this manner you will before long take a mouthful of my discharge.'

No sooner had I spoke the words than I felt the rising surge of intense sensation that preludes ejaculation. I wound my fingers into the young lord's hair and pushed his head further on to my bursting cock. But at the very moment of release, I pulled his head back, so that the hot pearls of my sperm sprayed over his lordship's face.

Quinn found that he was undergoing a disturbing physical reaction: his face flushed with heat; sweat broke out on his forehead and on the palms of his hands. He closed the book hastily, tilting his head up for air.

'See what I mean, sir?'

Quinn nodded.

'You have to be very careful with books of that nature, sir. Contaminate the soul, they do. I've seen fine upstanding bobbies turn into nervous wrecks because of such filthy reading matter. Starts off they're just reading it because they have to. It's their duty. To find out what we're up against. You can't catch a criminal without apprising yourself of the nature of the crime. Fair enough. Before long they become addicted to it.

It's a kind of queer fascination takes them over. Very queer, if you take my meaning, sir. I'm talking about married men too. Married men with children. You're not married, are you, sir?' asked Inchball darkly.

'What's that got to do with anything?'

'I'm just saying, sir. Be careful. If you insist on reading it, do it here, in the department, with at least one of us present – Macadam or myself, or preferably both of us. On no account must you read it on your own, sir.'

'But I thought you refused to stay in the room when it was being read?'

'I have realized that I have a duty of protection towards a fellow officer, sir.'

'I think you're rather overstating the dangers. Besides, I am not convinced the book has any direct relevance to the case. It is not the book I was looking for. We mustn't get sidetracked. As far as I can see, its only usefulness lies in its limited capacity to afford us an insight into the mentality, and to a lesser extent the life and habits, of Jimmy, our victim. What I was looking for was an insight into the mind of the murderer. Of the man who chose to inscribe *To be entirely free* on the inside of a cigarette case he placed in the jacket of a bloodless corpse.'

'Did you have any joy there, sir?'

'Not much, Macadam, I confess. The other bookseller you mentioned, whom I visited after the French bookshop, was able to suggest a number of titles to me all of which involved words beginning D.P. However, the first of these words was invariably "domestic". Let me see if

I can remember. There was *Domestic Peace*. Oh, and I seem to remember *Domestic Problems*. And I think *Domestic Pleasures* came somewhere in between. He also recommended a children's book called *Dumpy Proverbs*. However, none of his suggestions struck me as likely candidates for the textbook of a murderer.'

'Square one, then, sir. As in, back to.'

'It would seem so, Inchball.'

Quinn looked down at the book on his desk. The emotion that he felt was unfamiliar to him. He thought that it was most akin to fear, though there was a strong undercurrent of revulsion mixed in.

'It is a strange world into which we are being drawn. We must pick our way through it with caution, never losing sight of the fact that we are investigating a murder. We may shrink in repugnance from the lives and habits of men like Jimmy. But it is our duty to pursue justice on his behalf. And to serve and protect other men like him who may find themselves endangered by his killer. If it helps, let us think of them as sick – sufferers of a morbid and diseased psychology. Yes, they are sick. But the man who did this –' Here Quinn pointed to the photographs that were still tacked to the wall, showing the gaping wound on Jimmy's neck. 'The man who did this is a monster. We must concentrate our energies on tracking him down. We cannot rest until we have done so.'

Quinn folded the brown paper once again around the book. The air felt lighter and cleaner now that it was out of sight. But he could not get out of his mind what he had read, and the images it had conjured up. Had the contamination Inchball warned him about begun?

The Strange Capital

Quinn closed the front door behind him with tensioned care.

Tonight he had more reason than usual for not wanting to draw the attention of Mrs Ibbott. He was conscious of his throbbing nose. He was confident it wasn't broken, and the arnica tablets Macadam had given him seemed to be keeping the bruising down. But still, the last thing he wanted was the solicitude of his landlady.

God knows where that might lead! thought Quinn.

He pictured her calling out to Miss Dillard to come and see the terrible state of Mr Quinn's nose. Perhaps Mr Timberley and Mr Appleby would come too, and perform an impromptu skit on it.

In all his years of sneaking in, he believed he had only ever been able to suppress the door's shrieking exuberance once. The satisfaction it had afforded was something like that felt by a cricketer playing a perfect stroke.

Tonight he very nearly pulled it off, producing only a quick stab of protest in the air.

Standing motionless in the hallway, a brown

paper parcel clutched to his chest and concealed behind his bowler, he strained to listen to the voices from the dining room. There was no disruption to the flow of conversation. As far as he could tell, he had got away with it.

He could make out Messrs Timberley and Appleby's boisterous, competitive ribbing, as well as the predictably aghast reactions it provoked from the other lodgers: the older men's rumbling basses; the shriller piping of the women. In Miss Dillard's bewildered warble he discerned a pathetic cadence. Without being able to make out her words, he knew that she had somehow contrived to miss the point spectacularly. Mrs Ibbott calmly sought to restore order, her reasoned remonstrations only slightly edged with impatience. All the time, her daughter's flirtatious giggle undermined her efforts.

He took it all in and was thankful he had avoided that particular hour of torment.

Who was the flirtatious giggle for? he wondered. *Appleby or Timberley?*

Never for him, that was for sure. It was inconceivable under any circumstances that she would direct such laughter towards Quinn. The depth of his bitterness at such a reflection shocked him at first, until he had absorbed it and added it to his mounting stock of similar feeling.

He wondered if he had divined the cause of Mr Timberley's emotional disturbance of the previous night. Was there a rivalry between the two friends over Miss Ibbott's affections? And had the matter been decided in Mr Appleby's favour?

As he stood eavesdropping on the people who

shared the house in which he lived, he was taken back to another time, and to another young girl's laughter.

The prickly sweat of remembered shame broke out beneath his clothes. He felt it first on his back. But within seconds he was sure that it covered every square inch of his skin. How could something that happened so long ago still have the power to reduce him to this hot, drenched wretch?

Quinn heard the scrape of a chair against boards. Fearing discovery, he bounded towards the stairs. Now preferring speed over stealth, his steps thundered at his ascent. The door to the dining room – also a creaker – groaned open below him. He had turned the corner at the first landing before he heard his name called out questioningly.

Once inside his room, he stood for a moment with his ear against the door. He thought he heard the dining-room door close once more, a little more disconsolately than it had opened. *Poor Mrs Ibbott*, he thought. He hated to bring disappointment into her life. She deserved better from him. But it could not be helped.

Quinn inhaled decisively through his nostrils and moved away from the door. He dropped the parcel on to his bed, immediately regretting placing it there but feeling that to move it would compromise him even more in the eyes of an imaginary observer, the function performed now as it usually was by Sergeant Inchball.

For a moment undecided, Quinn at last placed his bowler hat on top of the object.

Released from the book's thrall, he threw himself down into his armchair. He tapped his left breast. Petter's portrait of Jimmy was still there in his pocket. From another pocket he produced the tin of Set cigarettes.

He studied the picture of the Egyptian deity distractedly.

Just before leaving the Yard for the evening Quinn had managed to secure an interview with Sir Edward Henry. He had wanted to put in a request for extra men to watch the *Librairie des amis de la littérature.* In order to strengthen his case, he had taken the book, so that Sir Edward would be in no doubt what kind of establishment they were dealing with. He had also taken the cigarettes so that Sir Edward might be reassured that they were making progress.

Sir Edward certainly seemed shaken by the character of the material on sale at the French bookshop. However, he did not find that Quinn had established a strong enough evidential link to warrant the expense of a surveillance operation, not to mention the strain this would place on other manpower requirements. In Sir Edward's words, the whole thing had about it 'the whiff of a wild goose chase'.

And so it was that Quinn came to have in his possession at home the book and the cigarettes.

It was an accident, in other words.

He took out one of the cigarettes, his pulse accelerating at the strange husk-like emptiness of its mass. He held it to his nose and inhaled the aroma, potent and laden with unnerving promise even though unlit.

Quinn placed the cigarette in his mouth and took in a breath of tobacco-flavoured air. He decided there was no reason why he should not light it. Retrieving the box of England's Glory from his pocket, he thought back to the moment he had lit the cigarette for the renter Tommy earlier that day. He experienced the same tremble in his hand when he lit his own cigarette now.

He breathed in the heavy smoke and felt it form a hand that gripped his heart.

The cigarette left him feeling nauseous and over-stimulated. But it was necessary for him to have smoked at least one of the noxious things in private, before he attempted to pass for a habitual smoker of Set cigarettes.

His room appeared stranger than ever to him now. The haze of smoke lay over it like a fine gauze. The objects of his room – the dark wood furniture, the cold ceramic ornaments, sharp-edged picture frames and metallic light fittings – softened as if they were on the verge of melting. He became convinced that if he tried to pick up the jug on his washstand, his hand would pass right through it.

He rose from the armchair, dipping at the knees, testing the solidity of the floor.

At the washstand, he became distracted by the looking-glass. He was interested to see whether the same change had been wrought in his face.

Certainly the face he confronted was as distant and removed from him as the other objects in the room. The bruise on his nose was hardly notice-able, laughably insignificant. He could not put his self-estrangement down to that.

The fact was, he felt that he had aged im-measurably since he had checked his reflection on the way out that morning. But it was not simply a question of ageing. He looked intently into the eyes in the mirror and could not for the life of him fathom what lay behind them.

He retrieved his bowler from the bed and looked again into the mirror. Unnervingly, the effect of the hat was to make him even more un-recognizable to himself.

He smoked a second Set on the open deck of the number nine omnibus, the heady smoke mixing with the dusk as it trailed off behind him. The night was warm and clear. He looked down at Hyde Park and saw a dance of shadows along Rotten Row. Isolated figures came together and separated. Some moved constantly. Others held their ground and drew clots of other shadows around them. Occasionally something sparked in the gloom. The amber tip of a burning cigarette; the glint of a brass button on a military uniform.

The steam-engined omnibus drew him away from these mysteries and bore him towards the blazing lights of Piccadilly.

The darkness thickened above him, pouring into the void of Green Park. At the same time, the street lamps and shop windows dazzled him with their brilliance. He had the sense that the great thoroughfare existed in its own dimension, independently of the rest of the city. He felt that it was taking him not into the centre of London, but deep into the heart of a strange and exotic capital in some unnamed foreign land.

They passed the Ritz Hotel, at its entrance a restless swarm of evening-suited men and expensively dressed women. As they laughed, their teeth flashed in competition with their diamonds. If they were prostitutes, they were the best that money could buy.

Quinn felt a vague and angry heartache and got to his feet. He would smoke the rest of his cigarette on the boarding platform.

He threw the stub out into the night and then jumped after it. He timed his jump badly. His legs shook as he landed and he had to run with flailing arms to regain his balance. The thump at his heart from the shock of physical danger chased away the woozy effect of the drug-infused smoke.

The illuminated signs of Piccadilly Circus served as a reminder of why he was there. Jimmy had been found beneath a similar sign, though in a place so different it felt like another country, another world. The invented brand names – BOVRIL, PROSET – seemed like coded words, clues that might hold the secret of Jimmy's death, if only he could unravel the puzzle of their meaning.

His hand pushed forward on the revolving doors at the entrance to the Criterion, the momentum drawing him inside.

He was quickly immersed in the din of countless overlapping conversations echoing beneath the glittering tiles of the coved ceiling. His entrance caused hardly a ripple. No doubt there were glances cast in his direction, but he had the sense that he was quickly discounted. And the sense too that, for all their braying gaiety, those gathered here were engaged in something urgent, something which would brook no interruption.

All the brilliance of Piccadilly was refracted into the interior of the Criterion. Here was the heart of that strange capital he had imagined earlier. The vaguely oriental styling of the decor, with its pillared walls and arched recesses, suggested somewhere in North Africa, a place he had never visited, except in his imagination.

The Long Bar itself was crowded, exclusively with men. Some wore lustrous top hats, others brushed bowlers. Some were bearded or moustachioed, others clean-shaven. Some were middle-aged or even old; others were young – barely more than youths. Some swaggered and preened, others hung back warily.

Yet all had some unnameable quality, a secret kinship discernible in the subtle ways they interacted. A hand held too long on another's arm. One body pressed too intimately on to the next. A smutty tone in the laughter provoked by a whispered indelicacy.

At the sight of one man lighting his companion's cigarette, his hand held steady in the other man's tender grip, Quinn spun on his heels.

No, it was too much. He couldn't go through with it. Even though its yellowish paper suggested the cigarette was a Set.

The glint in their eyes betrayed a fierce hunger that sickened him. He needed fresh air again.

As he was ineluctably turned out by the revolving doors, another party burst boisterously in.

A Party in the Criterion

'To marriage!' Sir Michael Esslyn raised his glass of Dagonet champagne towards a chandelier. The clear, creamy liquid glittered as if a thousand tiny diamonds were suspended in it. Esslyn's crystal-edged voice cut through the din of the Criterion. A startled lull descended, brought to an end by a wave of cynical hilarity.

'Good heavens, Esslyn.' Pinky's monocle flew from its precarious resting place in his eye socket. 'What an extraordinary toast to propose! What on earth can *you* have to say in favour of marriage?'

'It is true that I have never married myself, Pinky. However, that is not due to any principled objection to the institution itself. It is rather the result of a want of opportunity. I blame the service. In fact, you may say that I *have* been married – to my career. I fear that any actual bodily wife would have had more than sufficient grounds for a complaint of neglect. Also, I cannot help thinking that my devotion to my work would have provoked such a rage of jealousy in said putative wife as to make a *crime passionelle* inevitable. She would have assumed the worst – a mistress. In which case, I am sure, I would be dead by now. But the pleasures and consolations incumbent in a loving companion-ship with a member of the fairer sex are not to be lightly brushed aside. There are times, I assure you, when I have deeply regretted their absence from my life. It is too late for me, I fear, but not for Marjoribanks.'

'What's this?' cried Count Lázár Erdélyi, his eyes widening with sincere delight as he picked up Sir Michael's hint.

'Yes, it's true,' said the fourth member of their party, Lord Tobias Marjoribanks. A thin, barely present smile tensed on his mouth. He tossed his head, shaking the loose lock of hair at the front out of his eyes, but only for a moment. 'Jane and I are engaged.'

'Congratulations, Toby!' cried Erdélyi warmly. 'Wonderful news!' He held out his hand to shake Lord Marjoribanks'.

'Is it?' said Pinky.

'Yes, it is,' said Marjoribanks. 'I'm not like you, Pinky. I need stability in my life.'

'Nonsense, my boy! You're an artist!'

'Do you know how long it is since I picked up a paintbrush?'

'Now now,' said Sir Michael. 'Let's not spoil the celebration with all this self-pity.'

'Oh, I'm not sorry for myself. I was glad when I stopped. It liberated me. I could put my ener-gies into other things.'

'Such as your love for Jane,' said Lázár.

'Let us drink to that!' said Sir Michael. 'To love!'

'Oh, well, if you insist,' said Pinky, rather churlishly. He took a slow, thoughtful sip of his champagne. 'Of course I'm pleased for you. Her father is so tremendously rich.'

'I say, Pinky, there's no need for that.' The objection was voiced by Count Erdélyi. 'Why can't you just be happy for Toby?'

'On the contrary, I'm very happy for him. His financial security is assured for the rest of his life.'

'I would be grateful to you if you would keep such unworthy thoughts to yourself, especially as I have invited Jane and her father to dine with me here tonight.'

'Here?'

'Yes.'

Pinky's monocle dislodged itself again as he made a show of taking in his surroundings. 'Well, that's very bold of you, I must say.'

'I don't know what you mean. I know you use this place to pick up renters, but the Criterion is a perfectly respectable restaurant.'

'That's true. I've seen cabinet ministers dine here,' said Sir Michael.

As if to disprove Sir Michael, a young man with an unlit yellow-tinged cigarette in his mouth came over to accost Pinky.

Pinky refused to look at him. 'Go away. I won't talk to you here. I'm with my friends.'

The young man let out a peal of laughter. 'I thought *I* was your friend,' he complained.

'You are nothing but a vampire. I've given you all the money you're going to get out of me, so you may as well be gone. Leave us alone.'

Tommy made a moue of petulance. 'I only came over for a light.'

'You have no right to expect even that from me.'

Count Erdélyi picked up a matchbox from the bar. 'Here.'

Tommy leaned forward for his cigarette to be lit.

'No. You may take it and find somewhere else to smoke. Now you have what you came for, you will be so good as to leave us in peace.'

'You ain't seen the last of me,' said Tommy as he snatched the matches from Count Erdélyi.

Sir Michael followed his progress across the bar, his lips pursed in distaste. 'Is it not possible for you to find an outlet for your appetites among members of your own class?'

'You have certainly managed it, Esslyn. Married to your career, my eye! What keeps you chained to the department year after year is the constant stream of eager junior secretaries passing through. We are not all fortunate enough to have our own supply of compliant young acolytes at our beck and call. Some of us have to take our pleasures where we can. That inevitably requires us to deal with rough trade now and then.'

'You could follow Lázár's example,' suggested Lord Marjoribanks. 'Develop a hobby. Take your mind off ... all that.'

'Chastity does not become me. And I don't really think it sits well on Lázár, if I am perfectly honest. Have you not noticed how pale and nervous he is looking these days? He's worse than the *nosferatu* he spends his time chasing.'

'Please don't use that term,' said Count

154

Erdélyi. 'It's meaningless.'

'At any rate, a little self-control on your part would not go amiss. If you will insist on associating with such low types it can only end in scandal – or worse. Tragedy.'

'Don't be absurd, Esslyn. You know I am incapable of self-control. You might as well ask...' Pinky cast about for a suitably impressive turn of phrase. His hand hovered about him as if to pluck it from the air. Finally it came to him: 'A panther not to kill.'

'There are two problems with your analogy,' objected Lord Marjoribanks. 'First, you are the prey and not the panther. Second, you only said it because we have just now come from the Panther Club. And as you will know from the sorry specimen they keep caged up there, it's perfectly possible to persuade a panther not to kill. All you have to do is ensure that it is well-fed. Then it simply becomes a rather large pussy cat.'

'How horribly pedantic you are, Toby. I'm disappointed in you.'

Lord Marjoribanks sprang away from the bar and headed towards the door. The magnet for his energy was a young woman who had just entered in the company of a middle-aged man. She was wearing a midnight-blue evening gown with a high waist and hobble skirt. The dress was cut from lustrous satin, covered with a translucent drape, which was held in place between her breasts by a large metal brooch of Egyptian design.

A high nervous excitability showed in her

expression – the hint of a tendency towards waywardness. Her face was striking rather than pretty. The boldness of her eye was a challenge; any man who valued convention over adventure was bound to feel unequal to it.

Lord Marjoribanks was evidently not such a man. At the sight of her, his gaze became enlivened; the habitual ennui of his demeanour was shed. Whatever Pinky might say, it was clear that something other than the promise of her father's fortune drew Marjoribanks to Jane Lennox.

He took both her hands in his. 'Darling. You look ravishing. I love the ankh.'

'Dah-ling.' She delivered each syllable on either side of a greeting kiss. 'I love my ankh too. It was a present from Daddy.'

Marjoribanks turned his attention to the man who had come in with his fiancée. 'I didn't know you took an interest in Egyptian symbolism, Lennox.'

'I have no idea what you're talking about.' Harry Lennox spoke with the hint of an Irish brogue that his daughter lacked. He was a short man, and of slight build. His top hat seemed comically large on his head. But there was no doubting his power. He surveyed the room with the steady disdainful gaze of a man who believed he could buy everything and everyone in it several times over.

'Jane's brooch.'

'Oh, that. Jane picked it out. I merely paid for it.' If it sounded like a complaint, it was softened by his accent. But there was good humour in

Lennox's voice, and the smile for his daughter was indulgent. 'It is the father's prerogative,' he added.

Jane Lennox looked around distractedly, fascinated by the strange and undeniably attractive beings around her. 'This is an intriguing place, dah-ling. Quite delightful. Some of these men are practically beautiful.'

'It looks very Turkish,' said Lennox, taking in the golden tiles on the ceiling. 'Like a hareem.' Lennox now considered the clientele crowding the bar. 'Only without the women.'

'You're so funny, Daddy.' Jane Lennox adopted a patronizing, slyly mocking tone towards her father.

'Will Jane be quite safe in here, Marjoribanks?' asked Lennox. 'Some of these men are looking at her in the most peculiar way.'

'Quite safe,' said Marjoribanks. 'I can assure you that we are surrounded by ... gentlemen.' The pause was perfectly timed to raise Harry Lennox's eyebrow, and a giggle from his daughter.

Marjoribanks dipped his head towards a bow, before casting an uneasy glance over to the others at the bar. Sir Michael raised his glass in greeting. 'The bar is rather crowded. I suggest we go through to the restaurant. They should have our table ready for us by now.'

But Lennox had caught the welcoming salute from Sir Michael Esslyn. 'You said you would introduce me to Michael Esslyn, remember? They say he has the ear of the Home Secretary. It is an ear I would very much like to speak into.'

'Please, Daddy, don't talk business tonight!'

The indulgent smile returned to Harry Lennox's lips. 'My dear, if you won't let me talk business then I may as well leave right now!'

Marjoribanks turned his head sharply, suggesting this was an outcome to which he would not have objected. But he bit his tongue as he led his fiancée and her father towards the bar.

The Panther Club

Outside, Quinn lit another cigarette. He cast a half-hearted glance through the glass of the revolving door, surprised to catch sight of the satin-clad back of a woman moving through the press of men.

He looked at the cigarette in his hand. Set cigarettes had led him here. But his nerve had failed him at the last.

Quinn adjusted the position of his bowler on his head. It was as if he believed that setting himself to rights was as simple as straightening his hat. But a deeper shift of alignment had taken place inside him. Something fundamental had fallen out of kilter. As unsettling as this was, there was no doubt that the presence of his hat on his head went some way to reassuring him.

But he could not go back inside. He would direct his attention instead to the other place that Inchball had marked out on his list. On paper, a respectable gentlemen's club: he would surely have nothing to fear there.

There was no sign, nothing to indicate either the street number or the name of the establishment. This seemed to be common practice among the Georgian mansions of Pall Mall. Quinn spent several moments pacing up and down the pavement, calculating numbers from those few buildings that displayed one. The door upon which he finally settled was discreet, compared to the other clubs he had remarked, most of which were graced with grand, neoclassical entrances complete with columns and porter's lodges.

The bell-knob was ornately moulded in the shape of a scarab beetle nestling in a shallow bowl. Quinn gripped the metal insect with his fingertips and pulled it on its wire a few inches towards him. The mechanism tripped a bell somewhere deep within. The bell rang again as the beetle retracted.

The door was a panel of liquid blackness poured into the night. The lights of Pall Mall danced wildly in it as it swung open.

A liveried servant peered out. When he had taken the measure of Quinn, his look of enquiry changed to one of disdain.

'Is this the Panther Club?'

'If you need to ask, the answer can be of no interest to you.'

Quinn produced his warrant badge. 'Detective Inspector Quinn of the Special Crimes Department. Who's in charge here?' He didn't wait for an answer before pushing the door fully open and striding past the doorman.

His actions had a restorative effect on Quinn. Making brusque demands, forcing entry, putting servants' noses out of joint: it felt good to be behaving like a police officer again.

He did not remove his hat. In part, it was a deliberate gesture of defiance, a refusal to be cowed by the marbled opulence and Palladian scale of the grand foyer. His surroundings almost screamed at him to doff his hat, and – while he was at it – touch his forelock. In addition, Quinn was disconcerted by a pungent animal smell, so tangible and abrupt that it almost pounced on him the moment he was inside. There could be no thought of any act of deference in the presence of something so brutal.

The source of the smell was immediately apparent. In a gilded cage at the rear of the foyer a large black cat lay sleeping, its head tucked into the curve of its body.

Quinn gave the club servant a look of quizzical disbelief.

'Wait here,' said the doorman. 'I shall fetch Mr Stannard.'

Quinn crossed to the back of the foyer to study the slumbering beast. It seemed placid enough now, but Quinn doubted the flimsy wires of the cage could hold it if it were roused to anger. A sign at the base of the cage read:

Any member entering the cage does so at his own risk. Keys are available at reception.

As if it sensed that it was being observed, the animal lifted its head. Quinn need not have worried: it was evidently rather old, with a

160

sprouting of grey whiskers around the snout, and clearly used to human company. It sniffed the air myopically but failed to look directly at him. Before long, it nestled its head between its front legs and closed its eyes again.

'Hello? May I help you?'

Quinn turned to see a tall, upright man of about forty, dressed in formal evening wear. 'You are?'

'Stannard. I am the major domo. I presume you are the policeman.'

Quinn nodded. 'Detective Inspector Quinn. Special Crimes. What is the cat for?'

'Bertie is our panther.'

'I see. Because you are the Panther Club, you must have a panther?'

'There has always been a panther at the Panther Club. Indeed, we keep it in honour of the club's founders.'

'In what way does it honour them?'

'The Panther Club was established in 1764 by a group of young aristocrats who had been expelled en masse from Boodle's. They were fired for releasing a panther into that club's precincts. I believe one of the club's servants died as a result of the mauling he received. And one of the elderly members died from a heart attack. The Panther Club was founded as a place where such wildness would be welcome, even encouraged. They brought the panther with them, as it had naturally been blackballed from Boodle's.'

Quinn ignored the major domo's joke. 'Were they not punished?'

'They were barred from their club. That was

thought to be punishment enough.'

'These days, the law is rather more severe on those who cause the death of others.'

'Indeed?' The interrogative tone Stannard gave the word suggested that this came as news to him.

'And so, do you get many venturing into the cage?'

'I should say that every member has feasted with Bertie at least once.'

'I see. It is some kind of initiation ceremony?'

'Not at all, Inspector. However, the members do take a rather dim view of any new member who declines the open invitation.'

'He looks rather harmless,' said Quinn, glancing back at the panther.

'She. The current Bertie is female.'

'What do you mean, *current* Bertie?'

'Every panther is traditionally called Bertie. In honour of the original.'

'These traditions are no doubt very quaint,' said Quinn. 'But is this still a place where acts of reckless endangerment are encouraged?'

'As far as we are aware, our members obey the laws of the land when they are outside the confines of the club. Indeed, many of them lead lives of the utmost probity. But a certain atmosphere of licence prevails within the club's walls. These days it is manifested in what we might call Dionysian revels. Our members are fond of the grape.'

'And other intoxicants too, I am led to believe. You are responsible for the procurement of such things?'

'I am in charge of the cellar, if that's what you mean.'

'And what about tobacco purchases?'

'Yes, I oversee that too.'

'So you placed the order with Featherly's for a regular supply of opium-infiltrated cigarettes?'

'We do have a standing order with Featherly's, that's true. Offhand, I cannot recall the details of it.'

'It's an Egyptian brand. Set.' Quinn produced the cigarette tin from his breast pocket.

'Yes, I recognize the brand. It's very popular with our members.'

'I will require a list from you of all the members who favour this brand.'

'I can't do that! Such indiscretion would get me fired.'

'No one need ever know. I too can be discreet.'

'But the simple matter is that practically everyone here smokes them.'

'Very well, then. You will give me a list of all your members.'

'No, no, no. You do not know what you're asking! How can I make you understand? We have high court judges and even members of the government. I am sworn to preserve their anonymity. If it were known ... if their wives knew – even just the very fact that they are members here! There is only one rule at the Panther Club. What goes on within the confines of the Panther Club remains within the confines of the Panther Club. That applies even to the identities of members.'

'I don't see how you can ensure that. They

must see one another.'

'Of course, the members themselves would not reveal one another's identity, if it were known to them. However, our members – and their guests – are masked, and refer to one another by assumed names. Naturally, some of them recognize each other from outside. It is largely a formality...'

'Another of your quaint *traditions*?'

'You could say that. But it serves a useful purpose. There is a symbolic significance to the masks.'

'Mr Stannard, I am investigating an event that took place on the outside. If, as you say, your members behave impeccably when they are not here, then they have nothing to fear.'

'But they are not *my* members! *I* am employed by *them*. I am their servant. I cannot betray their trust.'

It was at this point that Quinn realized the man was afraid. 'I could arrest you. Are you prepared to go to prison for them?'

'If that is necessary ... then so be it.'

'Very well. I understand. In that case, I shall return. With men. To raid the premises.'

The major domo screwed up his face as if he was about to burst into tears. 'No, no. No – please! You mustn't do that.'

'Naturally, I would prefer not to. I hate to be a nuisance. But I *can*, you see. That's the point. Look at it this way, Mr Stannard. I am looking for one man. A vicious killer who has committed an act of such wildness and depravity that even the founders of the Panther Club would have

164

recoiled in horror from it. One man. One very vile and nasty man. The last thing I wish to do is inconvenience everyone here. Believe me, the most likely outcome of your furnishing me with that list is that nothing more will ever be heard of this matter. I will be gone and you will never see me again. Your members will be left alone to live their exemplary lives. I will no doubt discover that there is no connection between the members of the Panther Club and the crime I am investigating. No one need ever know – that is the point. But if you choose *not* give it to me, there will be a raid. Your members will be unmasked, their identities revealed and I will personally see to it that their names are known to every editor in Fleet Street. I can destroy this club and if necessary I will.'

The look of impending tears returned to Stannard's face. In her cage, Bertie started as if disturbed by a bad dream. She lifted her head and gave a querulous growl.

Voices in the Darkness

Quinn stepped out. The panel of liquid blackness slipped back into place behind him. He lifted his face up to the night and sniffed the air, a strangely animal gesture. The stench of Bertie's cage was replaced by the familiar street smells of horse droppings and automobile exhausts.

He felt restored by his success at the Panther Club. The major domo had undertaken to deliver a copy of the list of members to New Scotland Yard the following day.

He lit a Set cigarette and began to retrace his steps to Piccadilly Circus.

But at the sight of the Criterion's revolving doors, all his renewed confidence left him. The snatches of laughter that escaped in the turn of the doors were harsh and braying, as if the crowd assembled was made up of savage, dog-headed deities.

Perhaps Inchball had been right. He should dispense with all the subterfuge and simply show his warrant badge. How quickly the bar would empty then!

He peered in, trying to locate the satin-clad woman he had noticed earlier. He told himself that if he saw her, he would go inside.

'Don't be shy, dearie.'

Quinn turned to see a young man – a youth really, no older than seventeen, probably not even that – grinning rather foolishly at him. The youth was dressed in a flashy, though poorly tailored, suit. A pale grey bowler, or billycock hat, with the brim rolled tight to the sides, was set back on his head. It seemed to be several sizes too small for him.

'What do you mean?' said Quinn, his voice charged with hostility.

'I can see you want to go in. Yer first time, is it?'

'It's not like that.' Quinn bridled to think that this effeminate creature had mistaken him for one of his own type. 'You don't understand.'

'You get all sorts here, you know. You might think that it's not for you, but I know what it's like. Get lonely, don't yer?'

'I don't know what you mean.'

'Got a lady friend, have yer?' The question was delivered with a loathsome sneer.

'That's none of your business.'

'Thought not.'

'As a matter of fact, there is someone.'

'A lady friend?' The incredulity in the youth's voice was positively insulting. 'What's her name?'

'Miss Dillard,' said Quinn, without a moment's hesitation.

'Well, if you've got your Miss Dillard, wha'-cha doing 'ere? Like it both ways, do you? Best of both worlds. My friend tole me about men like you.'

'How dare you!'

'Aw'wigh'! Aw'wigh'! Keep yer hair on. It's jiss the way you was looking in there. Like you really wanted to go in but were afraid to.'

'No, I...' Quinn winced at his own stupidity. He had forgotten the role he was supposed to be playing. 'Yes, you're right. I came here because I'd heard that one could meet fellows, sympathetic fellows.'

'Wha' about your Miss Dillard?'

'There is no Miss Dillard.'

'Thought so.'

'I met a fellow once,' ventured Quinn. He drew too deeply on the cigarette and began to cough.

'Oh, yeah?'

It was a moment before Quinn could speak, his voice high-pitched and out of control. 'He gave me his picture.' Quinn dropped the stub of the Set and ground it into the pavement with his heel.

'That's nice.'

'His name's Jimmy.' The portrait of the unknown youth pulsated in the intermittent brilliance of Piccadilly Circus at night.

'Nice.'

'Do you know him?'

'Jimmy, you say?'

'Yes.'

'Hard to say, ain't it? You sees a lot of people in this game.'

'He ... has ... one ... very distinguishing feature, which you may have heard talked about.'

'Oh yeah, wha's tha'?'

Quinn swallowed. 'He's very well-endowed.

In the genital area.'

'Gentle area?'

'He has a big cock.'

'Oh, why din' you say so. You like that, do yer?'

'No. It's not like that. You misunderstand. We were friends.'

'I know. I know. There's no need to be coy wiv me, mister.'

'Do you know him?' insisted Quinn.

The youth took a step closer to Quinn. 'I know where to find 'im. Come wiv me an I'll take yer to him.'

'Really?'

'I wouldn't lie to yer, mister.' The youth jerked his head encouragingly.

'Where are we going?'

'That's for me to know and you to find out.' The young man turned slowly, keeping Quinn fixed with his gaze for as long as possible. At the last moment, he gave a suggestive hoist of his eyebrows and began to move away with sauntering steps.

Quinn waited for the backward glance with a pounding heart. When it came, it was poised and confident in its power to compel.

He followed at five paces. The youth led him away from the twinkling lights of Piccadilly Circus, back along Piccadilly. His pace was unhurried. Quinn had to slow his step to avoid catching him up.

Eventually they reached the entrance to the Ritz Hotel. He was in amongst the crowds he had looked down upon from the top deck of the

169

omnibus. The glamorous women, he saw now, could only be prostitutes. They cast their mercenary gaze on him, only to quickly dismiss him. Evidently, he passed muster as a renter's client.

In a moment of panic, he wondered if it was the youth's intention to take him into the Ritz and insist on a room. Of all the objections to this scheme that clamoured in his head, the loudest was the question of expense. But no. He was relieved to see the young man continue past the hotel.

Then suddenly, inexplicably, he vanished. One minute, he was there ahead of him, his stroll shimmering beneath the lights of Piccadilly. The next, he was gone.

Quinn drew to a bewildered halt.

'Psst, mister, over 'ere!'

The night fell away to nothing. The young man's voice came from the void.

A flare of orange light as a match was struck. The grinning face briefly revealed. He was holding out a hand to Quinn. 'Take me 'and. Then we won't get separated.'

The match burnt out. The youth vanished again.

'This way!'

Quinn groped towards the impatient hiss. A hand gripped his. A violent yank and he was pulled down from the pavement into the darkness of Green Park at night.

Quinn wrested his hand out of the other's. He heard the youth's footsteps ahead of him, cried out, 'Stop!'

'Shhh! You wanna bring the Ole Bill down on

170

us?' The youth spoke in an urgent whisper. 'I tole yer to hole on to me.'

'It's just that you nearly pulled me over.'

'Would you rather I pulled you off?'

Quinn was all at once surrounded by the sniggers of unseen men.

'Who else is here?'

'You don't arsk questions like that, mister.' It was the youth's voice. 'Let us get away from the thoroughfare so we can be about our business. 'Ere, put yer hand on me shoulder. I'm right in front of yer.'

Quinn's hand came down on something solid. 'That's it.'

The youth set off again. By now, Quinn's eyes were getting used to the darkness. He could see the moving silhouette in front of him. 'Are you taking me to Jimmy, or not?'

The youth stopped. There was some business in the darkness, as if he were pushing aside a curtain. All that was revealed was a deeper darkness. 'In 'ere. You first.'

Quinn stepped forward. The darkness closed around him. 'Where's Jimmy?'

'You don' need Jimmy. You got me now. I'll be your Jimmy now.'

Quinn felt the breath of another close to his face. Then a hand on his cheek. Another hand rummaging below. His own hands flew out to ward off the contact. The same hands, tensed into fists, lashed out wildly. One blow met bony resistance. There was a cry of surprise and pain.

'Whacha do that for?'

'Do you even know who Jimmy is, you bloody

171

pervert?'

'I ain't no more a pervert'n you, mister. Why d'ya come wiv me if that ain't what you wanted?'

A different voice came out of the darkness, somewhere to Quinn's left. 'Will you two pipe down? Are you trying to get us all arrested?'

'I got me a time-waster, 'ere. That's what it is,' said the youth. 'A time-waster an' a bully.'

'You wan' us to sort him out for yer?'

'I'm not a time-waster,' whispered Quinn. 'I've got money. I'll pay you money. I'm sorry I hit you. I couldn't see. It's so dark here.'

'That's the idea, mister. We carn't very well carry on like this in broad daylight, can we?'

'Pipe down!' urged another voice again.

'Lissen,' said the youth. 'Let's make this quick. Unbutton yer flies an' I'll suck you off fer half a crown.'

The youth must have been on his knees now. Quinn felt him groping at his groin.

'Good God!'

'You can imagine it's Miss Dillard doin' it, if it'll make yer feel better. All the same in the dark, ain't it?'

For Quinn, this was the last straw. He spun on his heels, pushed through the resisting curtain of branches and ran back towards the lights of Piccadilly.

Behind him he could hear the darkness hiss in urgent outrage. After a few paces, he crouched down behind a thickening of the night. He felt the unseen twigs of another bush scratch his face.

172

'Who was that?'

'Shall we go after 'im for yer? Sort him out?'

'Are you all right, dearie?'

'Did he hit you, the brute?'

'What was his game?'

'He was asking for Jimmy.'

'Ain't you 'eard? Jimmy's dead. Leastways that's what Tommy Venables said. He said he heard it from some copper who was going about with Jimmy's picture, asking questions.'

'This feller had a picture.'

'That'll be him. The copper.'

At the mention of that word, there was a sudden agitation in the darkness. Figures broke away, dark outlines running back towards the light.

'Now see what you done! You scared off all the gentlemen!'

'They'll be back.'

'Mine's still here, ain't cha, lover?'

A more educated voice, groaning with the strain of delayed gratification, answered: 'Would you mind terribly finishing me off? There's a good chap.'

The sound of an energetic pumping action gave a brisk rhythm to the speaker's words: 'According to Tommy Venables, this copper says someone done for Jimmy. Cut his throat.'

A moan of ecstasy was drowned out by a squeal of horror. 'No-o-o-o? Ooh, that's horrible!'

'You gotta be careful who you take in the bushes, dearie.'

'The coppers'll be crawling all over us now.'

173

'That's a pretty picture!'

'Seriously. Very bad for business.'

'So is getting yer throat cut, dearie.'

A cigarette was lit. Quinn recognized the aroma as Set. The more educated voice spoke again, calmer now: 'This boy that was killed. Jimmy. What was his full name, do you know?'

'Why do you wanna know?'

It was very much the question Quinn wanted answering.

'Listen, the police won't help you chaps. As far as they're concerned, if someone starts killing the odd renter here and there, that's one less pervert on the streets. Doesn't it strike you as fishy that a young man has been murdered, and yet there hasn't been a word about it in the papers? Now I don't know why that is, but I can tell you that if the police keep something like this out of the papers they usually have a damn good reason for doing so. The only way we'll get to the truth of what happened to your friend Jimmy is by shining the torch of independent inquiry. But look, we shouldn't talk about it here.' The speaker raised his voice pointedly: 'You never know who might be lurking in the bushes. And that fellow with the picture, you know, we can't be sure he's a policeman.'

His meaning was swiftly taken, and in silence.

The darkness stirred around Quinn. He heard footsteps on gravel. Then, with startling speed, the midnight park emptied and he felt himself alone.

A Place Beyond Fear

He could not believe it was so easy. Really, it should not be so easy.

They ought to see it in his eyes. There should be something in his eyes alerting them to what he was about.

Blood.

He imagined his eyes were filled with blood, as the eyes of victims of strangulation are reputed to be. He imagined the whites of his eyes turned a deep crimson.

A colour beyond beauty and ugliness, just as his acts were beyond good and evil. It was the colour of pain and joy, the colour of truth.

It amazed him that his eyes were not flooded with that colour.

Was it really possible that his eyes were indistinguishable from other men's?

As before, he had given this one every chance to get away. There would be no restraints, no binding, until the very last moment. By which time it would be too late. He would have made his choices. His fate would be decided. There would be nothing he, or anyone, could do.

When the first one had given him that imploring look at the last, mutely pleading for mercy as he took the blade to his throat, he reminded the

175

boy that he had come with him willingly. He had not forced him into the cab. A gentle guiding hand, perhaps, but if he had pulled away from his grip at any moment, he would have let him go. The operation required that both parties entered into it willingly.

The boy took that badly. Tears – of regret, no doubt, and self-recrimination. For it had to be said, he had no one to blame but himself.

And when they had reached the house, he had not held a gun against his head to force him inside. If the boy had refused to get out of the cab, he would have willingly paid his fare home for him. But he knew – they both knew – that there was never any question of that. The boy was always going to get out of the cab and follow him inside.

'This is your doing as much as mine,' he had said as he slid the steel into skin and allowed the hot gushing of blood to begin. He remembered the exultant shock against his naked tingling skin, his body tensed in anticipation, as he was bathed in the hot shower of the first boy's dying.

He did not create these situations – these works – so much as allow them to occur.

It began with the cigarette. That was the first test. He had decided that if they accept the cigarette – the symbol of our Lord Set, the Great Lord of Chaos and Confusion – then the work may be considered to have begun. If they decline the cigarette, they may go on their way. And so, that first choice, the choice that determines everything that follows, will always be theirs, and will always be freely made.

176

He had offered the cigarettes for a second time tonight. Once again, he had chosen his subject well. Just like before, this boy had taken one. These hungry, greedy boys could not resist. They would take anything offered to them. It was in their nature.

The work was simply the perfection of their nature.

As death is the perfection of a man's fate.

'Look at me,' he commanded, sitting up in the filthy bed. He held the lantern up to his face.

The boy, already stripped and sodomized, stirred in the bed. He was sleepy and confused, not used to the heavy smoke of the Set cigarettes.

The sheets had not been washed since he had entertained the first one there. The excrement stains had at first disgusted him. But now he accepted them as a necessary part of the work. And he knew that he would be washed clean by what was to come.

In his explorations of the esoteric arts he had read about the Alchemical Wedding. This part of his work corresponded to the stage of Nigredo in Alchemy. All the great philosophies were derived from a unified source. That was how he could be sure that his own method was divinely inspired. He had not made it up out of whole cloth. It had been revealed to him, in all likelihood by the Great Lord Set himself.

And so it was important that he should overcome his squeamishness and take strength, as well as delight, from his immersion in degradation and dirt. He was not a natural sodomizer. It was his knowledge of the strength he would gain from the work that aroused him, not the sight of a young man's buttocks.

The act, the work, required this of him. He would not shrink from it.

'What do you see?'

The boy frowned earnestly as he tried to make sense of what he was being asked. He shrugged.

'You see the world remade. Do you understand? The world purged of weakness and fear. A world that has undergone such tumult and mayhem that there is nothing left to fear. Do you know what fear is? Fear is the unknown. If you set yourself to know everything, you will fear nothing. I can take you to a place beyond fear. I will share with you my knowledge, and release you from fear. Come with me now, willingly. Take my hand and the two of us will go together, naked, to a place beyond fear. Will you do that?'

The boy nodded. He held out his hand and allowed himself to be led.

A Visitor to the Department

To look at him, Quinn would not have imagined he was given to the kind of practices undertaken in Green Park at night. With his strong jaw and confident gaze, there was no hint of the degenerate to his person. No flinch of shame. No telltale signs of weakness about his mouth or eyes. His handshake was firm and dry, his stance and features thoroughly masculine.

But as soon as the man opened his mouth, Quinn realized he was listening to the same well-educated voice that had come out of the darkness the night before.

'I think you know why I'm here, Inspector.' He handed Quinn a card as he sat down, bowler in hand:

George Bittlestone, Esq.
Investigative Journalist
The Daily Clarion
Fleet Street

'Let's not play games with each other. You are investigating the death of a renter. I have information that I believe would be helpful to your investigation. In return for this information, you will share with me what you know, in an exclusive arrangement.'

'My dear sir ... My dear –' Quinn deliberately

179

consulted the card. 'Mr Bittlestone. It doesn't work like that, I'm afraid. If you have any information about this matter, it's your duty to pass it on to the police. There can be no question of reciprocation. But kindly note that I have not yet acknowledged the existence of any such investigation. I am curious as to what led you to this department.'

'It wasn't hard to track you down. I have friends in the Met. You'd be surprised.'

'No doubt I would.'

'And how is your investigation going, Inspector? I must say, I find your methods rather unconventional. Picking up a renter of your own. Then assaulting him and running off to hide in the bushes. But perhaps that's the sort of thing we should expect from Quick-fire Quinn.'

Quinn glanced guiltily towards his sergeants. The look of aggressive scepticism on Inchball's face suggested that he was ready to defend his chief's honour.

'I was conducting an undercover operation.'

'And what did you uncover, undercover?' The arch tone did not go unnoticed by Quinn. It was the first hint he had picked up of the man's proclivities.

'For one thing, I witnessed you engage in an act of gross indecency.'

'Really? My recollection of last night was that I took a walk in Green Park with some friends. It was somewhat dark, I seem to remember. Impenetrably so. I am amazed that you were able to see anything.'

'I didn't have to see. I could hear.'

'Whatever you think you might have heard, Inspector, I rather suspect that you will have a hard time proving beyond reasonable doubt that I was involved in it. And as you will know, it is that question of reasonable doubt that decides the issue of guilt or innocence in any legal trial.'

'There can be no question of the police granting an exclusive to one newspaper over any other,' said Quinn, changing tack. 'Our duty is to protect the public. Therefore, if there is a need to involve the press, we will talk to as many newspapers as possible. We will treat everyone equally and fairly.'

'Now now, Inspector Quinn. You know that's not how the world works. The world revolves on the basis of one very simple principle. You scratch my back and I'll scratch yours. Here we are trying to find out who has the upper hand. You think you have, because you believe you heard some renter frig me last night. Whereas I think I have because I happen to know that your investigation has come to a grinding halt. And I am in possession of a piece of information that could move it forward.'

'Tell me what you know and you will not face charges over your behaviour last night. You know as well as I do that even to be charged with such an offence would be highly damaging. Especially for you, as a journalist at the *Daily Clarion*. How would your readers respond? Not to mention your employers. The *Clarion* in the past has taken rather a hard line against such offenders, I seem to remember.'

'Are you threatening me with blackmail,

Inspector? I am prepared to defend myself against any baseless accusation. I am also prepared to go to press with what I know already. Indeed, I have already written a story which I have left with my editor in a sealed envelope, with instructions to open it if I did not return from this interview. I anticipated that you might take this line.'

'I see.'

'Isn't it better for us to cooperate, Inspector? You show me yours and I'll show you mine. Figuratively speaking. You then can direct and control the release of information to the public. All I ask is that when the moment comes that the full story may be published, you remember who it was who came to you – voluntarily, I might add – with the identity of the victim.'

'That is what you have?'

'That is indeed what I have.'

'Very well. Who is he? I will remember who told me, do not fear.'

'His full name is James Albert Neville. Originally from Norfolk. The son of a farm labourer. He ran away as a youth to seek his fortune in London. Ended up living on the streets. Learnt fairly quickly that his fortune hung between his legs. He only had to look down to find it.'

'Most recent address? Known associates?'

'It's all here, Inspector.' Bittlestone produced a folded sheet which he handed to Quinn. 'He was living in a large house in the Primrose Hill area. My informant gave the address as ninety-six Adelaide Road, though he did express some uncertainty about the number. He was sure it had a nine and a six in it. He confessed it could have been sixty-nine, though he thought not, as he would have remembered *that* number, he said. Possibly one hundred and ninety-six? You should have no trouble finding it, however, as it is owned by a gentleman by the name of Henry Fanshaw, who is apparently well known locally as an eccentric. The house is home to a variable number of his friends. People come and go all the time, by all accounts. What you might call a transient household. James Neville's absence had been noted, but nothing much thought of it. It had happened before. He always came back after a few days – or possibly weeks, sometimes months – without so much as a by your leave.'

Quinn scanned the sheet. 'Thank you. This is most helpful.'

'Glad to be of service, I'm sure. Now, Inspector, I'm curious to know, if you don't mind, why this crime was kept from the press.'

'It has unusual features,' said Quinn.

'Such as?'

'Please, Mr Bittlestone, bear with me a while longer. I am grateful to you for this information, truly. And I promise you that your cooperation will not be forgotten. I am certainly inclined to overlook the events of last night. However, I must make enquiries of my own before I share anything with you. You will understand, too, that it is necessary for me to consult with my superiors before proceeding. One thing I will say: I am impressed with what you have been able to discover thus far. It speaks well for your abilities as an investigator.'

Bittlestone's expression closed down with disappointment. 'You seek to pay me off with flattery?'

'I have your card. I will be in touch. Please wait to hear from me before you rush to print.'

'I almost forgot, sir, what with the excitement of Mr Bittlestone coming in...'

'Yes, Macadam, what is it?'

'This arrived for you, sir.' Macadam handed over a plain white envelope addressed to *Inspector Quinn*. There was no postage stamp affixed, suggesting that it had been delivered by hand.

The envelope contained three folded sheets, each filled with lists of names, closely written on both sides. Most of the names were titled. There was no covering note.

'What is it, sir?'

'A list of members of the Panther Club. It was one of the places linked to Featherly's. I visited it last night. A strange establishment. They keep a live panther in the foyer.'

'Takes all sorts, sir. That's what I always say. A lot of names to go through there. You think one of them's the killer?'

'There is something strange about the place, that's for sure. I didn't like it at all. But whether they harbour a killer in their midst is another matter. However, I dare say that whenever there is a name of interest to us, it wouldn't do any harm to check it against this list. What we must be on the lookout for is a name that occurs in more than one connection to the case.'

'Is Bittlestone on there, sir?'

'Bittlestone?' Quinn checked the Bs. 'No. I cannot see him. I suspect he is not quite sufficiently elevated to enjoy membership of this particular establishment. He's only a Fleet Street hack, after all.' Quinn scanned the neatly written columns with a growing sense of disappointment. He realized that a part of him had entertained the desperate hope that the killer's name would somehow make itself known to him.

'Something else, sir, that you might be interested in. My friend Charlie Cale got something over from your friend Doctor Bugsby.'

Quinn lay down the list of names. 'I would hardly describe Doctor Bugsby as my friend. I have never met the man. But go on.'

'Some fibres, sir.'

'Rope fibres?'

'It would seem so, sir. Hemp.'

'That doesn't tell us much,' interjected Inchball gloomily. 'He was bound with rope. The rope was made of hemp. I could have told you that without looking through a bloody microscope.'

'Was he able to identify the particular hemp used?' asked Quinn, ignoring Inchball's objection.

'You must remember that Charlie Cale's particular speciality is tobacco, sir. He never made no claims about hemp. That's what he wanted me to tell you, sir.'

'Understood. But does he have anything for us at all?'

Macadam consulted a sheet of paper on his desk. 'He was able to say that the fibres contained strands taken from both the male and female plants of the *cannabis sativa*.'

'Is that unusual?'

'No, sir. It's normal practice. Very common. You would expect to find that in every hemp rope in the land. In the world, you might even say.'

'That gets us nowhere,' said Inchball.

Quinn had to agree. 'We're not looking for the usual, Macadam. I need something that distinguishes these fibres from others.'

'I was getting to that, sir, if you would only let me finish. Obviously, Charlie would be able to tell us more if we had had an actual length of the rope used. Quality of yarn, method of construction, number of strands, direction of cordage, et cetera ... Unfortunately, we only have a few tiny strands to go on. Not enough to form any decisive opinions about any of that.'

'Yes, Macadam. And so? What was he able to form decisive opinions about?'

'Well, one thing Charlie Cale can say is that the rope was not tarred, which suggests that it was not intended for use on a ship. We may even speculate that it was bought by a gentleman with no nautical connections whatsoever. Such a fellow would naturally prefer tarred rope, and if by some accident a length of the untarred variety came into his possession, well, his first instinct would be to treat it with tar himself, in order to protect it against the elements.'

'So it was not purchased by a sailor,' said Inchball sourly. 'That hardly narrows the field. There are more than enough men in the world who are not sailors.'

'That's not all,' said Macadam. 'Charlie Cale was able to detect in these fibres certain particles that are not usually connected with the manufacture of rope.'

'Go on,' urged Quinn. His impatience at Macadam's leisurely delivery was overridden by a growing excitement. He had the sense that a significant revelation was about to be made.

'Particles of lead, sir.'

'Lead?'

'Yes, sir. That is what Charlie Cale discovered, sir. If I might be so bold as to offer my own interpretation of his findings – Charlie Cale himself refrained from putting forward any interpretation, you understand – "That's for you boys to do", were his exact words to me ... So if I might be so bold, I'd say that the rope had been kept for some time outside, in a location close to a lead works. Might I suggest we make enquiries among ropemakers and chandlers thus situated, beginning with those closest to the spot where the body was found?'

'Excellent suggestion, Macadam.'

'I have taken the liberty of consulting the Post Office Street Directories for Whitechapel, Limehouse and Poplar. There happen to be two lead factories close together near West India Docks. A white lead factory on Garford Street and Locke's Lead Works on Bridge Road. There are a number of likely establishments nearby at which rope may be purchased – naturally, given the area's nautical importance. I daresay there are many sea captains and ship's bursars who favour these establishments with their business. But not so many individuals like the feller we are looking for – would you not agree, sir?'

'Indeed so, Macadam. Excellent work.' Quinn believed in stoking the rivalry between his sergeants in order to get the best out of both of them. 'What do you say to that, Inchball? I dare say even you will agree that that's a break-through.'

'Too early to say, sir. May turn out to be a dead end. It's often the way. Even if one of these places does remember selling rope to a non-nautical gent, there is no guarantee they will have made a note of the name, or even that they will be able to furnish us with a useful des-cription, unless our man turns out to have an animal head, like that there picture on the cigarette tin. And if that were the case, then I dare say he might have come to someone's atten-tion already.' Inchball sighed heavily, as if he shared the disappointment he imagined Mac-adam to be feeling. His face assumed an expres-sion of fatalism. He evidently judged it tactful to change the subject: 'What do you make of our friend Bittlestone, sir?'

'My first impression is not a good one, I am bound to say. I don't like to be presented with ultimatums. The letter left with his editor was little short of blackmail. And I suspect his friends in the Met will turn out to be bent cop-pers. I wouldn't be surprised if we may add brib-ery to the list of his moral shortcomings.'

'I have heard his name mentioned about the place,' put in Macadam, who seemed not the least bit discouraged by Inchball's pessimism. 'Though I myself have never had any dealings with him,' he added quickly. 'But the word is he's sound, as journalists go.'

Inchball allowed his face to express his scepticism; the gaping mouth and popping eyes a little overdone, Quinn thought.

'At any rate, the *Clarion* is held to be one of the papers we can trust,' continued Macadam, undeterred.

'Let us hope so,' said Quinn. 'I am afraid, whether Sir Edward likes it or not, we may have to have dealings with these newspaper types.'

'Bittlestone. Queer name, ain't it?' said Inchball. 'I've a feeling I've come across it somewhere recently.' Inchball flicked through the pages of his notepad. 'Thought so. There's a Mr Bittlestone listed here. One of the customers of that tobacconist's in Burlington Arcade. He may not be a member of that toffs' club, but he is nevertheless a smoker of the Set cigarette.'

'Interesting,' said Quinn. 'Incidentally, how did you get on checking your list against the files? Anyone come up?'

'Well, plenty of Jimmys, or Jameses, and Tommys or Thomases. Indeed, every blooming Christian name you care to mention is represented in our records of convicted buggers. But that don't get us nowhere, do it?'

'What about the surnames? Did any of them occur?'

'Bittlestone, for example?'

'Well, yes ... but any correspondence would do.'

189

'That would be too easy, wouldn't it, sir? And if this job was easy then anyone could do it.'

'At least we have the victim's name now, courtesy of Bittlestone.'

'I don't like to feel myself too much indebted to his sort,' said Inchball.

'We even have an address.' Quinn rose to his feet, bowing his head to avoid the ceiling. He crossed to Inchball's desk and handed him Bittlestone's sheet.

Inchball flicked the paper contemptuously. 'Ninety-six. Sixty-nine. One hundred and ninety-six. It could even be one hundred and sixty-nine, sir, with respect and all that.'

'That's only four doors to knock on, Inchball. It won't take you all day.'

'Me?'

'Yes. Macadam will be busy following up his rope lead. In the morning, I want you to go round to Adelaide Road and get statements from the occupants, once you've found the correct house.' Quinn took one of the photographs of the dead man down from the wall. 'Take this. At some point, we will need to show someone the corpse. Perhaps his landlord – if that's the right word – will oblige. This fellow, Fanshaw. First you'd better check that name against the list of Panther Club members. I wouldn't want to send you in there on your own if that were the case.'

Inchball scanned the lists. 'There's a Fan ... How do you say that? Fanli-*yoo*?'

Quinn glanced down at the name Inchball had his finger against. '*Fanlieu*? No, that's not it. Fanshaw is the name we're looking for.'

'There's no Fanshaw as I can see. Just that one you just said. Then Faversham. Then, blimey, how d'you say *this* one? Is it Fetherston-*huff* or Fetherston-*how*?'

'Here, let me see.' Quinn took the list. The name Inchball was struggling with was spelled Fetherstonhaugh, but Quinn had no confident suggestions as to how it should be pronounced. 'It doesn't matter. It's not the name we're look- ing for.' His eyes darted up the list. As Inchball had said, there was no Fanshaw. But Quinn's attention was snagged by the last name in the E entries: *Esslyn, Sir Michael.*

'Why do all these toffs have to have such blooming awkward names?' Inchball complain- ed. 'Can you tell me that?'

'Sir Michael Esslyn,' murmured Quinn.

'What was that, sir?' asked Macadam.

Inchball continued to grumble: 'Makes 'em feel superior, I daresay. Another way they can look down on the rest of us. It's like another little club of theirs. If you can say the name, you can belong. If not ... well, if not, you know what you can do. Proper gets my goat, it does.'

'Sir Michael Esslyn,' repeated Quinn. 'I saw him coming out of Sir Edward's office just before I was briefed on the case. And then again at the Royal Ethnological Society at a lecture on vampires.'

'You think he has something to do with this, sir?' wondered Macadam.

Quinn declined to answer the question. 'Inch- ball, before you go round to Adelaide Road, you may as well go back to the records and see if you can dig anything up on James Albert Neville. I have another name for you to check too: Tommy Venables. I heard it bandied around in the dark last night. Check him against crimes of vagrancy, gross indecency, sodomy...' Quinn's hand went up to his nose. It was still tender to the touch, but otherwise did not trouble him. 'Oh, and assault.'

A Wild Beast

Sir Edward's eyes started from his head as if he had just taken a bayonet to the kidneys. At first Quinn thought his pained expression was a reaction to his old wound making itself felt. But then he wasn't so sure. 'And so you are saying that the press have found out about this affair, after all?'

'Yes, Sir Edward.'

Now the bayonet had been twisted. 'I find that highly regrettable.'

'With respect, Sir Edward, it was bound to happen sooner or later. You cannot stop people talking.'

'What? Eh? I blame you, Quinn. You wanted it out in the first place and now you've got your way.'

'That's hardly fair, Sir Edward. When the journalist in question came to speak to me, I denied any knowledge of the matter. The story could have got out at any time, and in any way.

192

The dockworker who found the body could easily have spoken to a journalist.'

'Dockworkers and journalists? In what social sphere do they rub shoulders?'

'You know how journalists like to delve in all sorts of warrens for their stories.'

'But if they don't know there is a story to find in the first place, how do they know where to go looking? What took this journalist to the dockworker's hovel?'

'I'm not saying that the dockworker was the source. Only that they could have been. It could just as easily have been the caretaker at Poplar Mortuary, who incidentally struck me as being of very dubious character. However, I believe I know how this journalist got his information. He is ... he...'

'Come on, man, spit it out.'

'He is an invert himself, sir. He uses male prostitutes. And the fact that I ... that a police-man was making enquiries about the dead man was common knowledge amongst these people.'

'I knew it was your fault, Quinn.'

'But, with respect, sir, how am I meant to conduct an investigation without asking questions? I concocted a cover story. However, to gain some-one's trust, you have to be honest with them. I chose to be honest with one young man.'

'What did you tell him?'

'Isn't it more the issue what he told me?'

'What did you tell him, Quinn?' insisted Sir Edward.

'Merely that the man I was looking for had been murdered. I said nothing about the circumstances of the murder. Apart from the fact that he had had his throat slit. Naturally, I omitted to mention the exsanguinated state of the corpse.'

'I'm glad to hear it. You know what the press would make of that. It would not be long before the word *vampire* was bandied about. You can imagine what would ensue. The last thing I want is a moral panic on my hands. Once we know the facts, then we can decide what we tell the public. In consultation, I might add, with our masters.'

Quinn turned his head sharply away from Sir Edward. He briefly considered mentioning his discovery of Sir Michael Esslyn's name on the list of Panther Club members. And yet he found himself strangely reluctant to do so. He told himself that he did not wish to burden Sir Edward with a detail that would almost certainly turn out to be irrelevant. 'I'm sure it would be possible to keep the question of exsanguination out of the papers.'

'Don't count on it. The press is like a wild beast. Once you have released it, you cannot control it. And besides, this case is utterly distasteful from whichever angle one considers it. *But the men of Sodom were wicked and sinners before the Lord exceedingly.* Genesis, thirteen, thirteen.'

Quinn nodded sharply. 'My only intention, Sir Edward, is to do my job as well as I can. But I do think it may be necessary to get this journalist on our side. What if there is another murder? Will we keep that a secret too? Remember Jack the Ripper. There are certain particularities about the state of the body that suggest a ritual-

194

istic aspect to the crime. The draining of the blood. The careful cleansing of the corpse. There is every likelihood that he will strike again, and again, until he is stopped. How will it look if it comes out at a later time that we suppressed information that might have helped prevent future murders?'

'What? Eh? Are you trying to frighten me into agreeing with you, Quinn?'

'I am merely laying all the facts as I understand them before you. I should perhaps add that Bittlestone wants an exclusive arrangement when the time comes.'

'Is that all?' The question was sarcastic. Sir Edward drummed his fingers. 'The problem is, Quinn, he will want something from us. We may have to be completely frank with him in order to win his confidence. We may have to trust him.'

'I understand how alarming a prospect that may be, Sir Edward, really I do. However, I think it is a risk we are going to have to take. We have been caught out before, have we not? Whenever we have tried to conceal information from the public it has backfired on us. The press will either invent stories that are far worse than the reality, or they will not stop their probing until, by foul means or fair, they hit upon something close to the truth, which inevitably reflects badly on us. Our caution has only succeeded in provoking their hostility.'

'But we cannot tell them everything, Quinn. For one thing, it will jeopardize the investigation. In addition to that, as I believe I mentioned before, there is the question of national security.'

'Begging your pardon, Sir Edward, but I am afraid I fail to grasp the aspect of this case that touches upon national security.'

'Neville made his living by charging ghastly men for the dubious privilege of doing abominable things to him. He was a renter, in other words. It is this aspect of the crime that we are particularly desirous to withhold.'

'But why?' Quinn frowned. His focus, as always, was on solving the case; he had neither the time nor the inclination to consider the wider, political ramifications that disturbed his superiors. Sometimes that left him feeling hopelessly naive for a man in his position. He suspected this would be one of those occasions.

Sir Edward regarded him with a sharp grimace of pain. 'It is understood that the dissemination of information about such activities has a demoralizing and frankly corrupting influence on the populace at large, even when the information is communicated in terms of the severest disapprobation. As I have had occasion to point out to you before, Quinn, these are uncertain times, internationally. At home, the Irish problem looks likely to draw us into a civil war at any moment. There could be no worse time to shine the spotlight on degenerate practices at the heart of the Empire. Not only would it sap the morale of our young men, it would give strength and succour to our enemies. To put it bluntly, the Home Secretary is very keen to play down the queer angle.'

'There is the chance that Neville was killed *because* he was a queer,' said Quinn.

'What of it?'

'Therefore is there not also the chance that his killer will target other men who share his predilection?'

'We don't know that. As yet there has been only one death.'

'Even so, do we not have a duty to issue a warning? To encourage such men to modify their behaviour?'

'Such men are perfectly capable of desisting from their vile practices whenever they wish.'

'Perhaps there is some way, some coded way that will not offend public morality or give our enemies encouragement, some way we may deliver a subtle warning to these men?'

'What do you have in mind? Will any man who is fond of the colour lilac and the Ballets Russes kindly dress more soberly and seek out more masculine forms of entertainment?'

'No, sir, I can see that wouldn't work.'

'If we do cut a deal with this fellow Bittlestone – and I say *if* – there will be no mention of the victim's degeneracy. I would rather give him the exsanguination than the degeneracy.'

'Of course, Sir Edward. Although, as you know, Bittlestone himself is an invert. And he already knows that James Neville was a renter.'

'But he does not know that it may be significant to the case, and will have no reason to include it in any account. As far as he and the public are concerned, this fellow Neville was just some unlucky wretch who fell victim to an unknown monster.' Sir Edward sighed and stretched, only to flinch back from the sudden reminder of pain. 'I suppose there is no other way?'

'I fear not, Sir Edward. At least this way we will have one channel through which we can feed all the information we wish.'

Sir Edward winced. 'Very well. Arrange a meeting for us with this journalist and his editor. Here at the Yard. That will give us the initiative. We had better have the proprietor along too. It does no harm to get the top man on board. What paper did you say he writes for?'

'The *Daily Clarion*.'

'Ah, then that's Lennox. I've dealt with him before. Bit of an upstart among the proprietors, which means he's keen to make his mark. He should be flattered by the attention. If there is any problem, any question of this journalist fellow stepping out of line, we can throw the book at them all. Speak to Miss Latterly on your way out. She has my diary.'

'Very well, sir.'

'I warn you, Quinn, if this blows up in our faces, I shall hold you personally to account.'

It was Quinn's turn to wince. Apart from anything else, Sir Edward's choice of words brought to mind the passage he had read from the book *Profession of Shame*.

Quinn came out of Sir Edward's office and stood by the side of Miss Latterly's desk, waiting to be noticed. Once again, she was occupied in the operation of a typewriting machine. Quinn admired her upright posture and the speed of her fingers.

He admired, too, her powers of concentration.

198

He had no doubt she knew he was there. As before, her determination not to acknowledge his presence was absolute. There was no break in the fluid ripple of her fingers over the keys, no tremor of hesitation. She appeared so supremely unconscious of him that he began to doubt, if not his own reality, then at least their mutual existence in the same universe.

'Miss Latterly?' he ventured at last.

As he knew she would, she continued typing for a moment, before turning a puzzled frown on him.

'Sir Edward has requested that I speak to you.'

At first, she clearly found it difficult to countenance this startling information. But her expression quickly turned to one of horror. 'You're not going to talk to me about murderers, are you?' she cried.

'No. Sir Edward wishes to arrange a meeting. He says that you keep his diary and that I should consult with you.'

She closed her eyes and gasped in relief. 'Oh, if that's all...' Miss Latterly wheeled back on her chair and opened a drawer in the desk.

'It's what I do, you know,' said Quinn, stung to defend himself. 'My occupation. It's as natural for me to talk about it as it is for another man to talk about his day at the office pushing pieces of paper around.'

She had heard enough. 'I have Sir Edward's diary.'

'I am sorry that I said what I did the last time I was here. I don't normally ever say anything about my work to anyone. Least of all to ... well, to a young lady. It was unforgivable. I cannot think what came over me.'

'Let us say no more about it.'

'You will understand, I think, that this places a certain strain upon one. It makes it hard for one to be ... well, to be in polite company. And to be honest, I have never found that an easy thing. Even before I chose this occupation.'

'Please, you need not explain yourself to me.'

'Oh, but I do need to. I have offended you, I know. I am sincerely sorry. I had no right. I made the mistake of thinking that, because you work here, in the Yard, that you would be inured to such talk.'

She inhaled sharply and regarded him with a hostile, peevish glare. 'Really? That is all there was to it? It was merely that you were too stupid to realize that your conversation was distasteful to me? It was not that you deliberately sought to cause me distress?'

'How could you attribute such malicious motives to me?'

'I am sorry, I am sure, if I impugn your motives. I only know that that was how it seem-ed to me at the time. As if you wished to punish me for something.'

Quinn felt the heat rise to his face. It was shaming but true: he *had* wished to prick her demeanour of self-contained superiority; he *had* found her indifference provoking.

'I feel sorry for you, Inspector Quinn. It is clear that you are a woman-hater. Perhaps my very presence here in New Scotland Yard is what offends you. Let me tell you, I am here to stay, and your bullying will not shake me. I can see that I have hit a nerve.'

Quinn took it that she was referring to the colour he imagined his face to have now turned. He remembered that the reverse of her phrase – man-hater – had suggested itself to him when he had last been to Sir Edward's office. 'I am mortified that you think so badly of me.'

'Why should my opinion of you matter to you at all? I am surely so far beneath you that I am not worthy of the least consideration.'

There was something not wholly convincing about this abject self-negation. Quinn could not help but smile. 'I confess that once I imagined you had a similar opinion of me. That *I*, a mere plodding policeman, was so far beneath *you* as to be unworthy even of your contempt.'

'Why should you think that?' The question was harsh-edged with impatience.

'Oh, no reason.'

'I had imagined that you were making some attempt to be frank with me, Inspector. Therefore I consider it poor form for you to have recourse to evasions now.'

'Very well. Because I believe you have made quite a show of ignoring me.'

Miss Latterly's mouth fell open. 'Are you so conceited that you imagine every woman must look at you the moment you wander into view? It may have escaped your notice that I am kept very busy by Sir Edward.'

'So now I am conceited. A conceited woman-hater. And what else was it?'

'A bully.'

201

'If it is your view that I have been less than frank with you, Miss Latterly, then I apologize. However, I do not think anyone may accuse you of a similar failing.'

'You pushed me into saying what I have said. I repeatedly begged you to let the matter drop. But now that we have ventured into these waters, it is you who have been found wanting in courage.'

Quinn hung his head. It had suddenly struck him, with demoralizing force, how vast was the gulf between them. Not only that, he recognized it as the eternal gulf between the sexes. They were destined to misunderstand each other; to place the worst construction on each other's motives; each to simplify the other's psychology until it became a crude caricature.

Men and women were each a closed book to the other. That was the only conclusion.

'Perhaps in future it would be better if we confine our intercourse to matters pertaining strictly to police business,' said Quinn, in little more than a murmur.

'That is something we can agree upon,' said Miss Latterly, thumbing through the pages of Sir Edward's diary.

An Encounter with Miss Dillard

Quinn eased the front door shut with both hands. One to push it to, the other to strain against that momentum with a counterforce. The hinges behaved themselves for once: the merest creak, no louder than a mildly complaining stomach.

He could suggest to Mrs Ibbott that she put a dab of oil on the offending parts, even volunteer to do it himself. But wouldn't that look like he had something to hide? He half-suspected that Mrs Ibbott kept the hinges noisy deliberately, so that she could keep tabs on the comings and goings of her residents. Only a sneak or a spy, someone desirous of avoiding his fellow lodgers, someone who wanted to come and go like a thief in the night (only someone like Quinn, in other words) would take the trouble to argue for oiling.

But this business with other people, it fair wore him out. They wanted too much from him, with their questions and concern, their gentle manoeuvring, their insinuations and invitations. Far better to keep himself to himself.

Behind all this was his anxiety over Miss Dillard. To begin with, he was embarrassed about being made to look as though he had run away from dinner on her account the other night.

Far worse was the fact that he had allowed himself to use Miss Dillard's name in his exchanges with the renter last night. Not only that, he had given the impression that there was some sort of understanding between himself and Miss Dillard. An understanding of the worst sort.

Quinn felt the through-rush of shame. All his attempts at any kind of interrelationship with members of the opposite sex seemed to be configured by it.

He felt that he owed her some sort of apology. But how could he apologize for something he could never admit to? *My dear Miss Dillard, I do apologize but I happened to mention to a renter who was trying to pick me up that I had no need of his services because all my sexual requirements were taken care of by you. I hope that's all right. I know we don't have such an understanding, so I really shouldn't have said it – and perhaps I shouldn't have said it even if it were true. But for some reason, your name was the first that came into my head. I can't think why. Please be assured that I really have no desire for such an understanding with you – you need have no fear on that front. So I really am at a loss to explain why it was your name I thought of. I could have said Miss Latterly, or Miss Ibbott, because – to be honest – those are the ones about whom I really do entertain thoughts of that nature. The human mind is an unfathomable mystery. I feel sure I must have read that somewhere, but even so...*

The door to the front parlour opened and the lady herself came out, dressed as always in a dated and much-repaired gown. For one horrifying moment, Quinn thought he must have spoken aloud his strange monologue of apology. But her face was as mild and unassuming as ever, and as hopelessly unmoving to him.

Her gaze dipped modestly when she saw it was him, pathetically self-effacing. No, it was not true to say that her face didn't move him at all. But the only emotion it inspired was pity. He could not say what colour her eyes were. He did not dare look into them for long enough to find out. He had a vague impression of wateriness there. And about her face, a certain bloated slackness, as of a balloon that was beginning to deflate.

What saddened him, sickened him almost, about all this was that he was capable of entertaining such ungentlemanly thoughts.

You're no oil painting yourself, Quinn, he told himself.

Do you think your Miss Latterlys and your Miss Ibbotts would ever look twice at the likes of you?

Perhaps Mrs Ibbott was right to point him in the direction of Miss Dillard. Or perhaps all she was doing there was steering him away from her daughter. He couldn't blame her. In her shoes, he would do the same.

'Mr Quinn?' said Miss Dillard, with a note of surprise in her voice.

'Good evening to you, Miss Dillard.' Quinn removed his hat and gave a slight bow.

'You are late this evening. I was just going up.'

'Yes ... we are very busy at the office at the moment.'

'At the office, yes. One day you must explain to me exactly what it is you do at that office of yours, Mr Quinn.' Miss Dillard smiled slyly and lifted her eyes. He flinched away from her look of timid enquiry just as it turned into one of alarmed solicitude. 'Good heavens! What have you done to your nose?'

Her hand rose protectively towards his face, only to shrink back as she became aware of the involuntary and revealing gesture.

Quinn had forgotten entirely about his injury. It had not troubled him for some time, and thanks to Macadam's arnica tablets the bruising was almost entirely gone. Only someone who took an obsessive interest in the state of his face could have noticed the slight heightening of colour at the tip of his nose. 'Oh, it's nothing. A little accident.'

'You must take more care of yourself, Mr Quinn. We all worry about you, you know.'

Quinn found it hard to imagine Messrs Appleby and Timberley expressing any concern on his behalf, unless it were to do so ironically. And Miss Ibbott? He would have dearly liked to know if she was included in Miss Dillard's circle of worry. Even Quinn realized he could not ask the question directly, certainly not of Miss Dillard. He settled for a sceptical: 'All?'

'Oh yes, I am certain the others share my concern for your welfare.'

Ah! His image of the occupants of the lodging

206

house seated round the table earnestly sharing their anxieties over him evaporated.

'You must place a cold compress on it. If you like, I can...'

'No, no. That won't be necessary.'

Miss Dillard winced at the speed and sharpness of his rejection. 'I was only going to say I could speak to Mrs Ibbott about it. I am sure she has a compress somewhere that you can use.'

'It won't be necessary, I assure you.' Quinn endeavoured to soften his tone. 'It's very kind of you. Very kind.' The sense that he owed her something – if not an apology, something – suddenly overwhelmed him.

Slowly, deliberately, he directed his gaze towards her eyes.

Grey. So that was it. Grey.

The least he owed her was to look into her eyes and acknowledge the strangely beautiful pewter grey of her irises.

He could not say that he detected any great intelligence in those eyes. But he felt their compassion, and that was perhaps the quality he valued most of all.

'You are very kind,' he said, the focus of his gaze still locked on to her eyes. 'But really, it isn't necessary.'

She smiled, and for once he did not feel that her smile was pathetic and pitiable. He realized that when he looked into Miss Dillard's eyes, when he dared to do that, she made perfect sense to him. She was complete. She was not ridiculous at all, he realized. She was human.

The first thing he saw as he closed the door to

his room was the brown paper package on his bed. He couldn't believe he had left it in the open like that. Someone – anyone – could have come into his room, slipped the string, pulled apart the wrapping and seen the book inside. The offence of trespass would have been nothing compared to the opprobrium that would descend on him as one who read such material.

Betsy had clearly made the bed and replaced the book more or less where he had left it. Was there something pointed in this? A vile pornographic novel borne up on the homely neatness of a well-made bed? It struck him as a critical – perhaps even satirical – juxtaposition.

It was as if she was saying, *I know what you're up to, mister.*

But no, it was impossible to conceive of Betsy opening a private package belonging to one of the lodgers, especially one of the gentlemen lodgers. For one thing, she hadn't the time. Mrs Ibbott kept her far too busy. But more than that, Betsy was a good sort.

He looked at the inert package with loathing. Even when he turned from it, he felt its presence in his room, a kind of challenge. *Dare you read me?* it seemed to be saying to him.

He left it where it was and crossed to his table. The tin of Set cigarettes transmitted a similar mute message: *Dare you smoke me?*

Quinn had no eagerness to accept either challenge. The thought of the yellowish cigarette papers left him feeling physically nauseous. It brought to mind the deeper yellow cover of the book. The connection troubled him. It was as if there was some conspiracy at work here. He began to distrust the colour yellow. Although he had never thought so before, it seemed poisonous at its essence. He felt that the mere sight of the book would cause his mouth to flood with saliva, and his throat to begin the gag reflex.

As if to test himself, he picked up the tin and confronted the strange Egyptian figure depicted there. He could almost believe that this impossible being with a human body and animal head was the killer he was looking for, such was the antipathy it generated in him.

He remembered how the smoke from the cigarettes had estranged him from his room and himself. He had become someone else, under its drug-laden influence. Was it possible, he wondered, that it had a similar effect on the murderer? When the spirit of the cigarettes, the sinister Egyptian deity, entered that unknown person, did he become a creature capable of cutting and bleeding a young man till he died?

If that was the case, it was Quinn's duty to do what he had little stomach for. The enquiry demanded it.

He opened the tin, took out one of the fat yellow cigarettes and lit it.

Clearly, not everyone who smoked Set cigarettes became a murderer. But he knew from his own experience that they had a disorientating effect. It was more than that. They tended to loosen inhibitions. Perhaps this was why it was so common for inverts to smoke them. The great line that had to be crossed in order for them to commit their acts together required a virtual abandonment of inhibitions.

If your inner nature was that of an invert, then Set cigarettes would serve to bring it closer to the surface.

If your inner nature was that of a killer, then the same principle would apply.

Quinn inhaled. And closed his eyes. Strangely, he did not feel nauseous. He was becoming used to the effect of the cigarettes. Welcomed it now, even.

He crossed to the looking-glass on the wash-stand and confronted himself. The sense of estrangement was less than he had experienced the night before, as if he was becoming reconciled to the idea that his reflection did not match the image of himself that he carried in his head. Or perhaps it was more that the outer and the inner Quinn were growing closer together. Was that the power of the cigarettes, then?

He took a second, deeper inhalation of smoke. His pulse raced. The room swam a little, shifted from its moorings in the universe before being pulled back into place.

Quinn went to the bed and picked up the book. It seemed lighter than he remembered it. Perhaps the Set cigarettes gave the smoker strength too? Quinn had an uncle who was prone to sleep-walking, who had single-handedly moved a mahogany wardrobe laden with clothes, watched by his incredulous wife. In the morning, he had been unable to restore it to its original position. The wardrobe had to be completely emptied of clothes before the two of them together were able to shift it an inch.

Relating these observations back to the killer, it was conceivable that when he smoked the cigarettes he believed himself capable of anything. Physically, he might be able to make short work of hefting a body, for example.

Quinn took the package over to the armchair. It was harder than he had imagined to remove the string, almost as if it were jealous of what it bound. Then he remembered that he had tied the knot, so all it really represented was his own desire to keep the horrid secret of the book hidden from prying eyes.

He lifted away the paper calmly, as if he wanted to prove – to that imaginary observer again? – that he was in no hurry to see what lay beneath. That he could take it or leave it, in fact.

When finally it lay revealed on his lap in its nest of brown paper, the yellow of the cover still struck him as an unpleasant lurid hue. Its stridency still offended, like a hysterical scream in polite company. Quinn took this as a good sign. The cigarettes had not so poisoned his mind that he was capable of looking on such a book with anything other than disgust.

He opened it with a grimace, the Set cigarette held between his teeth as he drew on it.

Merely the sight of the type on the page induced a strange breathlessness, accompanied by a feeling like butterflies in the pit of his stomach. His body felt hollowed-out and volatile.

He read short passages at random, flicking the pages whenever he encountered a repulsive word:

211

cockstand
spendings
frig
arsehole
buttocks
prick
mancunt
pego
balls

Such words recurred with monotonous frequency. As he might have expected, the book lacked any literary merit whatsoever. Even on this cursory examination, he noticed numerous spelling mistakes and examples of slapdash punctuation. Coupled with its monotony of vocabulary and style, as a novel it was let down by its excessive repetition of incident. It was little more than a catalogue of the sexual encounters of the narrator. Of course, the power of the book lay in the shocking nature of these encounters. And, for Quinn, that power was deeply disturbing.

He remembered Inchball's warning. At the time, he had thought his sergeant was overstating the case. Inchball's fondness for blunt-speaking sometimes stepped over into gratuitous sensationalism. It seemed he relished the pleasure of shocking through his words.

But now Quinn realized that his dark hints of contamination, of policemen corrupted by such reading matter, were not without foundation.

If the human mind was an unfathomable mystery, as he had observed to an imaginary Miss Dillard, then the human body was a peculiar machine. He found himself, despite his deep disgust at what he was reading, sexually aroused.

Perhaps if one reads the word cockstand often enough, he thought, *one's cock is inevitably induced to stand. Whether one wills it or not.*

In his brief time as a medical student, he had been introduced to the physiological basis of sexual function. A cockstand, as the writer insisted on calling an erection, was caused by blood engorging the penis. Remarkable how the presence of a liquid could result in something so solid.

And so it was a matter of scientific fact that there was a link between sex and blood. A similar link seemed to be present in the murder of James Neville.

A sexually impotent man was one whose penis failed to engorge successfully with blood. The evidence of anal intercourse on the victim suggested that the murderer was not impotent, unless, of course, a third party had been involved. That was logically possible, though chilling. The idea that Neville may have been the plaything of two men had not occurred to Quinn before now. He preferred to discount it, at least for the time being.

Even so, the blood may still have been taken from Neville because of its association with ideas of potency. Just as a cock is steeled by the inrush of blood, so too, perhaps, the killer hoped to steel himself by summoning forth the blood of his victim. It may not have been simple sexual potency he sought, but something beyond that.

Quinn lay the book aside and stubbed out the cigarette. No longer aroused, queasy once again from the over-stimulation of the tobacco, he felt suddenly exhausted. He laid back his head where he was sitting and closed his eyes.

But images from the book would not let him be. He needed something else to take his mind off them. Remembering another book he had recently bought, Quinn stirred himself from his armchair. He withdrew from his bookshelf his copy of Lázár Erdélyi's ethnological study, *Killing the Dead: The Folk Beliefs and Rituals of Transylvania*.

The House of Pomegranates

Inchball looked up and scowled. The sky hung heavy with low grey cloud, promising another downpour. He had taken the precaution of setting out with an umbrella and his shoes were in good repair. His sour expression had nothing to do with the weather forecast.

The thought of the type of person he would encounter at the house in Adelaide Road made his skin crawl. The way they looked at him, sizing him up with their filthy eyes, imagining him in the buff, no doubt, licking their disgusting lips at the thought of their filthy hands all over him.

It was enough to make any decent man vomit.

If it rained, good. It might wash him clean afterwards. Perhaps God would even send a thunderbolt to burn the place down. After Inchball had got out of there, of course. That was a thought – what if God decided to punish the perverts while he was still in there interviewing them?

Bloody typical, he decided that would be. *Bloody typical of my luck.*

So it was just as well he didn't believe in God. Not when you got down to it. Not when you thought it through, good and proper. You see if your God existed, that's precisely what he would have done already. He would have smote them all down. As far as Inchball was concerned, the fact that your queer existed proved that your God did not.

It wasn't just your queers. Your queers were the least of it. Some of the things he'd seen working Special Crimes with Inspector Quinn, well, it fair made your blood curdle, it did. It was hard to hold on to a belief in a good and powerful God after you'd dug up the body of a nine-year-old girl who'd been raped and strangled by her own father.

Let it rain, was what he said. *Let it rain on them all. And let the thunderbolts fall.*

Fat chance.

Inchball looked around at the villas of Adelaide Road. His scowl deepened. It wasn't just that your God let your queers and suchlike exist. He set them up in neighbourhoods like this. By

215

the looks of some of these houses, it would take more than one thunderbolt to raze them to the ground.

It was enough to make you spit. When he thought about the little jerry-built cottage in Hornsey that he and the missus could just about afford to rent. An honest copper like him, working practically every hour God sent. Wearing out his shoe leather. And his knees. Oh, yes. And all them queers had to do was frig some toff and they could live it up in a mansion in Primrose Hill for the rest of their days.

As the governor had suspected, James Albert Neville turned out to have form. He'd served a month's hard labour in Pentonville for offences relating to the 1898 amendment of the Vagrancy Act. For soliciting, basically. Nothing worse, though that was bad enough in Inchball's book. He knew from his time in Vice how hard it was to nail these sods with anything more serious, such as gross indecency or sodomy. For that, you either had to catch them in the act, or get one party to inform on the other. The former had been known to happen, though it required surveillance of suspected premises, which was costly in terms of manpower and didn't always produce results. The latter was unlikely, for obvious reasons. To level such an accusation was by definition self-incriminating, unless you were talking about indecent assault, which was another matter.

There was a photograph in the file, which confirmed that the James Neville with a criminal record was the same James Neville whose body had been dumped in the London Docks. As far as an address was concerned, at the time of his arrest this was given as 'No Fixed Abode'. So any hope of saving his shoe leather proved vain.

Being on the even side of the street, the first of the possible houses he came to was number ninety-six. It was an imposing building. Inchball looked up bitterly at its four solid storeys, its cream stuccoed frontage immaculately maintained. But it turned out not to be the house he was looking for. He had to climb the steps to the front door before he discovered the discreet brass plaque announcing: *The Huguenot Home for French Governesses.*

Number 196 was on a similar scale but far less well-maintained. The front garden was overgrown. A long, untended ivy bush along the side fence obstructed the path. The stucco facade was cracked and streaked with coppery stains. A thick film of black grime dimmed the windows; the mismatched curtains were drawn in every one, even now in the middle of the day.

This had to be the place. *No plaque, this time*, Inchball noted with derision. He could see it now. *The Perverted Home for Brothers of the Bum.*

No, the people who lived here were not the sort to advertise themselves. Quite the contrary. They gave every sign of having something to hide.

He battled his way past the ivy, beating away its tendrils with his umbrella. It was as if he feared the touch of the plant as somehow contaminating. This fear of contact stayed with him after he had climbed the front steps. He aimed

217

the tip of his umbrella at the bell button and pressed.

A shrill metallic scream sounded somewhere in the depths of the house. He kept his weight leaning on to the umbrella. *No point being the shrinking violet.*

The sound of the electric bell began to grate; its harsh, unnatural monotony grew hideous. It was as if someone had found a nerve beneath his skin and was holding the point of a needle against it.

He released the pressure on his umbrella, only to find that the tip had become lodged. The bell's ugly peal continued. He tugged and wrenched the umbrella until it came away in a lurch. But still the bell sounded. It seemed he had jammed the button in.

The door opened against a chain, not far enough to reveal much of the person on the other side, but far enough to release the distinct whiff of the house's interior, a vaguely vegetal ripeness. 'There's no need to keep ringing it. I've heard you!' The voice was male, well-to-do, educated – the voice of privilege.

'It's jammed,' said Inchball, repeatedly ramming the button with the tip of his umbrella, in the hope that the violent action would work it loose.

'That isn't going to help matters. Wait here while I fetch a screwdriver.'

The door closed again.

The bell kept up its shriek of artificial panic.

The door opened again, still on the chain. A screwdriver was passed out to him, handle first.

218

'Here.'

'And what am I to do with this?'

'You can use it to release the button.'

Inchball could see that the button had been pushed beneath the rim of its brass surround. By loosening the four screws in the surround, he was able to ease out the button with the tip of the screwdriver. It was strangely satisfying to witness its pop of release. The clatter of the bell ceased abruptly. Inchball tightened the screws before returning the screwdriver. At the same time he lodged the toe of his boot, conveniently steel-capped, into the gap.

'You've just had your doorbell fixed by the Old Bill,' he said.

'What is this about?' The voice was brusque and imperious.

'I'm looking for Mr Fanshaw. Mr Henry Fanshaw. Would that be you, sir?'

'I know the law. I don't have to let you in. Not unless you have a warrant.'

'Now now, sir. Why should I need a warrant? I've only come here for a chat.'

'Very likely.'

'About a friend of yours. Mr James Neville is a friend of yours, ain't he, sir?'

'Jimmy? What about Jimmy? Has he got himself into trouble?'

'You could say that, sir. If you call being dead trouble.'

'Dead? What do you mean?'

'Ain't you heard? I thought it was common knowledge with you lot. Your friend Jimmy has only gone and got his throat slashed.'

'Oh my God.'

'Sorry and all that.'

'Poor, dear Jimmy.'

'Yeah, well, I dare say, and all that. Now listen, ain't you going to let me in, so as we can talk about this properly? My job is to find out who done for him, you see.'

Inchball felt the door squeeze against his foot.

'Kindly remove your foot so that I may close the door to release the chain.'

'If you try any funny business, sir, you will regret it.'

The vaguely vegetal smell Inchball had noticed earlier came at him in a ripe, fruity waft as the door was opened fully. The man who was now revealed was dressed respectably enough in a tweed suit, his auburn hair neatly cut, his face impeccably clean-shaven. Aged in his late forties, he had something of the air of a school-teacher. There was a certain fussy impatience to his movements, which was the only sign Inchball could detect of his sexual inversion. Because it was his job to remark such details, he noted the colour of the man's eyes, a muddy, pond-water green.

Before he closed the door, the man peered out warily, as if he suspected the house of being watched.

The hall was wide but gloomy. Inchball remembered all the windows at the front were curtained. He speculated that the same must be true of the back. The house felt completely sealed off.

Inchball took out his notepad and pencil. 'Just

to be clear, sir. You are Henry Fanshaw? Can you confirm that for me, please?'

'Yes.' It seemed to pain him to make this admission.

'And is there anybody else in the house at present?'

'I don't know. There may well be. The children come and go as they please. I don't keep tabs.'

'The *children*, sir? Children live here?'

'Oh, I call them my children, but they are all adults, I assure you.'

Inchball sniffed the cloying air suspiciously and licked the end of his pencil. He squinted in an effort to distinguish the blank page of his notepad from the soft grey felt of the darkness. 'Would it be possible to go somewhere with a bit more light, sir? I can hardly see the hand in front of my face.'

Neville's landlord led him along the hallway, down some steps towards the back of the house and into a room furnished with a long dining table and chairs. The bayed French windows at the far end were not curtained, but obscured from the outside by the overgrown foliage in the garden. Some light seeped in, but was somehow altered by its passage through the dense leaves. *Corrupted*, was a word that came into Inchball's mind.

The fruity smell was even stronger here. Inchball quickly ascertained the source. There was a stack of greengrocer's crates against one wall. A pyramid of shiny red fruit with star-like stalks rose out of the box on the top.

'Pomegranates!' cried Inchball. 'Takes me

221

back. My old man was a porter in Covent Garden fruit market. He used to bring us a pomegranate every now and then. Strange fruit, ain't it? All them seeds. But if you get a juicy one, it's delicious. Very good for you ... leastways that's what my old man used to say.'

'Indeed, we eat them mainly for their salutary qualities, though I do also enjoy their mythological associations. Some scholars believe that the forbidden fruit in the bible was not an apple but a pomegranate. And of course, we all know about Persephone.'

Inchball narrowed his eyes, as if he was wondering whether this Persephone was someone he ought to take in for questioning.

'Is there enough light in here for you to make your notes?'

The long walnut table had seen better days. Its once highly polished surface was covered with scratches, chips and stains. It was also strewn with newspapers, some of which had been cut up. Ribbons of cuttings littered the floor. There were towers of newspapers waiting to be ransacked at one end.

The other man moved hurriedly to close a drawer that had been left open in an antique escritoire on one side of the room. He turned to face Inchball, blocking his view of the escritoire. 'Won't you sit down?'

Inchball did not accept the invitation. Indeed, he had no intention of making himself comfortable in this house. But the business with the drawer intrigued him. 'A cup of tea wouldn't go amiss. I'm spitting feathers here. Thirsty work pounding the streets of London on the trail of a killer.'

His reluctant host frowned suspiciously. 'I don't employ staff here. For a number of reasons. In the first place, I believe in equality between the classes. In the second ... well, suffice it to say that I have had some unhappy experiences with servants.'

'But you do possess a teapot?'

'Yes, of course.'

'Excellent.' Inchball crossed to the far end of the room, his boots resounding on the bare boards. 'Don't mind me. I shall read the newspaper while I wait.'

'But they are all old.' A note of alarm sounded in the protest.

Inchball picked up an edition of the *Daily Clarion* from four years earlier. He opened it and peered with one eye through an elongated gap where a column of type had once been. 'I don't mind that. Three sugars, there's a good chap.' Inchball winked through the vertical slot in the paper.

The Scrapbook

As soon as he was alone, Inchball dropped the paper on the table and opened the drawer in the escritoire. It contained a thick scrapbook. Inchball pulled the drawer out to its full extent, so that he was able to lift the cover. As he flipped through the pages, it became quickly apparent that the general theme of the scrap collection was 'Crime'. There were accounts of bodies found, of premises burgled, of city frauds and criminal gangs, of rapes and assaults, common and indecent, crimes of passion, of poverty, greed and desperation; together with narratives of the subsequent arrests made, of the trials, the imprisonments and occasional executions. As far as Inchball could tell, in this necessarily cursory review, there seemed to be a preponderance of stories about guardsmen arrested in Hyde Park. A number of photographs pasted in had a certain familiar uniformity to them. They were head and shoulder shots showing the subject either from the front or in profile. The pose was always formal to the point of rigidity.

Sometimes, of course, the crimes lacked any sequels of justice and punishment, as the perpetrators were never caught.

The theme was only loosely held to. In

amongst the editorials and accounts were advertisements, notices and reviews for plays, books, lectures, artistic exhibitions, music hall performances, and moving picture shows. Only some of these could be said to have any clear connection with crime.

The scrapbook began in 1888. The first case for which articles had been collated – the case that seemed to have triggered the collection – was that of the Whitechapel murderer commonly known as Jack the Ripper.

A large portion of the scrapbook was given over to the various trials of Oscar Wilde. The section began with a short clipping pasted beneath the heading HOW THE WORLD WAGS. The clipping itself was brief:

The Marquess of Queensberry was on Saturday last charged at Marlborough Street with libelling Mr Oscar Wilde by leaving for him at a club a visiting card on which were words imputing serious misconduct. The defendant was remanded on bail.

He thumbed the pages, turning the scrapbook on its side to consider the front page of the *Illustrated Police News* for Saturday, May 4, 1895, which had been pasted in whole. It showed an artist's impression of THE CLOSING SCENE AT THE OLD BAILEY in the final trial of Oscar Wilde. There were contrasting sketches of Wilde at the height of his success on a lecture tour in America and now as a prisoner in Bow Street.

A little further on, the torn-out page from a book was pasted in. Beneath the heading DE PROFUNDIS, Inchball read:

...SUFFERING is one very long moment. We cannot divide it by seasons. We can only record its moods, and chronicle their return. With us time itself does not progress. It revolves. It seems to circle round one centre of pain.

Inchball quickly flicked the pages to the last entry: an advertisement for a talk. The title of the lecture, *Killing the Dead*, drew Inchball's attention but made little sense to him. Before he was able to read more, he heard footsteps in the hall.

He pushed the drawer closed and turned as the other man came back into the room. The bone-china cup rattled in its saucer.

'Thank you. That's most kind. You don't know how much I need that. Just put it on the table for me, will you? That's a good feller.'

The other man gave a surly look but complied. The saucer was swilling with a beige reservoir of tea. Inchball smacked his lips and looked longingly at the cup. It had not been his intention to drink it. In fact, the thought of letting something that a queer had prepared pass his lips filled him with a visceral revulsion. He had merely wanted him out of the room.

But now he found that the mere presence of the cup induced a thirst that he could not resist.

The tea was weak and sugary and the strong smell of pomegranates in the room seemed to overpower its flavour. Inchball took a second, deeper quaff. As he placed the cup down, he noticed an astringent aftertaste.

'Now then, let us get back to the matter in hand. When did you last see James Neville?'

'About a week ... ago? Perhaps more.' His tone

226

was distracted, uncertain.

'Can you not be more precise than that, sir? It may turn out to be important.'

The other man frowned as he tried to recollect. But he seemed more intent on watching Inchball closely. 'It was a Saturday, I think. Because I went to the British Museum. I often go to the British Museum on Saturday afternoon. I am interested in antiquities, you see. I take a particular interest in the Classical Greek period.'

'I expect you do, sir.'

'Jimmy sometimes went there too. But it was not there that I saw him that day. It was at the house before I left.'

'A Saturday, very good, sir. Which Saturday would that be? Last Saturday?'

'No. I didn't go to the British Museum last Saturday. It was the Saturday before.'

Inchball counted on his fingers. 'That would be the fourteenth?'

'If you say so. I don't have a calendar in front of me.'

'So the fourteenth of March was the last day you saw James Neville alive?'

Inchball's blunt statement struck a fresh blow. The other man let out a sob and held on to the back of a chair. 'Are you sure it was Jimmy? There can be no mistake?'

Inchball screwed up his face in dismay. 'Blimey, I nearly forgot. That business with the doorbell clean put it out of my mind. That and the pomegranates.' He reached inside his jacket. 'I was supposed to show you this.'

Neville's landlord clamped a hand to his

mouth and closed his eyes.

Inchball took another mouthful of tea, swilling it round his teeth noisily before gulping it down. 'That the feller?'

'Poor Jimmy.'

'I'll take that as a yes.'

'I warned him.'

'You warned him, you say? What about?'

'To be careful. But Jimmy knew better. He wouldn't listen. He didn't need anyone. It was Jimmy against the world. I told him ... that there is strength in fellowship, in brotherhood...'

'Brotherhood?' Inchball raised an eyebrow.

'I don't expect you to understand.'

Inchball saw the other man's expression change from one of anguish to distaste in the sweep of a glance. 'Are you saying that you believed Jimmy was in some kind of danger?'

'Of course! We are all in danger.'

'*We*? What do you mean by we?'

'You know what I mean. Men like Jimmy.'

'Men like Jimmy and *you*, you mean? Queers, you mean?'

'What do you expect me to say to that? I will not incriminate myself.'

'You needn't worry about that. I've been instructed to leave you alone about *that*. Now then, why did you think you was all in danger?'

'Jimmy and I, we are members of a brotherhood. Jimmy wouldn't acknowledge it, denied it in fact, but it doesn't make any difference. He was still a member. You do not *choose* to be a member of this brotherhood. You are born to it. He was born to it.'

228

'What *brotherhood* is this, sir?' Inchball couldn't quite believe it was the brotherhood he had in mind.

'I've said too much already.'

'Do you want us to find out who killed your friend?'

'If only it were as simple as that. Jimmy is dead. It's too late for him. I must think of the countless others who are still alive.'

'Very well,' said Inchball, snapping shut his notepad. He drained his teacup in a series of greedy swallows. 'Can't say I didn't try. If you don't wish to help me, I can't force you.'

The other man allowed a bitter smile of vindication to shape his lips. '*You're* not interested in helping us. You're just going through the motions. We have always had our enemies. Those who wish us harm. Who wish us dead, even. We must look to ourselves for protection, drawing our strength from the love that draws us together, as did the Sacred Band of Thebes in former times. We can expect no protection from the authorities. Indeed, it would not surprise me if it turned out that this crime had been perpetrated by an agent of the law.'

'What a load of rot. Agents of the law do not go around killing people. Not even queers.'

'Of course you would not admit it. You may not even know it. There are agencies within the police of which even the police are not aware.'

'But we ain't got no reason to!' objected Inchball forcibly.

'I can think of many reasons. The murder has brought you here, has it not? Asking your questions. Worming your way into my confidence.'

'Let me tell you, I have no desire to worm my way into anything of yours. I am here because I have a job to do. And the quicker I can get it done and get out of here, the better.' Inchball put a hand to his face, to rub away a sudden weariness. Despite what he had just said, he pulled out a chair and took a seat. The earlier effort of pounding the streets was at last making itself felt in his legs. 'And another thing I can tell you, though I probably shouldn't. It was very likely one of your own kind what killed your friend. How do I know that? Buggery. The doctor said your friend Jimmy's arse was in a very sorry state. Do you seriously expect me to believe that a policeman would do such a thing?'

'I will not disabuse you.'

'I'm very glad to hear it.'

'But does it not occur to you that the same individual may be both a policeman and a sod?'

'Good God! How dare you say such a thing? It's bad enough having to come here and take statements off you buggers. It's more than my job's worth to take your insults too.' Inchball was conscious of the impulse to rise to his feet in rage. But however much he tried to do so, he was unable to wrench himself out of the seat. The weight of exhaustion that he had earlier felt in his legs was spreading up through his torso.

'Believe me, it was not meant as an insult.'

'I've a good mind to box your ears.' But no matter how much he might desire to put his threat into action, Inchball found that his arms resisted any attempt on his part to move them. He excused himself by adding: 'Though I fear you would enjoy it too much.'

'From childhood, we are taught that the only possible physical contact between males is expressed through violence, or at the very least through the rough and tumble of the sports field. I have often thought it ironic that the Marquess of Queensberry was a great patron of boxing. In boxing, you see, the unacknowledged male-to-male attraction is sublimated and turned into aggression. The natural desire to possess another man sexually is perverted into an unnatural desire to beat him to a pulp.'

Inchball tried to speak. But he found he did not know where to begin voicing his objections to the speech he had just heard. He formed the intention of saying: *'You have your natural and your unnatural all mixed up.'* But the words that came out from his mouth did not sound quite right, even to him.

The weight that had spread from his legs to his torso was now squatting on his tongue. He felt it pulling his head down.

The last thing he heard before he hit his head on the table was: 'But do you not think it strange that Queensberry had not one but two sons who were Uranians?'

A Meeting of Minds

Quinn stood at the window in Sir Edward Henry's office. The view faced east, towards the cluster of cranes and scaffolding that squatted like an infestation of giant angular spiders on the opposite bank of the Thames. This was the site of the new County Hall building, which as yet existed mostly as a network of girders, and stacks of glistening stone ready to be put in place. There seemed to be no work going on today. Indeed, the project grew in fits and starts, with extended periods of apparent inactivity followed by bursts of frenzied construction.

A little like the progress of an investigation, it occurred to Quinn.

The river was low. A barge was beached at the bottom of the embankment wall, beneath the suspended arm of a crane. To Quinn's imagination, it seemed as though the crane was groping for the barge, which was hiding out of view and out of reach. But then he dismissed the idea as fanciful. His sense of metaphor had taken over from his grasp of reality.

He turned as he heard the door to the office open. Sir Edward came in with three men, one of whom was Bittlestone.

'Ah, here we are,' said Sir Edward. 'May I

introduce you gentlemen to Inspector Quinn? Quinn, this is Mr Lennox, owner of the *Daily Clarion*.'

'Good day to you, Inspector.' The short, middle-aged man offering Quinn his hand spoke with a soft Irish accent. 'So, this is the famous Quick-fire Quinn! What a pleasure to meet you.'

'I –'

'The less said about that, the better,' cut in Sir Edward. 'And this is Mr Finch, the editor.'

White-haired and wily-eyed, every bit the Fleet Street old hand, Finch avoided Quinn's gaze as he nodded a curt greeting. 'Inspector.' His evasive eye glanced about the room, looking for titbits.

'And Mr Bittlestone I think you already know.' Quinn experienced a frisson of revulsion when he looked at Bittlestone that he had not experienced before. It was perhaps informed by his reading matter of the previous night.

His dreams had been peopled by vampiric homosexuals and he did not feel easy about it.

Sir Edward gestured to the circular meeting table. 'First may I say how grateful we are to you gentlemen for coming in so promptly to see us?'

'One does not refuse an invitation from the Commissioner of the Metropolitan Police,' said Harry Lennox smoothly. 'Especially when the gentleman in question is a fellow Irishman.'

'My parents were Irish, yes,' said Sir Edward. A fond smile animated his face. For a moment it seemed that all the pain of his old gunshot wound had left him and he was a boy again. 'But I was born in Shadwell.'

233

'Shadwell! Then you come from humble origins too,' said Lennox with a sly smile. 'All the more impressive that you have scaled such heights in your career.'

'Not really. My father was a doctor there.'

Quinn's surprise at this revelation caused him to blurt out: 'My father was a doctor too!'

'What? Eh?' Sir Edward's brows contracted in impatience. 'Shall we get on with business? I understand that Mr Bittlestone approached Inspector Quinn with information that has proved useful in an investigation that is currently under way. It seems likely that he has confirmed the identity of a murder victim.'

'I more than confirmed it,' said Bittlestone. 'You had no idea who he was.'

'We certainly appreciate the contribution made by Mr Bittlestone,' said Sir Edward. 'And are willing to offer some tangible acknowledgement of our appreciation. Now that we know the victim's identity, we feel the time is right to make the story public.'

'But surely the time to do that would have been *before* you knew his identity?' said Finch, his gaze flitting wildly around the room. 'Then, perhaps, someone would have come forward and identified him sooner?'

Quinn and Sir Edward exchanged a glance. Sir Edward went on: 'Not every crime that is committed finds its way into the newspapers, as you well know.'

'But a murder?'

'Not even every murder. There were aspects of this case that we were anxious to keep from the public. This was a decision taken at the very highest level, you understand.'

'What aspects?' asked Finch.

Quinn noted with interest how it was the editor who had taken on the role of negotiating with Sir Edward. Clearly, Bittlestone was deferring to his superior. For the opposite reason – to maintain his elevated distance from the proceedings – Lennox also held his peace. Quinn was sure that the three men had carefully agreed their strategy before they came into the building.

'The body was found in Whitechapel. You'll be aware that Whitechapel was the location of a series of sensational crimes some years ago. Now I shall be frank with you: the press coverage of those crimes left a lot to be desired. Then, as now, there were certain details that it was necessary to keep out of the public domain. But the public's hunger for information had to be fed. And so, the newspapermen of the time, deprived of the true facts, decided to fall back on their powers of imagination. The wildest rumours were elevated to the status of undeniable truth. Baseless nonsense was peddled. It was not a glorious time for your profession, gentlemen.'

'The police must take their share of the blame,' said Finch in vague retaliation. 'If you had been open from the start, none of that would have been necessary.'

'That is certainly one way of looking at it,' said Sir Edward. 'The view that was taken by my political masters was that the mistake lay in telling the press anything. It was decided that if any future crimes were ever perpetrated of a

235

similar nature, we would keep the press and the public in the dark for as long as possible, allowing the police to get on with their very important work of catching the perpetrator. Given the information that has fallen into Mr Bittlestone's hands, it is no longer possible to maintain press silence. The story will break, whether we will or we won't. We accept that. That is why we have called you here today, to lay before you the full particulars of the case and to seek your co-operation in controlling what goes before the public.'

'You cannot censor a free press!' cried Bittlestone.

'What? Eh? I have no intention of censoring you. I merely wish to be allowed to present my case to you and to ask you to consider the full implications of whatever you publish.'

'You are inciting us to censor ourselves, which amounts to the same thing.'

'Quiet, Bittlestone,' said Lennox. 'Let the grown-ups talk.'

Sir Edward tactfully made no comment on this exchange, which had drawn a crimson blush to Bittlestone's face. 'I don't pretend to know anything about the economics – or the ethics – of newspaper publishing. I suspect the former is the determiner of the latter, but that is by the by. I know you gentlemen have a newspaper to publish, and to succeed, you need to sell more copies than your rivals. And one way to do that is to be in possession of more accurate – and let's be frank, salacious – information. That is what I am offering you. That and the enduring gratitude of the government.'

Sir Edward was canny enough to exchange a glance with Harry Lennox, whom he knew to be the only proprietor of a major newspaper without a peerage.

'All I am asking you to do is exercise responsibility which, when I think about it, is clearly a superfluous request, because I am sure that is what you would do anyway.'

'Quite,' said Lennox.

'So, what do you have for us, Sir Edward?' demanded Finch.

'The body of a young man was found in the East London Docks, near the Dewar Whisky sign on the eighteenth of March. His throat had been cut and ... the blood drained from his body.'

'Good God!' cried Lennox.

'That's ... sensational,' said Bittlestone, his eyes wide with wonder.

'I hope it is not that that you are asking us to suppress?' said Finch.

For the moment, Sir Edward let the question go unanswered. 'Mr Bittlestone has provided us with an identity of the victim, which as we speak is in the process of being confirmed by one of Inspector Quinn's men. But we are confident that the dead man is James Albert Neville.'

There was a knock at the door. Sir Edward winced as if he had taken a bullet. 'I do apologize. I gave strict instructions that we were not to be disturbed. Come in!'

The door opened minimally. Somehow Miss Latterly managed to slip through the gap. She whispered something into Sir Edward's ear. Sir

Edward's eyes started from his head and his complexion flooded with colour. 'Good heavens.'

He rose from his chair. 'If you will excuse me, gentlemen, I have to take this telephone call.'

As soon as he and Miss Latterly were out of the room, Bittlestone began the speculation as to what had called him away. 'There's been another one.'

'Nonsense.' Quinn's denial was immediate and instinctive. But he knew that Bittlestone was right. The look of horrified indignation – as if whatever had happened was a personal affront to him – on Sir Edward's face was unmistakable. 'It could be any number of things. Sir Edward has more to deal with than this one case. He is often called to deal with matters of national security. The seat of government falls inside his patch, after all.'

'No. Bittlestone's right. It's another murder,' said Finch decisively.

The door opened and Sir Edward returned. They watched him in silence as he took his seat again, his eyes squeezed tight against pain; whether emotional or physical pain, it was clearly savage.

It seemed to Quinn that in the interval he had been out of the room, Sir Edward had aged perceptibly.

Bittlestone was remorseless. 'There's been another one, hasn't there?'

Sir Edward buried his head in his hands. Then sat up to look Bittlestone in the eye. 'No, Mr Bittlestone. There have been another three.'

Mr Finch is Detained

'Three!' cried Finch, almost gleefully. 'This is sensational!'

'And here we are! The *Clarion*, right at the heart of things, just as the story breaks!' exulted Lennox. 'This is one in the eye for Rothermere!'

'It's better than that,' said Finch. 'We are part of the story! We must turn this into a crusade.'

'Tremendous idea, Finch!' cried Lennox. 'I can always count on you to come up with the goods. Incidentally, what are we crusading for – or against?'

'It's usual in these cases, Mr Lennox, to be against the incompetency of the police,' said Finch. 'That's generally held to be a safe position.'

Lennox gave a hearty laugh before remembering himself. 'Apologies, Sir Edward. We mean nothing by it, of course. You can count on us. We'll be stalwart in your defence.' If he didn't quite give a colluding wink to his editor, he may as well have.

Of the three newspapermen, only Bittlestone seemed chastened by the news.

Quinn was stunned. He could see Sir Edward's grim countenance grow increasingly dark and threatening. He was clearly disgusted by the

239

editor and proprietor's cold-blooded delight. It went some way beyond schadenfreude. And their open contempt for the police did nothing to endear them to him.

'What of the victims, Sir Edward?' said Quinn. 'What do we know of them?'

Bittlestone's glance was appreciative. The question needed asking.

'We have no details about them yet. As before, there are no clues as to their identity. But they are all male, aged between sixteen and twenty-five.'

'Are they ... renters too?' asked Bittlestone.

Finch was quick to pick up the hint. 'What's this?'

'Jimmy Neville was a renter,' said Bittlestone quietly.

'Please! Kindly show more respect to the dead!'

Quinn recognized Sir Edward's sudden outrage as a ruse to throw Bittlestone off the scent.

'But it's *true*,' insisted Bittlestone.

'A lot of things are true, Mr Bittlestone,' said Sir Edward, 'but they are not always relevant. For his sake, and for the sake of his family, I think we need not dwell on this. As for these three new victims, so far as I know, there is nothing to suggest they shared his lamentable occupation.'

Bittlestone was unconvinced. *'So far as you know,'* he echoed sarcastically. Then a new idea seemed to dawn on him. 'There is a chance I might know them.'

Sir Edward said nothing. But he gave Quinn a

look that acknowledged the plausibility, as well as the interest, of Bittlestone's remark.

'Do you want me to see if I can identify the bodies?'

'Excellent idea!' cried Finch enthusiastically. 'You can help them with their enquiry. Our Man in the Met! That's how we'll bill you.'

'Now now,' said Sir Edward discouragingly. 'There will be no need for that. Indeed, this strikes me as an example of precisely the kind of wild supposition that I was afraid of. There is absolutely no reason to assume that Mr Bittlestone will know the victims.'

'But if it *is* someone I know...' Bittlestone persisted. He seemed to have been struck by a dawning horror.

'It's different when it's someone you know, isn't it?' said Quinn quietly, to Bittlestone alone. 'It's not just a story any more.'

'I would ask you all, gentlemen, to remember what we were discussing earlier. Responsibility, that is. Until we know the details of these bodies, I would implore you to limit your reporting to the bare facts. In particular, I would urge you not to indulge in wild speculation. And, one more thing: what I told you earlier, about the blood, was not intended for publication.'

'But this changes everything, Commissioner,' said Finch flatly. 'All deals are off. There will be no keeping this out of the papers, with or without our cooperation. Don't delude yourself. There are too many disgruntled, underpaid coppers with half a dozen hungry kids already, and the missus up the duff with another one. Who can blame them if, every now and then, they meet a friendly hack over a pot of ale for a gossip and a bundle of banknotes tied up with string. I used to run several such "Met Pets" myself when I was a reporter. If one of these enterprising officers hasn't yet come in contact with one of your – what is it now? – *four* dead bodies...' Finch grinned in amazement, '...well, they very soon will. Then all Hell will break loose, I can tell you. So, you had better tell us everything you know, and get Bittlestone over to the mortuary right now so that he can begin writing his story without further delay.'

'Inspector Quinn,' said Sir Edward calmly, 'arrest Mr Finch.'

'Have you gone insane? You can't arrest the editor of a major newspaper.'

'It doesn't matter whether you are the editor of a major newspaper or the vendor of a minor one; you have just confessed, in front of witnesses – one of whom is the Commissioner of the Metropolitan Police Force – to corrupting the authority of a police officer. It is a criminal offence which I personally take very seriously. Inspector Quinn.'

Quinn stood up and bowed to Finch. 'Mr Finch, sir, I am arresting you on suspicion of corrupting a police officer. You have the right to remain silent.'

'No, no, no! You don't understand! If you arrest me, you'll have to arrest every editor in Fleet Street. And half the Metropolitan Police Force!'

'Is there not some way out of this, Sir

Edward?' said Lennox. He was no doubt distressed at the thought of losing his editor, but Quinn suspected it was the prospect of a peerage slipping away from him that really rattled him. 'I am sure that Mr Finch was in fact engaging in a little harmless braggadocio. Seeking to impress you, one might almost say bamboozle you, or possibly browbeat you into complying with his wishes. It was empty boasting. He didn't mean a word of it – did you, Finch?'

Finch shook his head fearfully.

'There are no corrupt police officers in the Metropolitan Police Force,' continued Lennox, his Irish lilt a little more pronounced than before, and his words flowing all the more mellifluously for it. 'We all know that. He overplayed his hand. We can tell he's not a gambler! Ah, to be sure, journalists and police officers like to stop for a natter now and then. But no money ever changes hands, does it, Finch? You made that all up, didn't you now, to try and get Sir Edward to give in to you?'

'Yes, that's right. That's what happened.'

'What about the Met Pets?'

'Well, I cannot swear there are no coppers with large families and fecund wives,' went on Lennox. 'But I find it hard to believe that they are ... what was the word you used, Finch? Disgruntled? Isn't that enough to tell you he was spinning you a yarn?'

'You've certainly kissed the Blarney Stone, Mr Lennox,' said Sir Edward. The flicker of a smile rippled across his mask of severity. 'But we are not playing games here.'

243

'Fair point.'

Sir Edward turned to Finch. 'Do you retract your confession? And withdraw the allegations you made against unnamed officers?'

'I do.'

'This places me in a very difficult position. Clearly you are incapable of plain-dealing. Therefore you have forfeited any claim to favoured treatment that Mr Bittlestone's assistance earned you. We will prepare a statement about the bodies which we will release simultaneously to all the London newspapers. You will be held here, incommunicado, until the statement is ready, then you may take a copy away with you. For now, we will not press charges concerning the matter of corrupting police officers. However, if any new evidence comes to light suggesting that anyone employed by the *Clarion* has ever been involved in such activities, then clearly it behoves us to come down with the full force of the law on that individual. And, I might add, on anyone else who is guilty of conspiring with him in committing the offence. That would include, for example, an editor who encouraged such practices and a proprietor who provided the funds for them.'

Lennox could not hide his dismay. It was evident that all the charm, all the professional Irishness, that he had invested in winning Sir Edward over had been wasted. And Harry Lennox was clearly not a man who liked to see his investments come to nothing. He scowled at his editor.

'Now,' continued Sir Edward, 'you will wait here while Inspector Quinn and I retire to another room to prepare the statement. I shall ask Miss Latterly to furnish you with some refreshments while you wait. And I shall have a constable wait with you to ensure that you ... have everything you need.'

Quinn found Sir Edward impressively calm when they sat down together in a small windowless room across the corridor. The only comment he allowed himself on the recent wrangling was: *'Be not deceived: evil communications corrupt good manners*. One Corinthians, fifteen, twenty-three.'

The sealed-off room, with its single bare electric light bulb hanging on twisted wires from a cracked ceiling, was designed to focus the mind. There was no view of the river, no conduit for their thoughts to flow along. Away from the thing they were forced to consider.

Three more dead.

'Are the victims exsanguinated?' asked Quinn.

'We don't know yet. The post-mortem examinations have not been completed. The bodies are being held at Golden Lane. You may want to go over there and speak to the surgeon yourself.'

Quinn did not acknowledge Sir Edward's suggestion. To inspect one corpse might be considered an unappealing duty; the prospect of confronting three together was surely beyond the call. 'How do we know they are victims of the same killer?'

'The throats were cut in the same way. The positioning of the bodies was similar. They were

245

dressed and clean. Spotless.'

'Was ... anything ... found on them?'

'Yes.'

'Cigarette cases?'

'Yes.'

'Inscribed?'

'It would seem so.'

'Same message? *To be entirely free*?'

'No. The wording of each is different. I made a note of it.' Sir Edward passed Quinn a sheet on which was written:

Seek entrance to the House of Pain!
D.P.
Where there is sorrow there is holy ground.
D.P.
Suffering is one very long moment.
D.P.

'May I keep this?'

'Of course.'

Quinn folded the sheet away. He sensed Sir Edward watching him expectantly. But Quinn was not ready to consider the messages yet. He bore the words to his heart, as if they were secret missives from a lover to be read alone later. Sir Edward seemed to sense his need for privacy. He did not push the matter. 'You will receive photographs of the cigarette cases themselves as soon as they are ready.'

'The ages of the victims,' began Quinn abruptly. 'What did you say? Sixteen to twenty-five?'

'Approximately. We cannot know for sure until we are able to identify them.'

'Bittlestone is probably right, isn't he? They are likely to be renters.'

'What I said to him is perfectly true. We don't know that. We may never know that. We cannot assume that it is relevant. Concentrate on the facts, Quinn. I am surprised I have to remind you of this.'

'Where were the bodies found?'

'That's better. They were all in the City Police District. Which makes managing the release of news even more difficult. We can barely control our own *disgruntled coppers*, let alone those of another force.' Sir Edward gave Finch's phrase a sardonic emphasis.

'What about the case? Don't they want to take it over? After all, the majority of the bodies now have been found on their turf.'

'The call I took was from Sir William, whom I had already fully briefed about the first murder. Whitechapel is, after all, adjoining the City district, so it was likely that we would need their cooperation at some point. He acknowledges – with demonstrable relief, I might add – that you have started work on this, and should therefore be allowed to carry on leading it. He is perfectly prepared to make men and whatever other resources we need available to us. Fortunately, I took the precaution when setting up your department of getting my counterpart in the City on board. I presented Special Crimes as a resource both forces could draw on. Sir William even contributes to your budget, don't you know. Indeed, I think I may have persuaded him that the whole thing was his idea.'

'That was very clever of you, sir.'

'As for the precise locations of the bodies,

well, see what you make of this, Quinn. The first was found at the south end of the Minories, just inside the City District. It had been positioned to face the Tower of London. The second was found on Threadneedle Street, facing the Bank of England. The third was found...'

'Outside Saint Paul's Cathedral,' said Quinn. The flatness of his voice belied the wild, destabilizing emotion that was overwhelming him. At last he was beginning to think like the killer. It marked a crucial progression in the conduct of a case, but it was also a move away from his precarious sense of self towards something he could never wholly control. He knew this from experience.

'Good heavens! How did you know?'

'Moving east to west, as the killer seems to be, it was the next major monument.'

'But these are more than mere monuments, Quinn.'

Quinn nodded slowly, as he considered the significance of the locations. 'They are institutions. And more than that, even. They are symbols of our nationhood. The killer is mocking the foundations of our state.'

Sir Edward pointed an arm accusingly towards one of the walls of the featureless room. 'And what will *they* make of that?' Whether he meant the three newspapermen, or the world at large, Quinn was not sure.

The detective tried to recover his train of thought. He had never used Sir Edward as a foil for his theories before. Being a career civil servant and not a policeman, the commissioner lacked the investigative discipline of a trained officer. 'Or perhaps it is more complex than mockery. Let us think back to where the first victim was found. Jimmy Neville. Body found in the London Docks, beneath a Dewar Whisky sign.'

'That doesn't fit in with these other ones,' said Sir Edward, glumly, clasping his hands together with an air of defeat.

'At first sight, no. The Dewar sign is no great monument, that's for sure. But it does symbolize something.'

'The demon drink?'

'Or perhaps it is more to do with our nation's dependence on commerce. The situation may signify more than the sign, if I may put it like that. The fact that it is in the Docklands, where the cargo ships of the Empire arrive to be unloaded. Did you not once remind me of the vital importance of the Thames to the capital? The food and materials we need to survive flow in through it. It is our lifeblood. The first crime poisons it, as these other crimes tarnish those great institutions.'

'If this gets out ... Why, it is the very worst that we feared!'

'We cannot prevent it from getting out, Sir Edward. I hate to say it, but that man Finch is right. Some disgruntled copper somewhere *will* let it slip. Whether he gets paid for it or not is immaterial. We must take the initiative.'

Sir Edward seemed to collapse physically as he accepted the truth of what Quinn was saying. He was the picture of a man not so much bowing to as buckling under the inevitable. 'Yes, of course. There is no avoiding it. Indeed, one thing I have not told you is that Sir William is preparing a press statement of his own. His right, I suppose, as the three bodies were found in the City. That rather forces the issue, if it hadn't been forced already. We shall of course compare notes before releasing a jointly signed communiqué.'

'Couldn't this all take rather a long time?'

'If you're worried about those three scoundrels in there, let them stew. I shall keep them as long as I need to.'

'In truth, I was thinking more about the progress of the case.'

'Oh, yes, of course. Leave the statement to me. I only really wanted an excuse to brief you in private. You must do whatever you need to do.'

'Then you should know that I wish to take Bittlestone to the mortuary to see if he recognizes any of the latest victims.'

'But to do so would be tacitly to acknowledge that there is something in what he said.'

'Sir Edward, I simply cannot proceed in this case if I must be constantly guarding a falsehood. It is as if you are tying one hand behind my back and putting me in to box.'

'What? Oh. Yes, I see. It's difficult for us all, Quinn. I'm under pressure too, you know. I can't simply give you carte blanche, because it is not mine to give.'

'There are three more dead, Sir Edward. *Three more dead!* Go to the man who has the ear of the Home Secretary and whisper that into it.'

'He doesn't carry the ear around with him, you

250

know, Quinn.'

'They must see that we have to catch this killer. If we do not, it will be worse for them.'

Sir Edward gave a shudder, which seemed to set off a new twinge of pain. 'I shall see what I can do. I suppose if Mr Bittlestone is all you say he is, there is a chance he will have crossed paths with one or other of the dead men – if they are indeed renters as you suspect. Surely there can only be a very small number of these degenerates in the capital?'

'I cannot say, Sir Edward.'

'What? Eh? Well, at any rate, it seems that there are four fewer now.' Sir Edward rose to his feet and cast his gaze frantically about the room, as if he were looking for a means of escape.

At the Palace of the Dead

The city went by in a blur.

Macadam was where he liked to be: in the driving seat. Quinn was thankful for the good, calm fixity of his sergeant's concentration as he drove. He was the embodiment of stolidity. His movements measured and reassuring. On such men was Britain built. Salt of the earth, it went without saying. Dependable and loyal: the two necessary traits of a great subordinate. The killer might be able to tarnish the emblems of Empire, but as long as there were men like Macadam, as long as their spirit was strong and uncorrupted, then there was hope.

Next to Quinn, in the rear of the car, Bittlestone took out a fat yellow cigarette from a silver case and put it to his lips. Misreading Quinn's look, he proffered the cigarettes. Quinn declined wordlessly and watched as Bittlestone lit up.

At the time of its construction, nearly forty years ago now, the mortuary in Golden Lane was one of the largest and best equipped in the capital. Held to be a veritable 'palace of the dead' by critics and proponents alike, it had provided the model for the wave of modern mortuaries that were to follow, including the one at Poplar which Quinn had visited at the beginning of the week. As at Poplar, it was located behind a coroner's court, another imposing red brick building with neo-Gothic detailing.

Inside, the apartments were on a grand scale, as if those who had built it had been expecting a glut of death.

Had they foreseen this moment? wondered Quinn.

The post-mortem room was large enough to house three dissecting tables, on each of which lay a cadaver.

Quinn and Bittlestone removed their bowlers simultaneously, with the same hurried motion. It was almost as if some invisible force emanating from the dead had pulled the hats from their heads and they had only just caught them in time.

The pallor was the first thing that hit him, the same inescapable pallor that had overwhelmed him before. The harsh electric lights and gleaming white tiles magnified the unnatural incandescence of the skin.

The bodies were still clothed, so the pallor was concentrated in the face and hands. It seemed all the more intense for that. At the same time, Quinn had a sense of it as something that had leaked out from under the clothes. He knew that there was more of it concealed from view, like an undiscovered cancer.

Quinn held back and allowed Bittlestone to make the first approach. The journalist walked slowly from one to the other, pausing each time for his gaze to linger over the full length of their bodies.

Bittlestone's expression was uncertain as he came back towards Quinn, preoccupied rather than pained.

'Well?'

'I recognize two of the boys. I believe their names are Vincent and Eric. They are the ones on the first two tables.'

'Surnames?'

'Vincent I only knew by his Christian name. Eric, I think, is Eric Sealey. I believe he worked in the Telegraph Office. Perhaps Vincent did too. You might begin your enquiries there.'

Quinn nodded in appreciation. 'And the third one?'

'Perhaps you should take a look at the third one, Inspector.'

Quinn frowned at the journalist's ominous tone. He craned over Bittlestone's shoulder towards the dissecting tables. 'Why can you not simply tell me whether you recognize the third body or not?'

Bittlestone stood to one side.

Quinn realized that he could not postpone the moment any longer. He approached the tables, his heart beating hard, his legs trembling, a feeling of nausea rising in his throat.

The third of the bodies was the renter who had approached him outside the Criterion the night before last.

The man came into the room tentatively, as if he was expecting – or hoping – to be denied access. Seeing Quinn and Bittlestone there already, his face flushed a deep red and he hesitated at the threshold, as if the whole situation – the three dead bodies in the room – was a cause of great embarrassment to him. His eyes stood out strangely pale, drawing the gaze with their quivering panic. They seemed to have been formed from the same marble that had been used in the slabs on which the bodies rested.

If it hadn't been for the fact that he was wearing a surgeon's apron, Quinn might have challenged his presence. As it was, he introduced himself. 'Ah, good day. I am Inspector Quinn of the Special Crimes Department. I presume you have come to conduct the post-mortem examination?'

The man nodded. It seemed an involuntary movement, more of a shudder that almost took over his whole body. 'I am Doctor Yelland, acting police surgeon. Doctor Farqueharson is on leave.'

'He has picked a good time,' said Quinn.

Yelland swallowed noisily.

Surely he is not going to be sick? thought Quinn. 'Is everything quite all right, Doctor Yelland?'

'Three,' said Yelland. He shook his head. *'Three!'*

'Yes.'

Yelland glared at Quinn as if the excessive number of victims was his fault.

Of course, the man was out of his depth. Who wouldn't be? They all were.

Balding and grey, the doctor at least had age, and presumably also experience, on his side. But perhaps that made it worse. In all his long career, he could never have encountered anything like this. His faltering manner did not inspire confidence; there was about him the ingrained humility of a man who knew himself to be a mediocrity. The test he had been dreading all his life had finally come, and he knew in advance that he would not be equal to it.

'Who is this?' Yelland pointed at Bittlestone. Like many insecure people, Yelland expressed himself with a gauche abruptness that bordered on rudeness.

'This gentleman has been able to identify two of the bodies.'

'Two? Good God.'

Bittlestone held out his hand. 'George Bittlestone, of the *Daily Clarion*.'

A journalist in attendance was unlikely to put the doctor at his ease. The tremor of locked-in panic Quinn had noticed in Yelland's eyes earlier intensified.

'A journalist?'

'Mr Bittlestone is not here in that capacity. He is here as a witness.'

Yelland seemed unconvinced. 'A journalist is a journalist. I suppose it is only to be expected.' He shook his head again. 'Three! Three?' It seemed he could not get past the numbers, as if their abstract simplicity was the only comprehensible thing about the case. Or perhaps it was more that the numbers had become a focus for his horror. 'There can be no keeping three out of the papers.'

'Are you aware, Doctor, that another body was found in Shadwell? I wonder whether the Whitechapel police surgeon's report was made available to you?'

'Another body? That's four!'

Quinn could find no fault with the doctor's arithmetic. 'Would it be helpful for you to see the other report?'

Yelland was unexpectedly – and reassuringly – decisive. 'No. It might prejudice my own conclusions.'

'As you wish.' Quinn was prepared to believe he had misjudged the doctor. He saw that the flush had drained from his face. He seemed calmer too.

Perhaps, thought Quinn, *it is the living that unnerve him, not the dead.*

'I suppose you want to watch?'

The question took Quinn off his guard. 'I had not...' Suddenly it all came back to him: the lifeless shiver of an excised organ poured into a steel vessel, the choking fumes of formaldehyde and disinfectant, the scalpel shaking in his hand as it probes the shrivelled skin, searching out the suctioning darkness of taboo within. These were the flickering remnants of his once broken mind, snatches of memory, mangled dream fragments, pulsating with a febrile energy.

'Very well. But you must go up into the viewing gallery,' continued Dr Yelland, who naturally assumed Quinn's answer to be in the affirmative. 'It is strange. I have no desire to watch other men go about their work. A labourer dig a trench, for example. Or a policeman pound his beat, for that matter. And yet, there is no end of people who wish to watch me carve up cadavers.'

'It is rather gruesome,' said Bittlestone, with a shudder of macabre excitement. 'I don't know how I would feel to watch it. Perhaps I ought to find out.'

'No,' said Quinn sharply. 'I am afraid I cannot allow it. I must insist that you go back to the Yard and await your instructions from Sir Edward. Sergeant Macadam will drive you there. Kindly tell him that I shall make my own way back.'

'You intend to stay?' Bittlestone's tone was resentful.

'I do.'

'And observe the post-mortem?'

'That is my intention.'

'Why should you watch it and not I?'

'Because I am the detective in charge of the police investigation and you are...' Quinn hesitated as he ran through all the possible ways he might describe Bittlestone in contradistinction to himself. 'Not.'

Bittlestone opened his mouth as if to voice an objection but thought better of it. 'No matter. You have saved me from myself. I ought to be grateful to you.'

Quinn watched him out of the room before turning to Yelland. 'One of the victims – the one on the furthest table to the left – was alive on the night of the twenty-fourth. That may help with a time of death.'

'I see. How do you know that?'

'I spent some of the evening in his company.'

'You know him?'

'No. I would not say that. I met him in the course of my investigations.' Quinn glanced over to the third table. He remembered the young man's hand in his own, his breath on his face, his touch against his cheek. It was almost as if, by superimposing these memories on the body, he sought to will it back to life; just as – in his dreams – his father had been able to reanimate those other nameless dead. 'I should have warned him. I didn't even try to warn him.'

'You weren't to know.'

Quinn was startled by the voice. He had forgotten about Dr Yelland. He was thinking of his father. It was to his father that he had addressed his self-accusing remarks. He looked Yelland up and down thoroughly, as if searching for some small speck of his father on him. 'If I had warned him, he might still be alive.'

'I must get on with the examination,' said Yelland, who had evidently reached the limit of his capacity for consolation. His gaze kept flitting over to the cadavers, as if he were impatient to join them.

Angels

Yelland started with the body of the young renter who had propositioned Quinn. The first thing he had to do was remove the clothes.

Quinn thought of what Bittlestone had said before he had dismissed him. *I don't know how I would feel to watch it. Perhaps I ought to find out.*

Was that the only reason he was sitting there now, forcing himself to observe this act of legitimized violation?

No, the case required it. It was his duty as lead investigating officer to attend the medical examination of the victims' bodies, wherever possible.

The killer had dressed these young men. He had been the last one to gaze on their naked bodies before enclosing them in their own immaculate clothes. Quinn told himself that to witness the reversal of that process somehow took him closer to the killer. As Dr Yelland slowly peeled away the layers of material, Quinn could not help thinking that it was a more respectful and patient undressing at a stranger's hands than any they had been used to in life.

Quinn felt a sudden revulsion at his own detachment. How could he make such a cynical observation, even in the privacy of his own mind? But it wasn't long before he began to doubt the revulsion as counterfeit.

The fact was that he continued watching.

The doctor had the jacket open now and was carefully shifting the inert body to work the shoulders loose. Next, Yelland untied the necktie and removed the collar. How careful and seemingly loving were his ministrations. It was as if he believed the body was a sleeping baby who might awake if his movements were too abrupt.

Had the killer exercised a similar tenderness when dressing him?

The doctor folded each article of apparel and placed it in a pile on a table to one side. And so the undressing was infinitely drawn out, an act of measured patience as the doctor moved unhurriedly between the two tables.

As the pile of clothes grew on one table, more and more flesh was exposed on the other.

Quinn watched in grim fascination. He could not tear his eyes away from the spreading pallor. And so he discovered that he had moved through horror. He had reached a point where he waited eagerly for each new expanse of whiteness to be uncovered. He welcomed it, wanted it – was soothed by it.

He thought of how he had acquired a taste for Set cigarettes. And the thought induced a craving for one now. How decadent it would be to smoke an opium-soaked cigarette while watching the post-mortem dissection of a young renter!

Was it this easy to become corrupted?

Quinn felt a tingling sensation around his crown. He reached a hand up to his head, half-expecting to find his hat in place. It was a stupid thing to do, as he could see his hat resting on his knees.

Somehow the sensation, which was not dispelled by brushing his fingers through his hair, called him back to himself. He resisted the urge to light a Set, though he did find it calming to know that he had the tin in his pocket, should he need it.

And now the doctor was peeling the last item of clothing, a sock, from the body. The pallor was complete, unmitigated. It seemed to vibrate with menace and potential. Quinn's gaze drank it in.

Why did the killer choose to cover this up? Surely the natural instinct would be to flaunt it? To exult in an act of fierce candour? *See what I have done!*

Yes, there was no necessity for the bodies to be dressed at all, if one thought about it. It would in fact require a great deal of effort to clothe a dead body. You would have to struggle against the weight of the corpse, without the compliance or cooperation of the one being dressed. If the killer took such pains, he must have had good reason.

Was it a failure of nerve at the last, a sudden fear of what he had unleashed?

But Quinn could not believe that anyone capable of creating that terrible pallor would have baulked at displaying it. If he chose to dress the bodies, it was because he wanted them clothed. There was undoubtedly some significance in the act.

The pile of clothes was complete, at least in the sense that there was nothing else to be taken from the body and added to it. And yet Quinn could not shake off the sense that something was missing.

Quinn watched as Yelland conducted his external examination of the body. The doctor walked slowly around the dissecting table, from time to time holding a magnifying glass to an area of the epidermis. He lifted a hand and peered into the wound at the wrist. Then, taking a pair of tweezers, picked at the wound, extracting something invisible which he shook into a glass container. He repeated the process on the other wrist, then on each of the ankles.

At last the time had come for the doctor to turn the body. So vibrant was that pallor, a force or energy in its own right, that it seemed almost as though it would be able to turn itself. All it wanted was a tap on the shoulder from Dr Yelland.

But no. The doctor had to heave and pull at the dead weight of it, rolling it like an awkward log over itself. When the turning was done, Yelland cast a questioning glance up towards Quinn, as if he were demanding applause.

It's not that, thought Quinn. *He's seen the lack of external hypostases.*

Indeed, the unbroken pallor extended to the back of the body. Yelland pored over this with his magnifying glass, like a historian who has discovered a rare and ancient document. Quinn tried to imagine what the doctor must be experiencing: the strange, dark thrill of being confronted by something that should not be.

Yelland looked up at the gallery again, but now his expression was one of outrage.

You knew about this? was what the angry glare of his eyes transmitted.

Quinn had tried to warn him, by discreetly offering to share the findings of the previous police surgeon. But Yelland had wanted to discover it for himself. Perhaps that was the way it had to be.

The doctor rolled the corpse back over. And of course the front of the body was more unnerving than the back, more of a confrontation that one wanted to shy away from.

One practical consideration, in terms of the killer's clothing of the bodies, was simply that the clothes provided the vehicle in which the killer's messages were transmitted. Without clothes there would have been no pockets. And without pockets, where would he have put the cigarette cases?

But there were other ways the words could have been conveyed.

Quinn watched as Dr Yelland made the first incision in the dead youth's skin.

That was one method. The words could have been carved into the flesh. Quinn had seen that done before, a bloody scrawl of wounding words.

Once again Quinn tried to conjure up a sense

of self-revulsion, this time at his capacity for macabre speculation. He came nowhere close to succeeding.

He put it to himself that it was his job to engage in macabre speculation.

He concentrated again on the salient fact: the killer had chosen to reclothe the bodies of his victims. It was as if he was trying to restore them to how they were before the blood had been drained from them. As if it was only the blood he was interested in, only the blood he wanted from them. Once he had what he wanted, he put them back in the world, more or less as they were.

Quinn looked again at the pile of clothes. He could not shake off the impression that there was something missing from it.

The killer had put them back to spread the word for him. That was the important thing: the message. The words in the cigarette cases. He did not want anything to detract from his message.

The dead youths, they were his messengers. His angels.

Another possibility suggested itself to Quinn. The killer covered the pallor because he felt it was too precious – too sacred – to be shared with the vulgar crowd. The expression 'pearls before swine' came to mind. The young bodies, perfected by exsanguination, became pearls.

But it was not just blood that the killer wanted from them. It was blood and buggery.

He took their blood and gave them his seed – his spending – in return; although in fact the spending must have come first. Did the killer believe that he was engaged in some kind of transaction with these youths? That the pearls of his semen were the currency with which he paid for the shedding of their blood?

Quinn would need Yelland to confirm that the same act had been committed in the case of the three new victims. But his suspicion was that it had.

If it was an exchange, an act of commerce, then it was hardly a fair one. Unless the killer believed himself to be giving something so remarkably precious that he held those few ounces of spending to be equal to every last drop of blood in another man's body.

If so, it was an act of monstrous arrogance. Without doubt, arrogance would turn out to be the defining characteristic of this individual, the feature that drove him. He clearly considered himself to be above all laws, divine and man-made. Equally, his sense of his superiority to other men was shockingly clear.

By a similar token, perhaps he believed that he was conferring a signal honour by taking the blood. The victims should consider themselves privileged in having been chosen. In the killer's mind, these acts signified his great generosity, his magnanimity not his cruelty.

He would expect them to be grateful!

Quinn wondered, then, how he went about choosing his victims. Were they known to him already or was there some test that led to their selection?

And what of the cleansing? To achieve that spotless luminosity, every spatter and spill of blood had been wiped from the body. Were they being cleansed to make them more worthy of their role as disseminators of his message, as harbingers? Or was it simply a question of gathering every last drop of the spilled blood, because it was the blood that the killer coveted?

Quinn imagined the moment of the blade severing the artery, the spray of blood. The killer must have been bathed in the hot rush, the victim's own rather more costly 'spending'. And for the killer, perhaps, the blood itself was cleansing. Not literally, but ritually. This was a kind of baptism. A purification.

A bath tub. You could fit such a quantity of liquid in a bath tub. And bathe in it.

Or in flagons, which you could draw upon as your thirst dictated. Or if not thirst, some darker appetite.

Quinn thought he remembered that one of the new inscriptions Sir Edward had shared with him had contained the word 'holy'. It would have been a simple matter to check, as he still had the sheet of paper on him. But at that moment Dr Yelland was working away at the translucent veil of skin, lifting it slowly away from the torso.

It was impossible for Quinn to look away from that. Indeed, he could not consider doing anything until that was completed. His very thoughts were frozen.

At last the young man was opened up at the chest and abdomen, the undersides of skin lying in slack folds around the wide placid wound inflicted by the surgeon's scalpel. Quinn's gaze rushed in upon the confused mystery revealed, like water sucked into a drain. He had seen enough dissected bodies to know immediately that something was amiss. The predominant colour was a sapped grey, not the usual drenched red. Only the bones held on to their customary pink tinge.

It is difficult to drain a bone, concluded Quinn.

His mind resumed its work, churning macabre speculations, until such time as a rare, startling insight should float to the surface.

He came back to the idea that the killer believed himself to be engaged in some form of religious rite. The cleansing of the bodies had suggested it originally. But now he considered the possibility that the blood was imbibed in an act of unholy communion. It was the wine of a hellish Eucharist. The semen he had delivered stood for the flesh, taken through the fundament rather than the mouth. A perversion of everything holy. Blasphemy added to atrocity.

The dark taboo at the heart of the dead youth continued to be explored. What the murderer had begun, the good doctor was completing.

Bittlestone's words came back to him yet again: *I don't know how I would feel to watch it. Perhaps I ought to find out.*

Had the killer said something similar to himself? *I don't know how I would feel to kill him ... Perhaps I ought to find out.*

But if it was only about that, then why repeat the act?

Because he discovered that he liked the way it felt.

Was it even possible that Bittlestone was the killer? Quinn had seriously entertained the question for the first time in the car, when he had seen the journalist light his Set cigarette. Was it not curious that he had come forward when he had, providing them with the identity now of three of the victims, and only withholding the identity of the one with whom he knew Quinn had had dealings?

What was his game?

Of course, it made no sense that the killer would take such a risk. Unless his arrogance was even greater than Quinn had suspected.

To have three bodies come to light while he was in the office of the Commissioner of the Metropolitan Police, what a delicious thrill that must have given him! Had he somehow engineered the situation to create that moment?

What fools he must take them for, to dare to play such games.

He was impatient too. What had he said in Quinn's office that time? *'Your investigation has come to a grinding halt.'* And so he provided them with information to move the investigation on.

Certainly he had all the necessary arrogance to be the killer.

It was as if he were giving them a head start, so confident was he that they would not be able to catch him.

But no, he could not quite fit Bittlestone into the silhouetted shadow he was hunting. He suspected that the distaste he felt towards the man's sexual habits was clouding his judgement.

Leaving aside the evidence of sodomy, it was far more likely that the killings were perpetrated by someone who shared Quinn's disgust at men like Bittlestone, a disgust that Quinn felt all the more sharply now that he had read more of *The Profession of Shame*.

The murders were a judgement meted out on them.

Quinn was forced to consider the possibility that the murderer was not a natural sodomite. That he did what he did for a purpose other than sexual gratification. If this were so, what aroused him was not the excitement of a sexual act with a man; it was the power that he had over the life and death of another human. It was the thrill, the exultation of slaughter.

He became a god. A god like Set, the animal-headed monster on the cigarette tin. A being capable of anything; utterly amoral, unfettered by the considerations that restrained other men. In the words of the first inscription, *entirely free*.

The youth lay like an unwrapped parcel on the dissecting table. A gift; the killer's gift to the world.

Quinn had seen enough. As he stood up to leave, he felt something fall from his lap. Looking down, he saw his hat roll away from his feet.

Panic

He felt the dryness in his throat before he came to.

He felt it as a painful contraction of the darkness in which he was suspended. In fact, the tightness intensified at various points of his dimly growing awareness of himself. He felt the pain before he knew who he was. Or where he was. Or how he came to be there.

He felt himself trapped by the heaviest weight he had ever borne: some part of the darkness that had the weight of infinity bearing down on it. Some part of the darkness that was inside him. He mustered his strength to move this great weight but was defeated by the effort.

The darkness punished him. It pinched and bit him. It forced its invisible claws into him and scratched.

It pressed down on him from above. Beneath him, it formed itself into something solid and unyielding, a cold, hard, uncompromising otherness against which he began to sense the edges of his being. There was no comfort in this burgeoning awareness. Only pain.

He tried to swallow but could not. He realized that the great weight he had struggled to move was his tongue. But there was something else pushing down on that. Something in his mouth.

He opened his eyes. The darkness changed, became edged with the possibility of light. But it was still darkness.

He wondered if he were dead. The pain suggested he was not.

No, it was simply that he had been blindfolded. And when he tried to move a hand to pull the blindfold away, he discovered that his hands had been bound behind his back.

He was lying on his side, he realized. He felt the boards against his cheek. His left arm was numb, trapped under the weight of his body. The other arm was twisted round uncomfortably by the binding.

His knees were pulled up. Straightening his legs, he realized that he had been bound at the ankles too.

He rolled over on to his back. He tried kicking his legs apart. Put all his tensioned strength into the effort. His body rocked blindly in a great upheaval of writhing, but caused barely a ripple in the darkness. His bonds had been tightly knotted.

He was trussed up good and proper. The queer snob had got the better of him, all right.

It was then that Inchball gave some thought to the acts that might have been perpetrated on him while he had lain unconscious. It almost seemed as if he felt the fellow's hands all over him now. So vivid was the sensation that it was inconceivable that it was anything other than a memory.

His writhing became violent and convulsive, as if an electric current was being passed through him.

He opened his mouth to give voice to the revulsion that racked his body. But a soft spreading weight pressed down on his tongue and sucked the moisture from his palate, making it impossible for him to utter anything other than a few stifled cries.

The darkness remained undisturbed.

Quinn spread the morning's newspapers across his desk. Despite its neutral tone and scarcity of detail, the press communiqué jointly issued by Sir Edward and Sir William Nott-Bower, the commissioner of the City of London Police, had resulted in some predictably lurid headlines.

FOUR DEAD IN GHASTLY MURDERS ACROSS LONDON

GHASTLY SERIES OF MURDERS HITS CAPITAL

FOUR GHASTLY MURDERS! POLICE BAFFLED!

There was no mention of exsanguination, unless the frequent use of the word *bloodthirsty* was to be taken as a reference to it. The *Clarion* had managed to work it into a headline: BLOOD-THIRSTY MURDERER WREAKS HAVOC IN GHASTLY TRAIL OF DEATH. Given the method of dispatch, this was unexceptionable. However, Quinn baulked at their description of the victims as 'pallid youths'.

At least they did not attempt to make any coded allusions to unnatural sexual practices – not so far as Quinn could detect, at any rate. However, there seemed little doubt now that there was a homosexual aspect to the crimes. Dr Yelland's report had arrived on Quinn's desk first thing that morning. The presence of seminal deposits in the rectums of the three latest victims confirmed that they too had been recently sodomized.

Even without these details, the accounts were shocking enough: four violent deaths visited upon the city in close propinquity. It was deemed especially disturbing that the victims had had their throats cut. Quinn reflected that it was undoubtedly unpleasant to be murdered by any method, but the cutting of throats always seemed to release a peculiar frisson. Nightmares, haunted by razor-wielding phantoms, could no longer be contained in sleeping minds; they leached out on to the streets to fill the shadowed doorways.

Some of the papers speculated that the murders might have been carried out by criminal gangs. The cutthroat razor was held to be a favoured weapon of such types. There were dark hints about the putative criminality of the deceased in an attempt, no doubt, to reassure decent, law-abiding folk that they had nothing to fear. If it was a case of the criminal fraternity turning on itself, these events could be safely dismissed. It was almost as if they had taken place in another city, on the other side of the world.

It was made clear that little was known about the victims other than their youthfulness. No names were given, on the grounds that the police had not yet been able to establish their identities beyond doubt.

The *Clarion* wondered whether it was in fact a razor that had caused the fatal wounds. Could it not be a *dao* or a *kris*, or some other bladed weapon of eastern origin? For that matter, was it not well known that the Tribe of Israel used sharp knives in their ritual sacrifices?

The locations at which the bodies had been found seemed to have captured the collective imagination of Fleet Street. Certainly, it inspired the hacks when it came to the question of giving the murderer a name. The proximity to the Thames led the *Daily Mail* to dub him The Riverside Ripper. Quinn winced at that one. Could this killer really be described as a Ripper? Nothing had been ripped out. Slasher was more accurate, which was the word the *Daily Express* favoured, to whom the killer was The City Slasher.

At least there was no Queer Killer, or any mention of vampires, alliterative or otherwise.

As ever, the front page of the *Illustrated Police News* was given over to a pictorial representation of the salient points. The four bodies were shown in situ, in separate vignettes arranged around a silhouetted figure, presumably intended to be the murderer. The artist – on what basis, Quinn could not imagine – appeared to have given this shadowy phantom an opera cape and top hat. Quinn focused on the featureless black shape, willing an identifiable presence to step forward and reveal itself. He could not dispel the notion that the figure possessed the vague animalistic head of the Egyptian deity Set, its strange upright ears hidden beneath the top hat.

Naturally, in all papers, the police were portrayed as being utterly out of their depth. The usual appeal for members of the public who might have seen anything suspicious to come forward was held to be an admission of failure.

He could imagine how Sir Edward would receive all this. The 'moral panic' that he had wished to avoid was clearly under way. Well, it couldn't be helped. The important thing now was to press on with the case and find the murderer quickly before there were any more victims.

At Quinn's request, detectives from the City Police were making enquiries at the London Central Telegraph Office on St Martin's-le-Grand in order to confirm Bittlestone's identification of one of the victims as Eric Sealey, and to investigate the possibility that the other victims had some connection with the place. He was expecting their findings at any moment. Meanwhile, Macadam was in the East End pursuing his lead concerning the rope fibres. It was frustrating, to say the least, that Inchball had so far failed to report for duty this morning. Quinn was impatient to hear what he had discovered at the house on Adelaide Road. He could only think that his enquiries had resulted in another lead, which he had taken it upon himself to follow up.

Quinn turned the pages of the *Clarion* away from its typical – and galling – subheading: QUICK-FIRE QUINN IN A QUANDARY.

His eye at last settled on a photograph in the society pages. He was drawn to it because he recognized one of the people in it as Harry Lennox. With him was a young woman with a compelling face, though whether the quality that

275

compelled was beauty or cruelty he could not say. She was identified in the caption as Lennox's daughter, Jane.

The third figure in the photograph was a man whose age seemed to be between that of Lennox and his daughter, though arguably closer to the former. Quinn struggled to think where he had seen this man before. According to the caption, he was Lord Tobias Marjoribanks, 'once a noted society artist, who last year returned to these shores after a long residency in the United States of America'. Quinn thought that that 'once' must have hurt. However, his expression showed no sign of disappointment or rancour. If anything, he seemed rather pleased with himself. And so, if he had suffered the loss of an artistic career, the impression was that he had gained something far more valuable. Precisely what that something was, Quinn discovered when he read the short paragraph that accompanied the photograph: 'Marjoribanks had recently become engaged to Jane Lennox'. Quinn was not surprised. Despite the disparity in their ages, they looked made for one another.

Both Lennox and Marjoribanks were dressed in the type of attire that the *Illustrated Police News* artist had chosen for the mysterious perpetrator. But this was not an interesting coincidence in any way, because it was the standard evening wear of the well-to-do or aristocratic male about town. What was strange, however, was how differently the garb sat on each man. On Lennox, despite his undoubted confidence and ease, for which Quinn could personally attest, the outfit appeared awkward, as if it were a costume he had hired for the occasion hurriedly, without trying on first. Quinn had the impression that not only Lennox, but everyone, would be more comfortable if he wore tweeds. Lord Marjoribanks, on the other hand, carried off the formal attire as one who had been born to it.

Quinn folded away the newspapers and spread out a street map of London. Using a red pencil, he marked with an X the locations at which the bodies had been found. The statements and police reports he had read indicated that, as with the first murder, the victims had been killed elsewhere and placed where they were discovered. The killer must have access to an efficient mode of transportation – a motor car, for example. That suggested the murderer was either wealthy enough to own a car, or someone whose job it was to drive a vehicle, whether motor-powered or horse-drawn. Quinn had always thought that driving a taxi would be the perfect occupation for a murderer. Given the multiplicity of victims, a delivery driver was also a possibility. Quinn tried to picture the three bodies piled in the back of an unknown van, thrown together in a posthumous intimacy.

Unless one assumed the presence of an accomplice, the killer must have driven himself and his dead passengers about. An accomplice could not be ruled out, but for the time being Quinn proceeded on the basis that the killer was acting alone. It was far more likely, given the particularly horrendous and shameful aspect of the crimes. That said, he knew of cases where men had come together to conspire in the commission of the most dreadful acts.

It was not known in what order the last three victims had been killed. According to Dr Yelland, their deaths occurred at approximately the same time. Quinn imagined an orgy of destruction. The killer must have picked the three youths up together. Perhaps they had even been complicit in each other's murder. Two held the first one down while his throat was slit. Then one was persuaded to turn on his mate. The last one would be left to beg for mercy as he realized that his earlier cooperation would not save him.

It was also impossible to say in what order their bodies had been placed. However, the plotting of the marks on the map encouraged one to think of a movement from East to West. In which case, the question had to be asked: *Where next?*

Quinn imagined a line drawn roughly through the locations marked. Like points on a graph, they did not align exactly. However, they held together sufficiently well to suggest a consistent direction of travel. Extending this line at its westward end, the next prominent structure upon which his eye alighted was Lincoln's Inn. Beyond that, the line took him to the British Museum.

The former might be said to stand for the state's judicial apparatus, the latter for its cultural heritage. If Quinn was right in his theory that the murderer was in some way engaged in an attack upon the cornerstones of the Empire, these institutions might be considered plausible targets for his attention.

Where would it end? had to be the next question.

Quinn took a twelve-inch wooden ruler from his drawer. He laid it over the points and ran his finger along the edge, until it reached a rectangle of pale green at the north-west of the capital. The patch was labelled *Lord's Cricket Ground.*

Macadam returned to the department around midday, carrying a coil of rope which he dropped on to Quinn's desk. 'A present for you, sir.' There was an excited energy about Macadam's eyes.

'I take it from this that your morning has not been entirely wasted?'

Macadam smiled in acknowledgement. 'Indeed not, sir. I made enquiries at every rope maker's and chandler's in the Limehouse and Poplar area. As it turned out, it was at the very first establishment I visited, Willett's on Bridge Road, just next to the Locke's Lead Works, that I made my discovery.'

'Which is?'

'Willett the chandler recalled selling a quantity of rope to a fellow whom he described as...' Macadam consulted his notepad. *'Not the usual type we gets in 'ere.* I recorded his words verbatim, sir.'

'Very good, Macadam. Kindly continue.'

'When I asked him what was so very unusual about this fellow, he said that he was a toff. He went on to affirm that they do not get many toffs in there. In fact, he went so far as to say that he had never served a single toff in his life before this mysterious customer.'

'Hardly surprising, given his store's location in the East End.'

'Indeed, sir. I asked if he could remember whether the rope he sold was tarred or untarred, and he averred that it was the latter. He further remarked that while he was out back fetching the rope, the toff must have lit up a cigarette. He particularly noticed it when he came back because he disliked the smell, which he said fair stank out his shop. I asked him if there was anything else he remembered about the cigarette, and he said that it was *yeller*.' Macadam gave what Quinn assumed was an imitation of the chandler's delivery of that word, injecting it with a forceful contempt. 'He seemed to strongly object to the colour, but on what grounds, I could not ascertain.'

'Sounds like it could be our man, Macadam.'

'I took the liberty of purchasing a length of the same rope, which as you may have gathered is this here sample here. With your permission, sir, it was my intention to pass this on to my pal Charlie Cale to get him to compare it to the fibres that came from the first victim.'

'Of course. Doctor Yelland recovered similar fibres from the other victims, which I had him send to Cale. I await his report. You could perhaps find out how he is getting on if you mean to take that rope to him. If we can link all the murders to the rope bought at your chandler's, it would be a significant breakthrough. Especially if the chandler is able to cast light on the identity of our toff. Did he come up with a name, by any chance? A delivery address, even?'

'Sadly, no, sir. The gentleman paid in cash and took his purchase away with him.'

'Ah, well, it was too much to hope for, I suppose. Nonetheless, this is helping us to build up a picture. He doesn't sound like the sort of fellow who drives a taxi or a delivery van, for instance. More like a well-to-do individual in possession of his own motor car. I have been developing the theory that the murderer must have some means of transport to convey the bodies to the various locations at which he disposes of them.'

'I see, sir. That makes admirable sense.'

Quinn was appreciative of Macadam's attempt to support and bolster him. However, the sergeant's instinctive deference reminded Quinn of Inchball's equally instinctive contrariness. 'Where's Inchball, do we know?'

'I haven't seen him since yesterday. Not since he went off to investigate James Neville's last known address.'

At that moment, the look on Macadam's face seemed to express exactly the icy dread that Quinn was suddenly feeling in the pit of his stomach.

A Sojourn in Hades

There is a limit to how much physical pain the human body can endure. Release may come through loss of consciousness, or even death. In Inchball's case, the intense pain of his over-burdened bladder found release in the simple act of letting go. While it lasted, the deep, sweet bliss overwhelmed every other sensation or consideration. But the pleasure was short-lived. Immediately after, he was forced to lie in the pool of his own urine, his crotch and thighs chilled by his sodden trousers.

As he lay there, he thought of what he would do to Fanshaw when he caught up with him. He would make of his face a bloody pulp. He knew how much these queers valued their looks.

The clawing tightness at his throat was still with him. He felt a similar but more intense contraction in his head. It was as if his brain were being wrung dry by hands with long pointed fingernails. Some residue of the drug that had been used on him still had its hooks in him. He could feel it in the queasy gaseous sensation that had replaced his internal organs. Every so often the balloon of nausea floated up inside him, pushing the membrane of its extent against Inchball's oesophagus.

He was forced to breathe through his nose by the cloth that had been stuffed into his mouth: a cotton handkerchief, so far as he could tell. There was no possibility of keeping his mouth moist. Any saliva he produced was immediately absorbed. Indeed, it felt as though the rag had sucked all the moisture from his body, and with it every ounce of energy.

What he needed to do more than anything was drink some water. If only he could get water to his lips, he would be capable of anything.

And so the fantasies that sustained him alternated: now he was pounding his fists into Fanshaw's face; now he paused to gulp down a long glass of iced water, its exquisite clarity cutting through the wadding of his unbearable thirst. Each fantasy was inevitably unfulfilling. When he was let down by one, he would turn to the other. In his imagination, Fanshaw's face repeatedly renewed itself, so that it could be destroyed afresh. In the same way, the glass was magically refilled each time he had drained it.

When both fantasies lost the capacity to distract, waves of abstract, angry emotion would break over him. Every sinew of his trussed body became tensed at the same time, as he pushed against his bonds, willing them to snap apart. But, of course, the bindings stayed in place. He would collapse, defeated by frustration and self-pity, incredulous that he had allowed himself to be bettered by a man like Fanshaw. Yes, he could only blame himself. He had let his guard down. He had let his thirst, and his partiality to tea, get the better of him.

He could not say how many times this cycle of fantasy and self-reproach repeated itself before he heard the ringing of the electric bell. The button must have become stuck again, because the shrill peal showed no sign of stopping. The ringing was drowned out by an incessant hammering, which was followed by the shout: 'Open up! Police!'

A window shattered.

Once again, Inchball tried to initiate the muscular processes that would under any other circumstances result in a full-throated roar. But the cloth that was jammed in his mouth stifled the fierce vibration of his vocal cords. A muffled groan was all that he could produce. It didn't matter, though; he knew that they would find him.

And indeed, just then he heard the door burst open. Hands pulled at the blindfold around his head. All at once he was looking up into Macadam's glorious, ugly face. He felt his throat begin to convulse with emotion. He could not say whether it was laughter or sobbing that was being stifled.

Macadam now set to work to undo the gag. It was a laborious operation. The knot was tightly tied. And once that had been slipped, the cotton handkerchief had to be pulled from Inchball's mouth.

'You took your fucking time.' Inchball's voice quivered hoarsely, little more than a cracked whisper. His throat felt as though he was swallowing needles as he spoke. But still, it was important for him to get the first quip in.

'Yes, well, we were enjoying the peace and quiet,' said Macadam.

Inchball looked deeply into Macadam's face. He cursed as he felt himself begin to weep. When Inspector Quinn strode into the room, the sobbing took him over.

Now restored to his feet, and his usual gruff calm, Inchball handed back to Macadam the glass he had just drained of water. He shook his head forlornly. 'I bloody wet myself.'

'That's all right, Inchball,' said Quinn. 'Perfectly understandable.'

'When I get hold of that fucking queer ... I suppose he's scarpered?'

'There's no sign of anyone,' confirmed Quinn.

'He's gonna regret getting on the wrong side of me.'

'Can you tell us what happened?'

'He brought me some tea. It must have been drugged.'

'But why would he drug you? Why imprison a police officer? It's a very serious crime. Had you discovered something?'

Inchball rubbed his forehead tensely as he tried to remember. It left a blotchy imprint, which seemed to emphasize his sudden vulnerability.

The look of deep confusion gradually lifted. He glanced questioningly at the escritoire against one wall. He walked tentatively over to it and opened the drawer. 'Gone. I might have known.'

'What was it?'

'There was a scrapbook in here. He didn't want me to see it. Shut the drawer when we came in. But I did. I saw it while he was making the tea.'

'And?'

Inchball shrugged. 'Hard to say. There was a lot of stuff about queers in there. And murders. Jack the Ripper. Oscar Wilde. And mugshots that looked like they'd come straight from the Yard.'

'Do you think this Fanshaw feller's our man, sir?' asked Macadam dubiously.

''Course he is!' cried Inchball. 'Why else would he knock me out like that?'

'It could be because he is the murderer and he thought we were on to him,' said Quinn. 'Or there could have been some other reason. He clearly didn't want you to have this scrapbook and was prepared to commit a serious crime to prevent it.'

'If we could find a photograph of him, sir, I could take it back to my chandler pal and see if it's the fellow what bought the rope. In the meantime, I could have Charlie Cale take a look at Inchball's bindings to see if it's the same as the others.'

'Excellent idea, Macadam. I would also suggest that we circulate Inchball's description of this man to the ports. It may be his intention to leave the country.'

'If that's the case, then you are probably too late already,' said Inchball gloomily. 'He must have made a run for it last night. He'll be in France by now. I hear they welcome queers over there. If I'd done what he done, that's where I'd go. And I wouldn't hang about neither.'

'Undoubtedly the reason he drugged you was to buy himself time,' said Quinn. 'He could have

286

killed you, you know. But he chose not to.'

'Are you saying I should be grateful?'

'I'm merely trying to put myself in his shoes. He has committed what he may have considered the minimum necessary crime.' Quinn caught sight of the pile of greengrocer's crates. 'Are those pomegranates?'

'That's right.'

'How interesting. Like Persephone, you partook of Death's fare and sojourned in Hades.'

'Persephone? He mentioned her, you know.'

'It's a classical allusion.' Quinn thought back to the imaginary line he had imposed on the map of London. 'It may be that he considers his work here not yet done. In which case, he will not have left the country, or even the capital. He will simply have gone to ground.'

'Begging your pardon, sir. When you say his *work*?'

'The murders, Macadam. I have the feeling that there is a very specific point to these crimes, given the similarities between the victims. However, I would remind you that we have not yet established beyond doubt that Fanshaw is the killer. To that end, let us search the house for photographs and anything else that might cast light on this man. I noticed some mail on the doormat as we came in. Perhaps I will begin with that.' Quinn frowned as he cocked his head. The electric bell had not stopped ringing since they had broken in. 'That's rather annoying.'

'I can fix it,' said Inchball. He looked down glumly at himself. 'If only I had a clean pair of trousers.'

Your Devoted Pinky

As Quinn bent down to pick the letters up off the mat, he noticed a pair of eyes peering through the broken pane in the door.

'You?' The voice was familiar. So was the loutish laughter that came as the eyes disappeared from view.

Quinn unconsciously drew a hand protectively up to his nose before pulling open the door. 'Tommy! Don't run away.'

In truth, Tommy Venables showed no intention of moving from the front step. His bowler was pushed back at an insouciant angle, a sign of his lack of concern at seeing Quinn again. 'I ain't goin' nowhere. So what's this all abou'? We had a break-in?'

Quinn gazed distractedly at the shimmering silk scarf that Venables had around his neck. It was a moment before he recognized it as the cloth he had bought at the draper's, which Venables had stolen from him. *'We?* Do you mean to say that you live here?'

'That's not what I said at all. Sometimes I pop over to see if any of my friends will put me up for the night. Is the Right 'Enrable in?'

'The right what?'

'Hen-rable. Henry. That's what I call him. The

Right Henrable.'

'Henry Fanshaw?'

'That's right. The Right 'Enrable.'

'Henry Fanshaw is in serious trouble. He drugged and imprisoned a police officer. We had to break in to release him. Fanshaw is missing.'

'Bloody 'ell!'

'So any information you can give us as to his whereabouts would be gratefully received. We think he may have had something to do with Jimmy Neville's death. You knew Jimmy lived here. You could have saved us a lot of trouble if you'd told me this that day when we met.'

'But you wasn't straight with me, was you, Quentin. Dint tell me you was a rozzer. Not straight away. I din' know what you was up to.'

'There have been three more deaths. If you'd told me what you knew, those boys might still be alive.'

'You carn' lay that at my door.' Tommy Venables' face was suddenly drained of colour. He took out the silver cigarette case that Quinn had seen that day outside the bookshop. 'Everybody's talking about it. They're saying there's a madman on the loose.' Venables lit a fat yellow cigarette and pocketed the case again. 'They're saying we should stay off the streets. It's hard enough anyway, what with all the rozzers there are about the place. London's crawlin' with 'em.'

'It's for your protection. For the protection of men like you. We have naturally increased the police presence on the streets.'

'Yeah, well, there's no business to be had no

more. Not for love nor money. Which means I don' eat no more and I don' get the change for a night's lodgin'. That's why I was comin' over 'ere to see if anyone would give me a bunk up for the night.'

'This may well be the very worst place you could have come to.'

'You've got it wrong again, Quentin. 'Enry din' have nothing to do with them murders, if that's what you're thinkin'. 'Enry's a sweet man. Bit of a nutter, I'll give you that. But 'armless. He wouldn't hurt a fly. An' he certainly wouldn't hurt another queer. He thought we all had to stick together. Look out for one another. It was a crusade with him. A war, you might say. In his head, there was a great army of queers marching against the rest of the world. A brother'ood. That's what he called it. I bet that's why he done what he done. To the rozzer, like. The police was always the enemy to 'Enry.'

'But we're trying to catch the man who has committed these terrible crimes against homo-sexuals. We're on *your side*!'

'Thass wha' you say. 'Enry wouldn't see it like that. He was always tellin' us to watch out for the Ole Bill. He probably thought the rozzer had come to round up the brother'ood.'

'Then he's a very stupid man. Do you know anything about his scrapbook?'

'I seen it, like. Borin', if you arsk me.'

'Was it anything to do with this brotherhood?'

'Everything was to do with the brother'ood. And 'Enry would have done anything to protect it. Except the crazy thing was ... It din' exist.

290

There was nothing *to* protect. It was all in his 'ead.' Venables looked over his shoulder nervously. His habitual stance of cocky defiance had lost some of its conviction. When he turned back to Quinn, there was a look of open appeal in his eyes. 'Listen, can't I come in, Quentin? I got nowhere else to go.'

'I'm afraid that won't be possible. We're conducting a search of the premises.'

'I'll stay out of your way, honest I will.'

Quinn hesitated before standing aside. 'Very well. You may come in, but on the condition that you go only where I say you may. And you must promise to answer any questions I put to you.'

'Whatever you say, Quentin.'

'You'd better not call me Quentin either. It's Inspector Quinn from now on.'

'Quentin Quinn? Cor blimey, your parents were having a larf, weren' they?'

'That need not concern you.' Quinn looked down at the letters in his hand as Venables walked past him into the hallway. He noticed that most were addressed to one *H. Fetherstonhaugh, Esq.* He remembered the name from the list of members of the Panther Club.

'So, where do you want me?' asked Venables pertly. His usual coarse laughter was not long in coming, prompting an inquisitive appearance from Macadam.

Quinn dismissed his sergeant with a nod. To Venables, he said: 'Less of that, do you hear me? If you don't behave yourself, you'll be out.'

'A'righ', Quentin. Keep yer 'air on. I mean, very well, Inspector Quinn. Whatever you say.'

'Now, besides Henry Fanshaw, do you know any of the other residents of this house? This man, for instance?' Quinn showed Venables one of the envelopes.

'That *is* Henry! That's how he spells his name. It's the nobs' way of spellin' Fanshaw. Did you not know that?'

'Are you sure about that?'

'Yeah, we used to josh him about it. He dint mind. He thought it was funny hisself.'

'I see. Did he, Fetherstonhaugh, own a motor car, as far as you know?'

'Nah – you jokin', ain't yer? The Right 'Enrable in a motor? He dint trust 'em. Used to cycle everywhere.'

'Show me that cigarette case, will you?'

'Yer what? Why you so bothered about my fag case?'

'All the victims were found with a silver cigarette case on them.'

Venables' expression was once again stripped of any pretence of arrogance. 'Wha' are you sayin'?'

'I am saying that the murderer appears to mark out his victims by giving them cigarette cases very similar to the one you have on you.'

Venables looked for a moment as though he was considering a smart riposte. But something about Quinn's expression evidently deterred him. He reached again into his jacket and handed over the cigarette case.

Quinn pressed the catch. The aroma of unlit Set tobacco that was released stirred a pang of something like nostalgia. He inhaled deeply and held his breath, as if he was trying to hold on to the unnameable thing that he had lost.

There was an inscription on the inside of the lid: *Dearest Thomas, Keep this always next to your heart, as I shall keep you always next to mine, Your Devoted Pinky.*

'Pinky,' said Quinn. 'Devoted Pinky.'

'It don't mean he had anything 'a do with these murders. Lots of gentlemen give their friends cigarette cases as presents.'

Quinn clicked the cigarette case shut and handed it back to Venables. 'Perhaps you're right. However, there is something here that must be looked into. What is Pinky's real name?'

'Francis ... Percy ... Arundel. The Marquess of Roachford.' Venables drew himself up as he uttered Pinky's names and title, as if he believed they somehow conferred honour on him; or perhaps something more: invulnerability.

A Heady Fug

Quinn pinned the map of London to the wall. The locations at which bodies had been found – the London Docks, the Tower of London, the Bank of England and St Paul's Cathedral – were shown with red pencil crosses. With a blue pencil, Quinn had marked Lincoln's Inn, the British Museum and Lords Cricket Ground. A black

293

cross indicated the location of the Panther Club.

The photographs of the four victims sprawled out around the map. When Quinn was concentrating on the map, he felt their peripheral presence like a dark contagion seeping out from the city. In some way, his aversion to confronting the horror they represented focused his mind on the case as an abstract intellectual puzzle. The map was rational and organized. The photographs were insane and chaotic. It was understandable that he would prefer to concentrate on the former. And yet he had a sense that he would only find the solution when he found a way to contemplate both aspects of the case at once.

Quinn opened the tin of Set cigarettes. There were only three left now. He took one out and lit it. He considered the glowing tip as he retained the first lungful of smoke.

'What are they like?' Inchball's voice was suspicious. And yet the mere fact that he was asking the question betrayed his curiosity.

Quinn held out the tin. 'I find them both stimulating and soothing. Try one. It may help you to recover after your ordeal.'

Inchball leant back, recoiling from the proffered cigarettes. 'I don't need them. I'm right as rain. With respect and all that, sir.' It was certainly true that Inchball's spirits had revived since he had been able to change into clean trousers and underwear.

Quinn did not withdraw the tin. He smiled and gave a half-shrug. 'You're afraid they will turn you queer, is that it?'

'No chance of that happening.'

'Well then?'

'Maybe I don't see the point.'

'If I ordered you to smoke one...'

'And why would you do that?'

'Because I know that you want to try them but you don't want to be seen as *wanting* to try them. Therefore, if I order you...'

'If you order me, sir, then I would be obliged to smoke one.'

'I order you to smoke a Set cigarette, Inchball.'

As Quinn was seeing to the lighting of Inchball's cigarette, Sergeant Macadam came into the room.

Quinn held the tin towards him. 'Macadam?'

'N-no thank you, sir.'

'It's an order. I have ordered Inchball and I order you too.'

Macadam stooped to take the final Set cigarette. He held it under his nose and sniffed it gingerly.

'That reminds me, sir. I've just come from talking to Charlie Cale. He says there were traces of the same tobacco in the other cigarette cases. The ones found on the three latest victims, sir.'

Quinn struck an England's Glory match and held it towards Macadam, forcing him to go through with smoking the cigarette. 'What about the rope?'

A fit of coughing prevented Macadam from answering straightaway. 'He has not yet completed his analysis of that, sir,' he managed at last. 'Though he says that he can tell that the

295

rope used to restrain Sergeant Inchball is clearly not of the same batch, as it is self-evidently tarred, sir.'

Quinn threw the empty tin on to his desk and looked down on it with some contempt. He congratulated himself on triumphing over the cigarettes. He had finished them. But he had no intention – no desire – of buying a second tin and turning his experiment into a habit. Even so, he allowed himself to enjoy an exquisite stab of regret. He was aware of a sense of loss to which he was not wholly reconciled.

'I further regret to say that my enquiries at Willett's the chandler's have drawn a blank.' Macadam took out from his waistcoat pocket a photograph of Henry Fetherstonhaugh that had come to light at the house in Adelaide Road. With a nod from Quinn, he pinned it on to the wall. 'Fetherstonhaugh is not the toff who bought the rope. He was absolutely certain of that, I am afraid, sir.' With a disconsolate expression, Macadam inhaled once more on his cigarette, coughed and sat down at his desk.

It was not long before the small attic room was filled with a heady fug.

'Shall I open the window, sir?' wondered Macadam.

'I order you not to,' said Quinn.

Inchball sniggered briefly. Quinn's answering groan seemed weighted with reproach.

All three men fell back into silence and directed their gaze towards the wall.

The map Quinn was using was Bacon's Large-Scale Ordnance. It had Charing Cross as the

296

centre of London with concentric circles spreading out at half-mile intervals. As Quinn squinted through the shifting swirls of smoke, it seemed that these circles began to radiate, as if they were ripples thrown out by a pebble breaking the surface of a pond.

Now he had the impression that the circles had somehow become detached from the map. He visualized them radiating out beyond the confines of the map, extending over the whole wall. He felt that if he wished to, he would be able to move them at will.

It would not be too hard, he imagined, to shift the concentric circles so that they radiated out from the black X that marked the Panther Club on Pall Mall. This was about an inch to the left of Charing Cross, the mapmaker's chosen centre of London.

He did not attempt to do it. There was no need. What the strange perceptual distortion had suggested to him was the idea of the Panther Club as the centre of the case. The Xs of the other locations were points on various orbital rings around it, the planets to its sun. He understood now why the line connecting the points was not exactly straight: the planets in a solar system are never in complete alignment.

Of course, there was no strong evidential link between the Panther Club and the crimes. He ran through the chain of connection in his mind: flakes of tobacco from Set cigarettes had been found on the first victim, indeed on all the victims it was now confirmed; the Panther Club had a large regular order for that brand of cigarettes with one particular tobacconist's. It could be said that the lead that had taken Quinn to the Panther Club was as tenuous as the wisps of smoke swirling around his head.

Quinn knew that Set cigarettes were available at many other outlets in London; he had instigated enquiries, through external resources, at every establishment on Inchball's original list of Featherly's customers. So far, from that list, the only link with Jimmy Neville that had come to light was with the Panther Club: Henry Fetherstonhaugh – or Fanshaw, as they were used to thinking of him – was on the list of members.

The fact remained that Fetherstonhaugh had drugged and tied up Inchball, and followed that up by disappearing. All of which suggested that he had some reason to avoid contact with the police. That did not make him the murderer, of course. Indeed, the chandler's insistence that his unusually upper-class customer was *not* Fetherstonhaugh argued somewhat in his favour; as did Cale's opinion concerning the rope used on Inchball.

Nonetheless, Fetherstonhaugh was certainly someone Quinn was interested in talking to. And his interest in Fetherstonhaugh only served to strengthen his interest in the Panther Club.

Since returning to the department, Quinn had checked the list of Panther Club members again. It did not surprise him to find the Marquess of Roachford among them. He thought back to the first time he had seen Pinky, after Count Erdélyi's lecture at the Royal Ethnological Society. Sir Michael Esslyn had also been there, another member of the Panther Club.

He had to admit that he was disappointed not to find Count Erdélyi listed. But perhaps that would have been too much to hope for. And even if he had found the Hungarian's name there, it still proved nothing.

The only grounds he had for visiting the club again – even possibly for raiding it – was Fetherstonhaugh's disappearance. Given what Quinn knew about the Panther Club, it was not inconceivable that Fetherstonhaugh would be welcome there, no matter what crimes he might have committed outside its precincts.

But whether Fetherstonhaugh would risk going there was another question. On the one hand, he could not have known that the club was under suspicion or that his name had been linked to it. And a gentleman might very well look upon his club as a place of refuge, a sanctuary. On the other hand, would it not be preferable for a fugitive from the law to isolate himself entirely from all human contact? To seek out the company even of friends and fellow club members was to increase the chance of betrayal.

But Quinn believed he knew enough about how these clubs operated to understand that it would be possible for a man to go to ground in one. He remembered, too, what the major domo had said about the tradition of wearing masks at the Panther Club.

Quinn's concentration was disturbed by a sudden fit of coughing from Macadam. 'I beg you, let me open a window!' cried the sergeant, red in the face.

'Very well, Macadam. If you insist.'

A draught of fresh air began to disperse the clouds of smoke.

Inchball gave a shudder. 'No. It's no good.'

'What?' said Quinn.

'I was looking at them inscriptions.'

Quinn followed Inchball's slightly unfocused gaze. Enlarged photographs of the inscriptions from the latest three cigarette cases had been placed on the wall alongside the first. 'Something about one of them seemed familiar. I had a feeling I've seen it before somewhere. It was just coming to me and then Macadam had to go and spoil it.'

'Wasn't my fault! I can hardly breathe in here!'

'Which one was it?'

'Nah. It's gone. Completely gone.'

There was a knock at the door. Quinn sat up straight and wafted the smoke away from his face. 'Come in.' He was surprised to see the young artist Petter enter the room.

As before, Petter avoided looking Quinn in the eye, so assiduously that Quinn began to wonder whether he had acquired a facial disfigurement.

'What can we do for you?'

'Well, sir, begging your pardon, sir, but are you still wanting to go to the British Museum? Only you said you might want to go there with me. And it is Saturday tomorrow.'

Sergeant Inchball stirred. 'What's that you say? The British Museum. That queer what done for me ... He said something about the British Museum. Said he liked to go there. Said he went there the day Jimmy Neville disappeared.'

'I see.'

'Do you think he would go there again, sir?' asked Macadam.

The stub of Quinn's cigarette was so hot it burnt his fingers. But he took one last draw from it before grinding it out in a tin ashtray. 'There was something Tommy Venables said to me, about Fetherstonhaugh. About how he believed in some kind of brotherhood.'

'Yes, that's it! I remember something about a brotherhood too!' cried Inchball.

'The Greek and Roman galleries at the British Museum are a known haunt of inverts. The only reason Fetherstonhaugh might have for going there would be to communicate with other members of this brotherhood – perhaps to warn them of the danger that he believes is threatening them.'

'So you think he might go there tomorrow when the place will be filled with queers?' asked Inchball.

'It's true that there may be a higher than usual proportion of such individuals at the British Museum tomorrow. I learnt from Venables that many renters are keeping off the streets. However, the need to earn their rent does not go away. Neither do the unspeakable urges experienced by gentlemen who ought to know better. It may be that both sides consider the British Museum in the afternoon to be a safe place to seek liaisons. If Fetherstonhaugh has not left the country, there's a chance he might turn up there tomorrow.'

'So ... you *do* want me?' said Petter glumly.

'Do we want Petter?' asked Quinn.

'He's not my type,' said Inchball. He then frowned quizzically at the cigarette butt in his fingers before hurriedly stubbing it out.

'It may be beneficial to have him along,' said Quinn. 'He knows the conventions of the place. Given what Macadam has told us about the rope, we must face the possibility that Fetherston-haugh is not the murderer, after all. He may, however, be able to lead us to him. If Fetherston-haugh does put in an appearance, and attempts to make contact with anyone, Petter may be able to tell us if that individual had any connection with Jimmy Neville.'

'If this and may that!' cried Inchball impatiently. 'Face it, man, you've got nothing. You're chasing shadows!'

Quinn was taken aback, but he understood Inchball's frustration. 'Do you have any better suggestions, Sergeant?'

Inchball hung his head despondently. 'If only I could remember...'

The four men turned to consider the prints of the inscriptions that were pinned to the wall.

Quinn was aware of a sudden nervous agitation on the part of Petter. He was glancing repeatedly from the wall to Quinn, almost – uncharacteristically – meeting his gaze.

'What is it, Petter?'

'It's just that one there ... I'm sure I read it in a book.'

'I knew it!' said Quinn. 'Which one are you talking about?'

'That one. *Suffering is one very long moment.*

It's the first line, you see. That's why I remember it. I'm sure it's the first line.'

'Yes, man. The first line of what?'

'Of *De Profundis*, by Oscar Wilde.'

'That's it!' cried Inchball. 'That's what I read in the queer's scrapbook. Them were the very words. *De Perfumis*. Petter's right.'

'*De Profundis,*' corrected Quinn quietly. 'D.P. Do you have a copy?'

'Oh, yes,' said Petter.

Quinn rose from his seat in a burst of energy. 'Is it here, at the Yard? Can you get it now?'

'No. It's at my lodgings. In Streatham.'

'Sergeant Macadam, will you take Mr Petter to his lodgings.'

'In the Ford?' asked Macadam hopefully.

'Of course. We must waste no time getting to the bottom of this.' Quinn picked up the Set tin from his desk and flipped it open. Even though he knew there were no cigarettes left, he felt a strange disappointment to have its emptiness confirmed.

Ellipses

It was a slight volume, almost weightless in his hands. Indeed, he felt that there should be more to it. After all, he hoped it contained the solution to the case, which ought to have increased its substance and mass.

When he first felt its blue cloth hardcover, he was reluctant to open it. He acknowledged the possibility that he had set too much store by what this book might hold for him. While it was unopened, its potential to provide a solution was untested, and therefore intact. Once he began to examine its contents, he would have to confront the prospect of finding nothing; of failure, in other words.

Meanwhile, the book seemed to possess a talismanic power, and for the time being that was enough for Quinn.

And so he let his gaze, and his touch, swim across the small stretch of aquamarine, as if he would find the solutions he was looking for there. The gilt detailing stamped on the front cover snagged his attention: beneath the title and author's name, a bird stretched out its wings, behind the bars of a cage.

At last he opened the book up, greedily inhaling the scent of pages and dust that escaped, as if that were the secret he was looking for.

He lingered over the publisher's advertisement in the front of the book, before turning to the preface. The type was set large, with few words to a line, and few lines to a page. Quinn began to read:

For a long time considerable curiosity has been expressed concerning the manuscript of De Profundis, *which was known to be in my possession, the author having mentioned its existence to many other friends.*

Further on, the writer of the preface, Robert Ross, had inserted a letter from Oscar Wilde concerning his instructions for publication. It began:

I don't defend my conduct. I explain it.

Quinn wondered if this was the murderer's intention in quoting from *De Profundis*.

Oscar Wilde's letter to Ross ended with a sentimental image:

On the other side of the prison wall there are some poor black soot-besmirched trees which are just breaking out into buds of an almost shrill green. I know quite well what they are going through. They are finding expression.

Again Quinn tried to relate this to the murderer's intentions. Was he not also, through his crimes, finding expression? There was another sentence earlier in Wilde's letter:

I need not remind you that mere expression is to an artist the supreme and only mode of life.

Did the murderer consider himself to be an artist, therefore?

And so Quinn came to the first line of the *De*

Profundis itself, the words which Petter had identified in the inscription. As they appeared in the book, they were preceded by three points of ellipsis:

...SUFFERING is one very long moment.

Naturally, all Quinn could think about was what had been omitted from the text. This was the instinct of the detective: the solution, always, was in what was withheld. He turned the pages quickly and saw that the text was littered with such marks of ellipsis throughout. Turning back to the frontispiece, he could find no acknowledgement that the text had been abridged. Nor was there any indication in Wilde's note to Ross that he wished for sections of his work to be excised before publication.

Quinn turned back to the beginning. Whatever had been taken out, those six words remained, the six words that were so close to the heart of a murderer that he chose to have them engraved on an object left in the pocket of one of his victims:

Suffering is one very long moment.

In the passage from which these words were taken, Wilde was evidently referring to a prisoner's experience of time. But the killer's meaning was not necessarily the same as Wilde's.

But it was interesting to Quinn to see where Wilde took the idea. He spoke of time circling 'round one centre of pain'. Given the crimes perpetrated on the four young men, this was a telling phrase.

Did the murderer in some way seek to suspend time through these atrocities? To create centres of pain around which time would circle, without ever moving forward? In Wilde, time's immobility was presented as a negative concept. He spoke of 'each dreadful day in the very minutest detail like its brother'. But if one read the words without any empathy for the experience that lay behind them, could they be taken as some kind of instructional handbook, a guide to harnessing eternity? Or to put it another way, to achieving immortality?

No doubt it required the reader to invest Wilde's metaphors with a literal truth; to consider him more than just a disgraced writer: a god, or at the very least a prophet; and to look upon his literary self-justifications as holy writ. And to the question 'What kind of man would do that?' there was no meaningful answer other than 'a madman'.

Quinn continued reading. It was not long before he came upon a phrase that reinforced his interpretation, which at the same time brought to mind one of the other inscriptions:

For us there is only one season, the season of sorrow.

The inscription he had in mind had said:

Where there is sorrow there is holy ground.

Quinn read on. Within a few pages, he had found the phrase itself. His heart beat violently as he read and reread the passage in which it occurred:

...sorrow is the most sensitive of all created things. There is nothing that stirs in the whole world of thought to which sorrow does not vibrate in terrible and exquisite pulsation. The

307

thin, beaten-out leaf of tremulous gold that chronicles the direction of forces the eye cannot see is in comparison coarse. It is a wound that bleeds when any hand but the hand of love touches it, and even then must bleed again, though not in pain.

Where there is sorrow there is holy ground. Some day people will realize what that means. They will know nothing of life until they do...

That brief passage filled almost an entire page of the book. Quinn was able to tear through the pages in little over an hour. He was not reading it for Wilde's meaning, but for the murderer's. In particular, he was looking for the passages from which the other two inscriptions were taken.

He did not find them. He was forced to concede that *To be entirely free* and *Seek entrance to the House of Pain!* were not taken from *De Profundis*. At any rate, they were not present in the edition he had before him.

He turned to the front of the book, where he discovered that this was the eleventh edition, printed in 1908; the first edition was dated 1905. Some matter had undoubtedly been omitted, presumably on the grounds of public decency or for legal reasons. But how had the murderer had access to such material?

Quinn laid down the book. The empty Set tin was still on his desk. He regretted sharing his last few cigarettes with Inchball and Macadam. A Set cigarette was just what he needed, given what was required of him now: to imagine that he was the murderer, reading the book for passages that would inspire or affirm his sanguinary course.

As he read, he noted down passages that struck him.

Sorrow, then, and all that it teaches one, is my new world.

...the lessons hidden in the heart of pain.

Pain, unlike pleasure, wears no mask.

There is about sorrow an intense, an extraordinary reality.

...the voiceless world of pain...

...may beauty and sorrow be made one in their meaning and manifestation.

...he regarded sin and suffering as being in themselves beautiful and holy things and modes of perfection.

There were more, many more, along the same lines. Indubitably, it was a selective reading, which led to a distorted interpretation of Wilde's argument. His meaning was twisted round – inverted, one might almost say. As far as Quinn could tell, Wilde's theme was Christian repentance. His great idea – his 'dangerous' idea as he put it himself – was that sin and suffering were essential to Christian salvation and, in fact, central to the Christian experience. They were therefore beautiful in themselves. He insisted that suffering was not a mystery, as conventional clergymen might have it, but a revelation. One could not be a true Christian, unless one sinned, he seemed to be saying. And indeed, he came close to representing Christ as positively wanting us to be sinners. Another passage caught Quinn's eye:

But it is when he deals with a sinner that Christ is most romantic, in the sense of most real. The world had always loved the saint as being the nearest possible approach to the perfection of God. Christ, through some divine instinct in him, seems to have loved the sinner as being the nearest approach to perfection in man.

This could almost be taken for a manifesto for sin, with a Christian justification. True, Wilde went on to acknowledge the necessity of repentance, but it was almost in passing. Given his emphasis on sin and suffering, it was easy to overlook this part of his thesis.

'Will you be much longer, sir?' It was Macadam. He and Inchball were at the door, ready for home.

Quinn took out his fob watch. It was six o'clock. 'I still have more work to do here.' As well as the *De Profundis*, Petter had provided Quinn with two other books by the same author, *The Picture of Dorian Gray* and *Lord Arthur Savile's Crime and Other Stories*.

'May we help you with anything?' asked Macadam.

Inchball gave a snarl that indicated how little he appreciated the offer made on his behalf.

'No, no. You two may go. I must look at these

310

myself.'

'There's always tomorrow,' said Inchball.

'Yes, tomorrow,' echoed Quinn distractedly.

'If you're sure then, sir,' said Macadam.

'Quite sure.' But as his two sergeants left the room, Quinn was overcome by a wave of panic. The task ahead of him seemed insurmountable. In that instant, all his confidence drained from him. He was left only with the empty fluttering of apprehension. He had latched on to these books, as if he were certain they would yield secrets crucial to the case. But really, he had no way of knowing.

The solution could just as easily lie in evidence that was denied to him, like the ellipses in the text of *De Profundis*. And so the hours spent poring over the books would be wasted hours. In the meantime, the killer might even now be preparing to commit his next crime.

Quinn looked briefly, longingly, towards the window. He imagined himself on the other side, heading back to the lodging house in West Kensington, one small figure among the multitudes. Perhaps tonight he would dine with the others. Ignoring the sniggers of Messrs. Timberley and Appleby, he would look more closely into the pewter-grey eyes of Miss Dillard. And in that moment, he would know that he was not alone.

But he did not go home. He did not even cross to the window to look down upon his imagined self trudging into the settling dusk. He stayed at his post and felt his loneliness expand around him.

The Wings of Thanatos

The day began in a soft milky haze. Quinn stood at the window, flexing the hunched hours out of his spine. He looked down, as if he half-expected to see his imagined self scurrying back along the embankment into work. Flecks of silver were borne away on the river, a flotsam of cold brilliance. His capacity for imaginative identification, which served him so well in his work, stretched to the Thames itself. For a moment, he was a rolling weight of water, a blind, heedless force, impelled by a tidal compulsion.

His stomach grumbled testily, reminding him he was a man.

When he came back from the canteen, refreshed after a cup of tea and a toasted teacake, he found Macadam already at his desk. Inchball was hanging up his hat.

'What's the plan for today, sir?' said Macadam.

'Gimme a chance to get through the bloody door,' complained Inchball as he took his seat.

Quinn thought again what it would be like to be a river; in other words to live without the need for making plans and issuing commands. He rubbed his face vigorously, as if to pummel out his exhaustion. 'It is going to be a busy morning.' He felt the weight of everything they had to do suddenly pressing down on him. No amount of rolling his shoulders could dispel it.

By the afternoon, the rain had returned. There was a vengeful quality to its renewed persistence, as if it were punishing the world for enjoying its absence over the last few days. It was everywhere, inescapable; quickly drenching clothes, carried indoors in the damp, bedraggled auras of those taking shelter, dripping from eaves with a heavy patterned rhythm. As it fell, it swallowed up all the soot floating in the polluted air and threw it down in dirty gobbets. The spattered pigeons were outraged by the insult.

And it brought with it an unseasonal darkness. The intimations of spring were forgotten, summer's promise mocked; the year had skidded forward several months to a wintry misery.

Beyond the black railings on Great Russell Street, in the forecourt of the British Museum, an unusually resilient crowd was gathered. But if anyone had paused to study those milling there, it would have soon become apparent that a high preponderance of them were dressed in the black capes and helmets of policemen. The rain bounced off them. They gave every impression of being men who had stood up to far worse.

The Special Crimes Department's Ford Model T pulled up. The four men in it hesitated, a hunkered fixity rooting them to their seats. They looked out through the rain-streaked gloom towards the distant pagan glow coming from the museum interior.

'If the rain don't put him off, then the sight of all those bobbies will,' muttered Inchball, who was in the back of the car with the artist Petter. 'With respect and all that, sir.'

'Stay in the car, Inchball,' ordered Quinn without looking round. 'Fetherstonhaugh knows you.' Quinn seemed to be waiting for some signal, a change in the drumbeat of the rain on the canopy of the car, perhaps. At last, he must have heard whatever he was listening for. He adjusted the position of his bowler and checked the fastenings of his Ulster. 'Mr Petter, Macadam. Let us do this.'

Quinn launched himself out into the rain without looking back to see if he was followed.

Under the portico he waited for Petter and Macadam to catch him up.

'You know the disposition of the place, Mr Petter?'

'I do.'

'If you don't mind, I would appreciate the opportunity to browse the Egyptian gallery briefly on our way.'

Quinn could not have said what he hoped to gain from such a detour. He did not, of course, expect to find the murderer there. But perhaps, in a room full of animal-headed gods, he would confront the forces that drove such a monster as they were hunting.

It soon became clear to him that what he was looking for was a sighting of the god Set.

He glimpsed sphinxes, a giant scarab, lion-headed goddesses, a divine baboon serenely flaunting an erection, as well as a strange fat-

314

bellied creature carved from liver-spotted stone, which the accompanying card informed him was a pregnant hippopotamus. But there was no representation of the Egyptian god of chaos in the gallery that he could see. Instead, he sensed its presence stalking the rooms, a shadow moving at the periphery of his vision.

Quinn looked into the faces of the men and women wandering bemused among the out-landish statues. If one of them had snarled back at him with a dog-faced snout, or snapped shut a beak, he would not have been surprised.

They left the company of savage gods and stepped into a tableau of naked youths, their stony beauty only marred by the occasional missing body part.

Petter turned to Quinn expectantly.

'So, this is where...' Quinn cast a discreet glance around the gallery, '...where you come to draw?'

'Y-yes.'

'And you have your sketchpad with you today?'

Petter withdrew a small pad and graphite stick from a pocket.

Quinn glanced around. His eye was caught by the damaged figure of a winged youth, much like a Christian angel, which seemed to be emerging from a massive block of stone. It was described as a sculpted marble column drum from the fourth century BC, found at Ephesos. The figure was not an angel, but Thanatos.

Quinn nodded decisively. 'I think you should sketch this.'

'Do you want me to draw it as it is, or to reconstruct the missing part?'

Quinn spent a moment considering the time-ravaged form. 'Imagine it as it once was. Perfect.'

'What shall I do, sir?' asked Macadam.

'You have familiarized yourself with what our suspect looks like?'

'Yes, sir.'

'Then keep an eye out, Macadam.'

Macadam wandered off, with that tremulous drifting gaze that was typical of a highly alert police detective feigning inattention. Quinn cast his eye over the preliminary marks that Petter had made. He nodded approvingly and left the young artist to it.

As Quinn moved among the statues, he thought of the long-dead youths who had modelled for these placid remnants; of the passions and humours that had stirred their living limbs, of the blood that had coursed through their veins. The smooth, immovable stone stood for warm flesh that had once been caressed, perhaps by the hands as well as the eyes of the sculptor.

He knew how it was in those days and thought he understood why men like Fetherstonhaugh came here. Indeed, how it would be difficult for them to stay away. It was not simply for the aesthetic – or even sensuous – pleasure of gazing on sculptures of muscular young bodies. He supposed there had to be a kind of nostalgia in play too. Could a man feel nostalgic for an age he had never known? But for men of that type, Athens of the classical period – with its well-known acceptance of love between males – represented a lost homeland. Their longing for it would be all the stronger because they had never known it.

Quinn found himself in front of a semi-clad male figure holding a lyre. The loose robe was carved with great skill. It was frozen in the course of slipping from the otherwise naked body, suspended eternally at the top of the thighs, revealing a tantalizing glimpse of the penis. Although he had left Inchball in the car, he felt his disapproving presence at his shoulder. He could almost hear what he might say: *I bet they love that, the fucking queers.*

Quinn felt suddenly embarrassed. He wondered if he would be taken as a connoisseur of antiquities, or a pervert. He turned his attention to the placard at the base of the statue. He read that the statue apparently depicted a hybrid of two gods, Apollo and Dionysus.

'It represents the reconciliation of the two opposite sides of our nature, does it not?'

Quinn half-turned, reluctant to show his face to the man who had addressed him. It was enough to see not Inchball but a top-hatted Sir Michael Esslyn standing at his shoulder. Quinn turned his gaze quickly back to the statue. It was some time before he realized that he was looking directly at the god's penis.

Sir Michael went on: 'The supremely rational and the wildly irrational. The intellect and the passions. The Apollonian and the Dionysian.'

Quinn wondered if Esslyn knew who he was. The first time he had seen the mandarin, he had not thought that Esslyn had noticed him sitting outside Sir Edward's office. And there had been no flicker of recognition after Count Erdélyi's lecture.

Quinn preferred to think that Esslyn was merely addressing casual remarks to a stranger. But then it occurred to him that if that were the case he had to accept the rather shocking possibility that Sir Michael was attempting to pick him up.

'Rather a sophisticated idea, is it not? We tend to think of earlier civilizations as more primitive than our own, but this rather belies that, do you not think? Not simply in the excellence of the craftsmanship, which is the equal of anything by Michelangelo, but also in the psychological acuteness of the conception. What truth! What depth! What beauty!'

Quinn muttered that he did not know anything about that. When he risked a second glance in Sir Michael's direction, he saw that he had gone.

Now Quinn moved away from the statue, scanning faces for any that might be Fetherstonhaugh's. Inchball had confirmed that the photograph they had for reference was relatively recent; hairstyle and facial grooming were up to date. It was easy to discount the women. He then discounted any men who were too obviously old or young; Inchball had said that Fetherstonhaugh was around forty. Inchball had further briefed them on hair and eye colour. Hair colour could be changed, so Quinn looked first at the eyes. Inchball had described Fetherstonhaugh's irises as 'murky green'. Of course, it was a subjective

318

description, but it did enable Quinn at least to eliminate faces whose eyes were remote from green on the spectrum.

Quinn walked the length of the gallery, at least pretending an interest in the classical nudes. One, of a boy removing a thorn from his foot, genuinely engaged him. The boy's absorption in his task was timeless. It was a glimpse of a human moment that cut across the centuries. As far as Quinn was concerned, you could take the prancing satyrs, the headless goddesses and eternally poised athletes; he would swap them all for this one boy poring over his foot.

Quinn felt the sense of something about to happen. At first he thought it was related to the statue, which was so imbued with life that he was almost surprised not to see the boy twitch and fidget as he yanked his leg into a better position. He was eternally on the verge of coming to life.

After a moment, Quinn realized the source of his intimation was a commotion coming from the next gallery. Raised voices intensified into shouts. He ran towards them.

Macadam had the arm of an auburn-haired man of about forty years, dressed in a tweed suit, twisted up behind his back.

The other visitors to the gallery took the disruption in their stride. There were no shrieks. It was simply that the crowd parted around the grappling men, suddenly more interested in grappling centaurs.

Quinn looked into the eyes of the man Macadam had in a tensioned hold. 'Mr Fetherstonhaugh, I presume? I am Inspector Quinn of the Special Crimes Department. I was hoping I might run into you today.'

Fetherstonhaugh called out to the room: 'Murderers! These men are murderers!'

'Now now, sir, calm down. We're policemen, not murderers.'

'The police are waging a war against the love that dare not speak its name. The love between a man and a man. They are slaughtering those that love that way. They are seeking to purge society of us. Those they do not kill they seek to cow into submission. If you are here as a male lover of men, run for your life, I say. I am Henry Fetherstonhaugh. If you read about my death in the paper you will know that I am right!' Fetherstonhaugh gave out a sharp yelp of pain as Macadam twisted his arm further up his back.

'Enough of that! We only want to ask you some questions.'

'You can kill me, but you will never kill the love that dare not speak its name!'

'We ain't gonna kill you,' said Macadam. 'Wherever did you get that idea?'

'Four young men brutally murdered. The coroner's inquests held behind closed doors. No public, no press. Why else would the authorities do that unless they have something to hide?'

'Mr Fetherstonhaugh,' said Quinn. 'Your theories are interesting. May I suggest we discuss them back at the Yard?' To Macadam, he added: 'Get the cuffs on him then take him to the car. I shall just tell Petter we are finished here.'

Quinn retraced his steps. The marble column

drum came into view. There was no sign of Petter. Quinn felt a fluttering sensation, like a muscle going into spasm. Then the ripples hardened into the fierce hammering of a heart overwhelmed by the chemicals of panic.

He told himself that the artist might have been overtaken by a call of nature, or that he had grown bored of sketching that particular artefact and had moved on to something else. But the crowd in this gallery had thinned as everyone had rushed into the next room to view the fracas with the police. It was easy to see that Petter was not there.

Quinn noticed a discarded leaf from Petter's sketchpad, lying in a crumpled ball on the floor near the figure he had been sketching.

He straightened the paper to see a reasonable rendition of the winged figure of Death, perfected by the artist's imagination. Beneath it was written in a hurried scrawl:

to bring terrible events to a terrible issue

The Paul Reynolds Edition

Quinn pinned the sketch of Thanatos to the wall, as if he were putting up a child's picture for admiration.

'It doesn't mean he has been abducted by the murderer,' said Macadam. 'He could have just got bored. Or scared. You can't trust his type.'

But Quinn's pinched, bloodless lips brooked no reassurance.

'We cleared the galleries, one by one,' said Inchball. 'No sign.'

Quinn glanced at the map of London. 'I thought he might be intending to leave a body outside the museum. I did not consider the possibility that he would abduct his next victim from there. I ought to have.'

'Why did he choose Petter?' asked Macadam.

Quinn thought back to the moment he had directed Petter to sketch the figure of Thanatos in its pristine form. Had an unacknowledged part of his reasoning been the consideration that if he were the killer, he would prefer to see Death immaculate?

'What I mean,' continued Macadam, 'is that perhaps it is someone known to Petter. Petter knew we were going to the British Museum. He may have mentioned it to one of his ... friends. Why else would he go off with this individual, unless it was someone whom he knew? It is hard to imagine that he was forcibly abducted from a gallery in the British Museum in the middle of the afternoon.'

'Unless it took place when you were arresting Fetherstonhaugh,' Quinn pointed out. 'Which would make it, essentially, an opportunistic crime. But you are right. It could be someone known to Petter. Someone who knew he would be there. Someone, therefore, who was playing games with us.'

'The message...' began Macadam.

'*To bring terrible events to a terrible issue,*' read Quinn.

Inchball shook his head grimly. 'Doesn't look good for Petter,' he concluded.

'*He* may have written it,' suggested Macadam, a little more brightly.

'*Why?*' Inchball gave the word a disparaging force.

'To alert us to the fact that he had been abducted?' suggested Macadam hopefully.

Inchball screwed up his face. 'Why not just write, *Help! The murderer's got me!* Or even better, shout it?'

'He didn't want the murderer to know he was on to him.'

'Nah, nah, nah, it don't make sense,' insisted Inchball dismissively. 'I mean, if he thought it was the murderer, why would he go with him at all, even if it was someone he knew?'

'Maybe he decided to play amateur detective?' said Macadam tentatively. 'Hence the enigmatic note. That's how he believes detectives carry on from the books he's read. We know he is something of a book reader.'

'I believe the murderer wrote it,' said Quinn abruptly. 'It is a quote from *De Profundis*.'

All three men lapsed into thought.

Quinn crossed to the wall and began to take down the photographs of the existing victims, as if he were making space for those yet to come.

The photographs were face down on the table of the interview room, spread out like cards for a tarot reading. Quinn did not need to look at them to know what they depicted, or the order in which they were placed. The images had burnt themselves into his memory.

Fetherstonhaugh was directed into the room by Macadam.

'You are in a good deal of trouble, Mr Fetherstonhaugh. Did you think we would take lightly the drugging and false imprisonment of a police officer?'

Macadam rough-handed Fetherstonhaugh down on to the seat opposite Quinn.

'I did what I had to do.'

'You may be interested to know that Sergeant Inchball has recovered fully from his ordeal. Thank you for asking. He wanted to conduct the interview with you himself, but I could not allow it. We have a responsibility to protect those in our custody.'

'He wants me dead.'

'He's very angry with you. You can hardly

blame him. What would have happened if we hadn't found him? He might be dead himself.'

'Someone would have found him.'

'Where is the scrapbook?'

Fetherstonhaugh was momentarily thrown by the sudden change of tack. 'It is in a safe place.'

'At the Panther Club?'

Fetherstonhaugh gave a second start of surprise.

'Yes, we know all about the Panther Club. We also know about *De Profundis*.'

'What do you mean? What about *De Profundis*?'

'You have pasted a page from that book into your scrap collection.'

'What of it?'

'Why were you at the British Museum? Had you arranged to meet someone there?'

'There are always members of the Brotherhood there at that time.'

'Ah, yes. The Brotherhood. I have heard about this Brotherhood of yours. What is the link between the Brotherhood and *De Profundis*?'

'Why do you come back to that?'

Quinn knew the time had come to reveal his hand. He turned over the first of the photographs. Without glancing down, or taking his gaze off Fetherstonhaugh in any way, he said, 'James Neville. Perhaps you knew him better as Jimmy. A friend of yours, I believe.'

Fetherstonhaugh blanched.

Now was the time for Quinn to make a conscious display of sharing in what he had revealed to Fetherstonhaugh. *'May beauty and sorrow be*

325

made one in their meaning and manifestation,'
he recited. Even knowing the nature of Neville's
vices, it was hard to look upon the face in the
photograph without the word *angelic* coming to
mind. The luminous perfection of his features
was *beauty*; *sorrow* was the wound beneath
them. That slit in his flesh, inhuman in its swift
precision, furnished a fine glimpse into the
blackest part of the human soul.

Fetherstonhaugh flinched away from the
photograph, unable to bear either Neville's
beauty or his death.

'Look at it. You must look at it!' insisted
Quinn. His tone modulated from stern command
to the brimming excitement of an enthusiast
wishing to share his passion. His own gaze
eagerly obeyed the directive, drinking in the
potent image.

Fetherstonhaugh's head quivered as he turned
back to confront the dead man's photograph.
Quinn saw the tears spill from his eyes.

'There are more. You must look at them all.'

Quinn turned over the next three photographs,
revealing the other victims. Objectively, it was
clear that none of the other youths was Neville's
equal in looks. It did not take a connoisseur of
male beauty to see that. But their humanity was
equally present, and in their lifetime had been
every bit as fierce and fragile.

'Eric Sealey and Vincent Unsworth. Our investigations have confirmed that they were
clerks at the London Central Telegraph Office on
Saint Martin's-le-Grand. The fourth victim is an
associate of theirs called Leonard Mountjoy. He

did not work at the Telegraph Office but used to meet them there.' Quinn paused as he looked at Mountjoy's picture. 'I had the pleasure of Mr Mountjoy's company, briefly, on the night we believe he was killed. He picked me up outside the Criterion and took me into Green Park.'

'You?'

'I enjoy the occasional Set cigarette and am familiar with *The Profession of Shame*. I will not say it is a great work of literature, but it serves its purpose.'

'You are a member of the Brotherhood!'

'I have never formally been initiated.'

'It does not matter. There is no need. You are a member.'

Quinn smiled. If that was the way Fetherstonhaugh chose to think of him, then he would use it to his advantage. 'Very well. As a member of the Brotherhood, I appeal to you to help us find the man who did this.'

'I know nothing of these crimes.'

Quinn turned over four more photographs. 'Each of the victims was found with an empty cigarette case about their person. Inside the lid of each case was an inscription. As you can see, all the inscriptions end with the letters D.P. This one, *Suffering is one very long moment*, we have identified as the first line of *De Profundis*, which you will know is Oscar Wilde's letter to Lord Alfred Douglas written from Reading Gaol. You will know this because Sergeant Inchball recalls reading the same quote in your scrapbook.'

'But it is not the first line. There are many pages of Oscar's complaints to Bosie before that.'

'The dots?'

Fetherstonhaugh nodded. 'The first edition of the *De Profundis* was put out by Robbie Ross in 1905. It was very savagely abridged. He removed a lot of material that was particular to Oscar's relationship with Bosie. Perhaps he feared Bosie's reaction. Or perhaps he was worried that it made Oscar appear petty and self-pitying. A revised edition appeared a few years later with some additional material, but it was not until last year that the full text was finally published in English.'

'I see. So we have the wrong edition. I thought as much. Where can we get a copy of the full text?'

Fetherstonhaugh smiled ambiguously. 'The 1913 edition is very rare. Only sixteen copies were produced.'

'Sixteen? Why so few?'

'It was a legal manoeuvre on Ross's part. Bosie was threatening to publish his own version of the letter, which he claimed was his, as it was addressed to him, although Oscar had entrusted it to Ross for publication. Ross brought it out hurriedly in America, with Paul Reynolds as the publisher, simply in order to fulfil the requirements of American copyright law. Once that was done, Bosie could not publish.'

'What happened to the books? With so few copies produced, it should be possible to track down each one.'

'Indeed. Fifteen copies were donated to libraries or given to friends of Oscar Wilde.'

'And the sixteenth?'

'It was put on sale in the publisher's show-room in New York, as copyright law required. The price was fixed at five hundred dollars.'

'Good grief.'

'It was sold within a few days. To whom, it is not known. The purchaser paid in cash and took the book away with him.'

'Have you ever seen a copy of this edition?'

The ambiguous smile returned to Fetherston-haugh's face. 'I was fortunate enough to be counted among Oscar's friends. I have a copy at my house.'

'Why did you not say so before? Macadam, tell Inchball to take a cab round to Adelaide Road to pick up this book.' Quinn turned to Fetherstonhaugh. 'Where will he find it?'

'In the room on the left as you go in. There are bookshelves. The books are in alphabetical order, according to author's name.'

'While he's there, he can pick up Tommy Venables. Tell him to be nice to him. Tell him to say Quentin has an important job for him. And before you go, I have a job for you too.'

Quinn reached under his desk and pulled out a pile of newspapers. 'Your pal Cale has confirmed that rope fibres recovered from the three latest victims are likely to have come from your rope purchased at your chandler's in Lime-house.' Quinn pulled out one of the papers. He turned the pages in frantic haste. At last he found what he was looking for. He took the scissors from his drawer and made a cutting. Fetherston-haugh scrutinized the operation closely, like a

329

surgery professor examining a student's dissection. There was a certain impatience noticeable in his stance, as if he was desperate to snatch the scissors out of Quinn's hands to show him how it should be done.

'Therefore, I wish you to go back there to see if they can recognize their mystery toff rope buyer now.' Quinn handed the cutting to Macadam, who hurried from the room with it.

'We don't have time to track down every owner of the extended version of *De Profundis*,' said Quinn to Fetherstonhaugh. 'But the sixteenth copy was sold in New York, you say?'

'Yes.'

'Last year?'

'So I believe.'

Quinn nodded in satisfaction. 'While we are waiting for the outcome of those investigations, we may as well see what you can remember.' Quinn turned over the remaining three photographs. 'This inscription, *Where there is sorrow there is holy ground*, was also in the edition of *De Profundis* from which we were working. But the other two are not. It would be useful for us to be able to confirm if they are in the later edition.'

Fetherstonhaugh studied the photographs. *'To be entirely free* ... It is difficult to say with that one. It is rather a neutral phrase. You would have to check the text. But I can imagine Oscar writing that. It is a sentiment by which he aspired to live his life. And his life was his great masterpiece, you know. The other. *Seek entrance to the House of Pain!* Yes, I do remember that. It is the sort of phrase that sticks in the mind. You are lucky – I pride myself on my memory, you see. Of course, the truly memorable phrase from *De Profundis* is the one that refers to feasting with panthers.'

'What is that you say?'

'Oh, you know ... it was Oscar's description of entertaining renters. Like feasting with panthers, he said. The danger was half the excitement.'

'And so we come back to the Panther Club.'

'Everyone at the Panther Club holds Oscar's memory dear.'

Quinn nodded. 'You realize that I must charge you for the false imprisonment of Sergeant Inchball? You will be held in custody until your appearance before magistrates on Monday morning. In the meantime, there is something you can do which may help your case. There can be no guarantees, but if you cooperate with us on this matter I feel sure that it will be taken into account when it comes to sentencing. I will certainly put in a good word for you.'

'I don't care about that. I will accept my fate, whatever it may be. However, I will do it for the Brotherhood.'

'You have read the newspapers closely over the years, I believe?'

'Yes.'

Quinn produced from a pocket the list of Panther Club members. A handful of names were underlined. He passed the sheets across to Fetherstonhaugh. 'I would like you to tell me everything you can about the individuals marked.'

'You wish me to inform on fellow members of

the Panther Club? That would break the club's first rule.'

'Which is your greater loyalty? The one you owe to the Panther Club or the one you owe to the Brotherhood?'

Fetherstonhaugh looked down at the papers in his hand. 'What in particular do you wish to know?'

Return to the Panther Club

Quinn surrendered his bowler at the cloakroom and was given in exchange a white domino mask with trailing ribbons. Inside the mask was a number, 398, which served as a cloakroom ticket. Quinn stood patiently as Fetherstonhaugh tied it in place at the back of his head, and then reciprocated the favour. Fetherstonhaugh's mask was black; the difference in colour was the distinction between a member and his guest.

To see the world – or at least the interior of a particularly esoteric gentlemen's club – through the eye slits of a moulded celluloid mask, was a disorientating experience. It felt like the closest he had yet come to putting himself inside the skin of the murderer.

He had to move his head to look around. All the grandeur of the surroundings was reduced to a shaky, hazily edged ellipse. And so he understood that the mask worked in two ways: to conceal the identity of the wearer, but also to diminish and restrict the wearer's perception. The peculiar focus was conducive to acts of inhuman detachment. It made him both more conscious of, and less connected to, the objects that came into his view.

Certainly, his sense of the Panther Club was different to the last time he visited. He was there now as Fetherstonhaugh's guest. He was no longer the unwelcome intruder. To some extent, the club had appropriated him. By putting the mask on him, it made him one of its own.

'Now for your name,' said Fetherstonhaugh.

'My name?'

'You cannot be called by your real name within the precincts of the club. I, for example, am known as Phaedo.'

'Phaedo?'

'From the Platonic dialogue. You must choose a name by which you wish to be known.'

'I hadn't really...'

'If you cannot think of one, I will choose one for you. I have something of a talent when it comes to devising false names.'

'Quentin,' said Quinn peremptorily. 'You may introduce me as Quentin.'

Fetherstonhaugh seemed disappointed. 'This way then.'

He led Quinn back towards the snoring panther in her cage. A double staircase rose up on either side, merging into one as it reached the first landing. Through a half-open door Quinn glimpsed a large reading room. It had the good manners to conform to his idea of what the reading room of a gentlemen's club should be, except for the fact that all the gentlemen in leather armchairs were masked.

Quinn felt somewhat self-conscious. Unlike everyone else there, neither he nor Fetherstonhaugh were in evening dress. But the urgency of the situation had not allowed for a change of suit. Fetherstonhaugh had assured him that the lapse would be tolerated as a bohemian eccentricity. 'We had one member who turned up once dressed as a tramp.'

Fetherstonhaugh led him along a corridor, lined with cartoons and sketches, all portraits or caricatures of men in domino masks. Quinn stopped at one which showed the masked subject smoking a fat cigarette which had been faintly coloured yellow. The wisps of smoke formed themselves into an Egyptian-looking symbol. Quinn squinted at the signature and read it out.

'Möbius?'

'That is his name in here.'

Quinn looked down the corridor warily. 'Lead on.'

Quinn recognized the cigarettes the men were smoking as soon as he walked into the room. The pungent smoke was unmistakable. They could only be Sets.

There were five men seated in front of a crackling fire. Three wore black masks; two white. Even masked, Quinn was able to identify them as Sir Michael Esslyn, Pinky – or the Marquess of Roachford, Lord Tobias Marjoribanks, and the guests in white masks, Count Erdélyi and

Harry Lennox.

Not one of them looked towards him as he slipped into the room. He stood at the threshold, apparently unseen.

Quinn did not attempt to eavesdrop on the particulars of their conversation. He was more concerned with getting a sense of the group's internal relationships, to see who dominated, who deferred, and what the tensions were between them.

Sir Michael was clearly the most senior of the group, but any respect the others owed him was disguised by good-natured joshing. They reminded Quinn of a group of schoolboys being indulged by their well-liked form master. That is to say, there was a certain licence permitted, but Quinn had the sense that had he so wished, Sir Michael could have imposed a disciplined obedience to his will at any time.

Pinky was the form joker; it was clear he did not even take himself seriously, so how could anyone else be expected to? Count Erdélyi was the studious and sensitive one, in general respected by the other boys for his cleverness, but occasionally the recipient of their contempt for his bookish ways. Lord Marjoribanks (whose name, Quinn had learnt from Fetherstonhaugh, was pronounced Marchbanks) was the troublemaker, the rebellious but gifted individual constantly testing the boundaries. Lennox, perhaps, was the new boy, a little too eager to please.

Quinn allowed the conversation to continue for several moments, before the words he needed to say suddenly came to him: 'It's not as easy as you think to kill someone.'

If he had intended to silence the company with a remark, he achieved his objective spectacularly. They turned as one in the direction of his voice.

'Good heavens!' said Sir Michael on behalf of them all.

Quinn stepped forward through the smoke. He felt like a ghost taking on substance. 'May I join you gentlemen?'

A chair was produced for Quinn. His white mask signalled he was the guest of a fellow member, and so he was welcome anywhere in the club.

'You speak as if you know what you are talking about!' Lord Marjoribanks' laughter was forced, and betrayed a touch of fear.

Quinn's voice was peculiarly devoid of humour. 'Naturally. I am not in the habit of talking about things of which I have no knowledge.'

His remark provoked a sceptical chorus, led by Sir Michael.

'Now, now!'

'Steady on!'

'Surely not!'

'But you mean to say?'

'I mean to say precisely what I said,' cut in Quinn emphatically. 'It is not as easy as you think to kill someone.'

'Be careful, my friend. If I did not know you better, I would think you were confessing to murder.' The warning came from Sir Michael. He watched Silas Quinn closely, with an intensity of expression that mirrored Quinn's own.

The trace of a smile curled on Sir Michael's lips, like a snake finding repose on the branch of a tree.

Quinn did not smile. 'But you do not know me at all,' he observed, with a cold insistence on the factual.

Sir Michael indicated their surroundings with a sweeping hand gesture. His meaning seemed to be that Quinn's presence in the Panther Club told him everything he needed to know.

'So you have...? Murdered?' Was there a glimmer of respect in Pinky's tone, or was it perhaps an unseemly relish? Beneath his domino mask, his face flushed its usual deep colour. One eye had a glassy shine over it, his monocle held in place behind the mask.

Quinn considered for a while before replying, 'I have certainly given it a great deal of thought.'

'Ah, I see,' said Sir Michael, a hint of disappointment entering his voice. 'You are a theoretician of murder, rather than a practitioner?'

'Why is it you people always seek to rephrase what I have said in words that are not my own? Can you not see that you will inevitably distort my meaning?' The heat of Quinn's response was disproportionate, and therefore prompted a stir of disapproval. Perhaps he had revealed himself to be something less than a gentleman.

'My dear fellow, I am only trying to understand you better.'

'Is my meaning not clear enough? What is it about what I have said that you do not understand? *It is not as easy as you think to kill someone.*'

'But none of us has suggested that it is easy!' pointed out Harry Lennox, with a nervous laugh. He cast about to see how his remark had gone down with his fellows.

'And it is not so much what you have said as the manner in which you said it that gives rise to consternation,' said Count Lázár Erdélyi. 'It is almost as if you are defending the practice of murder on a point of honour.'

'Perhaps I am.'

'Well, I am not an exemplary moralist myself, but I rather think you should not.'

'Even to conceive of killing someone, and then to formulate a plan for how one may put the intention into action ... that in itself requires...' Quinn broke off, searching for the right word. 'Character,' he settled for at last. 'But to go through with it! To turn the intention into an act! That is something beyond character – that is evidence of a superhuman greatness!'

'My dear fellow, you will have to do better than that,' said Sir Michael wearily. 'The crime of murder is rather more commonplace than you suggest. And even some quite unexceptionable people have proven themselves capable of it. Downtrodden husbands and uppity wives. Members of the lower orders are particular prone to it – all it takes is a few drams of strong liquor for them to overcome whatever minuscule scruples they might have had in the first place. Why, even the middle classes have indulged in it on occasion.'

'All these people whom you so dismiss have proven themselves gods.'

'Oh, now you really are going too far!' objected Lord Marjoribanks. His mouth twitched into an uneasy smirk, as his eyes flashed nervously about.

'Have you ever tried to kill someone?' demanded Quinn in response. 'I mean you yourself, with your own hands, as it were?' Quinn held his hands in front of his face, and examined the splayed fingers with a look of horror. 'Have *you*?'

A violent spasm convulsed Silas Quinn. He looked into the young lord's eyes as if into a deep abyss into which he was in danger of falling. 'Yes, of course.'

At that moment there was a sound like a gun being discharged. Everyone, except for Quinn, jumped in their seats, startled. When they realized it was simply a coal exploding in the grate, laughter released the tension they were feeling. Quinn alone remained serious. His face had a dejected cast to it. 'I failed,' he said.

'You failed?' said Pinky, absent-mindedly turning from the flaring fire which had distracted them all from Quinn's last utterance. 'At what?'

'At killing.' Quinn felt the tremor of duplicity cross his face. If it was true that he had once failed at killing, his critics might say that he had certainly made up for it since. But he had always drawn a distinction between the deaths that regrettably occurred in the course of his investigations and the wanton crimes perpetrated by the cold-blooded murderers he hunted. Besides, for now it suited his purposes to appear inept at the art of killing. It flattered his audience – in particular the man he believed to be the killer.

Once again, all eyes were on Quinn. No one spoke. There was the sense that he had said something interesting. They wanted him to go on.

'It happened many years ago. I was a student at the time, of medicine, at Middlesex Hospital. I never completed my studies. It was said that I became ill, that I suffered a breakdown. Perhaps that is the truth. I don't know anything about that. I boarded in a lodging house in Camden. And it was there that I met the man I determined to kill. He was a fellow student, and he was everything I was not. Handsome, well-liked, athletic. But superficial – a man of surface, a glib, empty man. A bubble of a man. Surely it should not have been so hard to pop him?'

Quinn mimed a slight stabbing action, as if he was pushing a pin into a balloon. As he told his story, he became increasingly lost in the past he was recounting. It was almost as if he was no longer telling it for his audience, but because he was driven by the need to confess.

'The landlady had a daughter. My enemy had an easy way with the opposite sex and charmed the girl into an affectionate relationship. But I saw what he was really like. I could not allow him to ... I loved her, you see, genuinely – not like he did. My love for her was total, absolute, pure and deep. There was no one else for me. And so, I decided that the only solution to my problem was to eliminate my rival. But I tell you, it is not as easy as you think to kill some-one.' There was a despairing intensity to Quinn's

340

voice as he scanned his listeners, as if searching for sympathy.

'Did you try awfully hard?' Pinky's mocking tone prompted a round of sniggers.

Quinn was oblivious. Whatever purpose he had had in telling the story seemed forgotten. The story demanded to be told, and this audience, of strangers and suspects, was as good as any. 'First I had to decide upon the place where I would kill him – the scene of the crime, as it were. I did not want to do it at the lodging house. That would incriminate me too much. I needed to pick a neutral place, one not associated with me at all, and yet it had to be somewhere I could entice him to. It had to be a lonely spot, nowhere overlooked. And I had to be sure that I would not be interrupted. I decided to write a note in her name, in which she promised to give herself to him completely if he would meet her on the towpath, beneath the bridge near Camden Lock after dark. In her name, I commanded him to destroy the note once he had read it and to say nothing of the assignation to anyone.'

Quinn's voice took on a note of cold cunning. Certainly, his narration had started as a performance, a simulation. But he had gone beyond that now. He felt again all the raw emotions that had unhinged him all those years ago: the bitterness, the hatred and the grief.

'My medical studies were not so far advanced that I had learnt how to ease suffering or cure disease. But I had learnt enough to know how to inflict a fatal wound quickly and efficiently. My plan was to cut his throat with a barber's razor

341

and then push him off the towpath into the canal. The body would inevitably be found, but there would be nothing linking me to it. No one knew of my love for the landlady's daughter, not even the object of that love herself. It would be assumed that he was the victim of a violent robbery that had gone too far.'

'And so, how did this melodrama play out?' asked Harry Lennox, the newspaperman in him eager for detail.

The question had the effect of reminding Quinn where he was. He took in his audience as if he was surprised to see them there. But his voice was calmer now, for the moment, at least.

'As I think you can guess, I could not go through with it ... as soon as I heard his voice, calling out to her in the dark, instead of the hatred I thought I would feel – I ... I felt only horror. Horror at what I was about to do. I imagined the blade of the razor touching his throat. In my imagination, the skin of his throat was impossibly resistant. I could not make the blade cut through it. It was like thick leather. I imagined pressing the blade hard against the leathery skin, but the blade would not penetrate. I threw the razor into the canal and ran.'

'A lucky escape, for you as much as him,' said Sir Michael.

'But why could I not go through with it? It was not compassion. I still hated him. I still wanted him dead. That night, I dreamt of killing him. I was able to accomplish in my dreams what I had not managed to do in reality. The preternaturally sharp blade cut through his skin effortlessly. The blood spurted out from his neck. What a great sense of release and joy I felt, as it drenched me! A sense of ecstasy, almost. The blood gushed in an endless spray from his neck and filled the canal. Still he stood there, spraying blood from his wound. The canal ran with crimson liquid, the level of which continued to rise, until it flooded out and lapped around my feet. I looked in horror at the boy I had killed – for he was just a boy and in fact now seemed younger than ever – and saw that he was both dead and not dead at the same time. The life had gone from his eyes, but he continued to stand upright, and was even able to move his limbs, though lifelessly like an automaton. Suddenly, the wound in his neck stopped spurting blood and to my horror I saw the sides of the gaping flesh part. A terrible dread gripped my heart. I knew that the wound was about to speak to me, as indeed it did. Its sides opened like the lips of a mouth. "You killed me because you love *me*, not *her*," it said to me.'

'Good heavens!'

'I awoke from that vile dream and leapt raving from my bed. I ran through the lodging house screaming – and naked, it must be said. I fell into a faint outside the door of my hated rival. When I came to, I was in a hospital bed.' Quinn hung his head, as if in shame. 'I did not find peace then and I have not found it since. Sometimes it occurs to me that the only way I will ever find peace is if I hunt him down and kill him.'

'But why are you telling us all this?' Count Erdélyi yawned to show that he was not really interested in a reply.

There was a manic gleam to Quinn's eyes as he lifted his head and confronted each of them, one by one. 'Because I believe each and every one of you is capable of the very thing I am not.'

'Really?' said Sir Michael, raising an eyebrow when you might have expected him to cry out in outrage. 'You take us for a gang of murderers?'

Quinn felt calmer, once again in control, as he turned on Sir Michael. 'Did you not draft a memorandum that advised the use of baton charges against striking workers? This policy was responsible for the deaths of two workers in the Dublin Lock-Out.'

Sir Michael turned his head to one side sceptically but said nothing.

'Indeed, I rather think it is true to say that the cost in human lives is always your last consideration when it comes to shaping government policy. If there was a war, you would not hesitate to produce the documentation necessary to send millions to their deaths.'

'It's not my remit.'

'But if it were, you would.'

Lord Marjoribanks' mouth twitched. 'I don't think I could kill anyone, any more than you could, old fellow,' he protested.

'Does the name Sophie Armstrong not mean anything to you? She was once a young actress of promise.'

'What has she got to do with anything?'

'Did you never wonder what became of her?'

'She ... I severed all contact with her.'

'Yes, after she told you that she was carrying your child.'

'I gave her money.'

'For a certain illegal operation...'

'What of it?'

'Is that not murder, in your eyes?'

'It is unfortunate, but not murder.'

'And what of *her* death – Sophie's death – from an infection contracted during the operation?'

'I knew nothing of that. I feel awful, now that you have told me about it. But you cannot say it's murder.'

'Did you not put her in contact with the quack who performed the operation?'

'I...?'

'And did you not know that there were rumours about women who had died as a result of his ministrations? Did you not know that he was a drunk and a drug-fiend? Had you not seen the filthy premises in which he carried out his work? You caused her death as certainly as if you had pointed a gun at her head and pulled the trigger.'

'What choice did I have?'

'Please, there is no need to justify yourself to me! Don't you see, I admire you for what you were capable of doing! I merely want you to face up to what you are!'

'But I did not want her dead. That was not my intention.'

'You wanted her out of your life. You had ambitions. Was it not the case that in those days you dreamt of being an artist? Her continuing existence with some brat of a child could only have been an encumbrance to you. Her death was more than convenient, it was necessary – to the duty that you owed your Art. A pity then, that you put aside all such aspirations and turned instead to other distractions.'

'I discovered that I had no talent. It was better that I did so before wasting my life entirely.'

'That must have been painful for you. But the passage of time numbs the pain, does it not? Particularly when assisted by an opium habit. It was, after all, in a Limehouse opium den that you met the doctor concerned.'

'I have cured myself of my addiction,' protested Lord Marjoribanks, his thin lips clamped tightly together.

'I congratulate you. It is not an easy thing to do, to open yourself to pain again. But there will be pleasure too, for I hear that you are recently engaged to be married. Your betrothed is Jane Lennox, I believe. What a spectacular couple you will make! It is clear that you did the right thing eliminating Sophie Armstrong all those years ago. Just imagine what a frump she would be today had you allowed her to live.'

Marjoribanks' expression closed in on itself. Just as Sir Michael had, he remained silent.

Harry Lennox shifted uneasily in his seat. It was hard to gauge his expression beneath his mask, but he seemed to be reassessing his prospective son-in-law.

'And what of us?' said Count Erdélyi, gesturing to include Pinky. 'I am interested to hear why you think we are capable of murder.'

'You will have read of the recent spate of murders that are exercising our police here in the

346

capital,' answered Quinn. 'What is not generally known is that all the victims are homosexuals. You gentlemen are familiar with that term?'

Pinky and Count Erdélyi indicated vaguely that they were.

'The police have kept another detail out of the newspapers. All four victims were exsanguinated.'

'Exsanguinated?' hissed Pinky.

'Yes. Drained of blood.' Quinn turned back to Count Erdélyi. 'I believe that your presence here in London has something to do with that case.'

'Would you care to explain what you mean by that?'

'As your name – your outside name – suggests, you are a Transylvanian Hungarian.'

'What of it?'

'There are stories of creatures in Transylvania who prey on the blood of others.'

'I am familiar with such stories. Do you believe me to be a vampire?' Count Erdélyi asked mockingly. His shoulders shook with laughter. But strangely there was no humour in his eyes.

'I know you have hunted down and destroyed such creatures. Could it be that you are here, on your own account, to perform the same act on the monster perpetrating these crimes? The Exsanguinist, we might call him.'

'I am sure I don't know what you are talking about. And even if I did, it is nonsense. These murders are not, in point of fact, consistent with the behaviour of the vampire of Transylvanian lore, who do not slit the throat but bite it. And one need look for nothing more supernatural

347

than a bucket to explain the bloodlessness of these victims. Have you never seen a pig being drained of its blood, my friend?'

Quinn narrowed his eyes as though he were considering a response, which he declined to give.

'But what about me?' said Pinky, petulant, it seemed, at being overlooked. 'I couldn't hurt a fly.'

Quinn turned slowly to face the Marquess. 'All of the killer's victims have been young men of the labouring classes who have turned to prostitution to supplement their legitimate but meagre earnings. Is it not true that you have a predilection for such youths?'

'I have a predilection for beauty! What gentleman doesn't?'

'At any rate, you have a knack of persuading young men to go with you...'

'There is no knack. It is simply a question of offering them sufficient money.'

'But Pinky could not possibly be the murderer!' objected Count Erdélyi.

'Perhaps not,' said Quinn. 'But do you perhaps remember a youth called Algernon Foxe?'

'Algie? I say, there's no need to bring Algie up.'

'He killed himself, did he not?'

'I think you will find that the inquest delivered a verdict of death by misadventure.'

'Shot himself while on a hunting party.'

'The gun went off unexpectedly.'

'He separated from the rest of the party. There was the sound of gunshot. They found him in a secluded spot, hidden behind a wall, hunched over his gun, dead.'

'No one knows for certain what happened. We are dishonouring his memory if we assume it to be suicide.'

'His friends spoke of him as a young man of great promise and exceptional beauty. They also spoke of an older man who pressured him into a sexual relationship and then abandoned him.'

Pinky's nostrils twitched as if they had just been assailed by an unpleasant odour.

'Be careful, my friend. You have overstepped the mark. This is dangerous slander,' warned Sir Michael on the Marquess's behalf. Pinky himself remained tight-lipped; his characteristic colour drained from his face.

'Besides,' continued Count Erdélyi, 'the unfortunate youth's death hardly amounts to murder.'

'Perhaps not. But hours after Foxe's death, this gentleman was seen enjoying the company of a young estate worker of rugged physique.'

'I needed consoling!'

'Please, do not misunderstand me. I do not say this to condemn you. And it goes without saying that I would not repeat any of this to anyone other than ourselves. This is all, as it were, between friends.'

'You have not mentioned me yet,' said Harry Lennox uneasily. 'I have the feeling I know you. Have we met before?'

'Now now,' intervened Sir Michael. 'The rules of the club forbid you from even asking such a question.'

'But are you not curious to know how this fellow knows so much about us all?' protested Lennox.

'Everything that I have said is in the public domain,' said Quinn. 'Are you capable of murder? Perhaps not. But you are certainly capable of profiting from it. Which therefore gives you a motive for perpetrating it, or at least encouraging it. Perhaps it is absurd to suggest that you would commit murder in order to sell newspapers. However, you cannot escape the charge that newspapers like yours have created an atmosphere in which a man may achieve a degree of fame by pursuing such a course.'

'If that is all you have to accuse me of, then it is not very much.'

'Let me say again, I am not here to accuse but applaud. This is the Panther Club, after all.'

'Perhaps you are the murderer!' cried Count Erdélyi, turning on Quinn with vindictive glee. 'Yes, *you* are the – what was it? – the Exsanguinist!'

'I wondered who would be the first to suggest that.'

'I was recently in Vienna,' continued Count Erdélyi, turning to his companions delightedly, 'where I attended a series of interesting talks given by a noted specialist in dream interpretation.' He turned back to Quinn. 'I cannot help wondering what he would make of that dream you told us earlier.'

'Was it Doctor Freud?' asked Sir Michael. 'I rather fear that he sees phalluses everywhere.'

'How wonderful,' said Pinky, licking his lips.

'It was a disciple of Freud's,' admitted Count Erdélyi. 'And from what I understand of Freud's theories, our friend's dream suggests the repression of homosexual desire. Indeed, as you suggest, Ezzelino, the razor *can* be seen as standing for his phallus. He creates a wound in the other student's neck, which is to be interpreted as a surrogate vagina. The meaning is clear: that he wished to have sexual relations with the boy and not his landlady's daughter. The words spoken by the wound make this explicit. And the outpouring of blood is nothing less than an ecstatic ejaculation, which is transferred to the murdered youth, rather than experienced directly by the dreamer. None of this could be admitted by his conflicted psyche. In fact, to suppress the desire, he kills the object of his desire. But only in his dream. He failed to do so in real life. Hence his remark about not finding peace until he has tracked down and killed his erstwhile rival. Is it not conceivable that the crimes of the Exsanguinist are in some way playing out that intention? But instead of finding and killing the one he loved – who would by now have aged somewhat – he is repeatedly obliterating the idea of him *as he once was*, in the form of other youths.'

'It is an interesting theory,' said Quinn. He took out from his pocket a silver cigarette case. He opened the cigarette case and offered it around the company, allowing the inscription on the inside of the lid to be clearly seen:

The danger was half the excitement.
D.P.

Quinn noted the reactions of the men as they accepted a cigarette from him.

'Ah dear, dear Oscar,' said Pinky affectionately.

Sir Michael's 'Oh' was disapproving, as if he had borne witness to a lamentable breach of protocol.

'*Like feasting with panthers*,' said Count Erdélyi, completing the quote.

Harry Lennox frowned in confusion at the words. 'What *is* that?'

'It's a quote from a compatriot of yours, Oscar Wilde,' said Sir Michael. 'Of course, much as I admire Wilde, I cannot approve of him. Except when I am here, of course.'

The only one of the group who did not make a comment on the inscription was Lord Tobias Marjoribanks, who also declined to take a cigarette. His brows drew together in deep consternation. He rose slowly to his feet. 'Who are you?'

'Your nemesis.'

'That won't do.' Marjoribanks' voice rose to a whine. 'I don't believe in all that superstitious rot. There is no universal law that says a man must have a nemesis.'

'Are there any universal laws at all, I wonder? Other than, *that which is realized is right*? Or, *the only sin is shallowness*.'

'I cannot stay here talking to you. I have important work to do.'

'And all I ask is to be able to help you in it. To learn from you. Every great artist is a teacher. And you are a great artist. I will be Ruskin to your Turner. I will explain you to the world.'

'I don't need you.' And with that, Marjoribanks dashed from the room.

Quinn took out a Set cigarette and lit it before bowing to the assembly and calmly taking his leave.

The Exsanguination

He found Fetherstonhaugh on the floor of the landing, hunched against the wall near the entrance to the reading room. His domino mask was off. He was bleeding from a deep gash in his right cheek. Quinn crouched down and peered into the wound. 'That's nasty,' he said at last.

'I tried to stop him. Möbius. I didn't realize he had a razor. He lashed out at me.' The words came in a rush, as if the wound had released a torrent of speech as well as blood. There was an excited, enlivened glint in Fetherstonhaugh's eye.

'That was very foolish of you. However, you will live. We may take it that had he wished to kill you, he would have done so.'

Fetherstonhaugh almost seemed disappointed.

'I will get someone to take care of you. In the meantime, I must go after him.'

'Do it for the Brotherhood,' panted Fetherstonhaugh, the shock of the attack convulsing his body.

Quinn sprang to his feet and turned, just as the sound of panicked shouting reached him from the foyer below. He ran down the stairs to discover that the door to Bertie's cage had been opened and Bertie was prowling the foyer with a languid feline curiosity. Club members and servants scattered ahead of her, pushing one another out of the way and slamming doors in the faces of those behind them.

The panther seemed unperturbed by the commotion. She turned to Quinn and lifted her head to sniff the air. She was standing between him and the door, blocking his way out. Then suddenly she must have caught the scent of something that interested her far more than he did. She padded past him, gathering speed until she was bounding up the stairs. He realized too late what was drawing her.

Fetherstonhaugh's screams confirmed it. She had smelled blood.

Quinn chased up the stairs.

He found her pinning the man down with her front paws on his chest. She had her jaws around his face and shook his head as a domestic cat would shake a morsel of meat.

Quinn withdrew his revolver from its holster. He moved quickly, thrusting the muzzle against the side of the animal's head as he squeezed the trigger. The force of the shot threw Bertie's head to one side, as well as converting much of it to a spray of bloody matter. A sudden intensification of screaming suggested that the separation of teeth from his face had not been without pain for Fetherstonhaugh. He was slumped over completely now. In places, his face looked like raw minced meat.

Quinn felt for a pulse.

He looked up and saw a number of the club's servants surrounding him nervously. 'He is alive. Help him.'

As Lord Marjoribanks burst out of the Panther Club, he was accosted by a young man wrapped in a shimmering silk scarf.

'You're just the feller I was looking for,' said Tommy Venables.

'What do you mean by that?'

'Tall, good-lookin'. Wearin' a mask.' Venables let out a burst of coarse laughter.

Marjoribanks showed him the bloodied razor in his hand.

'Cut yerself shavin', didyer? Y'ought to be more careful.'

'Aren't you afraid of me?'

'Nah. I seen you with Pinky. If I were you, I'd put that away before a bobby sees it.'

Marjoribanks folded the blade away and pocketed it. 'Of course – Pinky. He knows all the queer lowlife.'

'There's no need to take that attitude.'

'Aren't you the renter who was trying to blackmail him?'

'Simple misunderstanding. All cleared up now.'

'The vampire.'

'I don' know wha' you mean.'

'You're like the scum that destroyed Oscar. You pull everything down to your own level.

Nothing fine or beautiful is possible while there are louts like you in the world.'

'If you're talking about Oscar Wilde, you should hear the tales some of the old 'uns tell. Nothing fine or beautiful about what he liked to get up to.'

'I don't have time for this.'

'Let me get you a taxi then.' Venables threw up his hand and whistled. 'It's the least I can do.'

A taxi pulled up with remarkable speed, as if the driver had been waiting for Venables' signal. Venables opened the rear door for Marjoribanks and then followed him in.

'What are you doing? I didn't invite you into my taxi.'

'Where to, sir?' asked the driver.

'I thought you and me could go somewhere nice,' said Venables.

'It doesn't work like that. I choose who goes with me. I am not chosen.'

'Tonight's different.'

'So where to, then?' came from the front.

'Very well,' said Marjoribanks. 'Limehouse.'

Venables smiled. 'Limehouse? Blimey! I thought we'd go to yours.'

'I keep a residence in Limehouse. For evenings such as this.'

The taxi lurched forwards and stalled. The driver cursed. 'Beggin' your pardon, gentlemen. I shall have to get out and start her up.'

'Don't mind us,' said Venables. 'Take all the time you need.'

But the hand he put up to Marjoribanks' cheek was brushed roughly away.

* * *

When Quinn came out of the club he saw Macadam at the front of the taxi, readying himself to crank the starter; at least, that was what he was pretending to do. In fact, he was keeping an eye out for his guv'nor.

'You managed to get a taxi, I see.'

'Yes. Requisitioned it for the night from a pal of mine. It's a Unic. French model. Takes a bit of getting used to after the Ford.'

'We are fortunate you have so many pals, Macadam.'

Macadam raised his hands and formed circles with his fingers which he held over his goggles. 'You've got a mask on, sir.'

'Does he still wear his?'

'Yes, sir. Black one.'

'Then I will keep on this one.' What this meant, of course, was that Quinn had not retrieved his bowler. Perhaps it was for the best.

Quinn moved round to the far side of the taxi and got in, sandwiching Marjoribanks between himself and Neville.

'What's this?' cried Marjoribanks. 'You?'

'You left Phaedo in a bad way back there.'

'Anything is permitted at the Panther Club. He knows that. He will have no complaints.'

'If he lives.'

The taxi's engine rattled into life.

Macadam got back in. 'Sorry for the delay, gentlemen. Ah, I see you have gained an additional friend. Still Limehouse, is it?'

'Limehouse?' said Quinn. 'Of course.'

The vehicle pulled away.

357

Quinn thought back to the beginning of the case, when Macadam had driven him east to Shadwell Police Station. He looked at Marjoribanks' masked face. His attention focused on the other man's mouth, which fell away weakly on one side. 'You were the beggar who laughed at me.'

'Perhaps,' said Marjoribanks. 'I sometimes don a costume, in order to move among the locals without arousing suspicion.'

'You should have worn it when you went shopping for rope,' said Quinn. Marjoribanks started in his seat.

The taxi headed east along the Strand and on to Fleet Street. Silas Quinn settled back. Marjoribanks seemed little inclined to talk, and so Quinn began a speculative monologue, trusting that Marjoribanks would interrupt him whenever he got a detail wrong:

'When did it begin – the pain? When you weaned yourself off opium? How courageous an act that was, to let the pain back into your life? But oh, the toll that it must have taken on you. Not only did you allow yourself to suffer physical agonies once more, there were the memories too. Everything that had been numbed and buried in the years of addiction, now came rushing back into life.

'And with your emergence from opium addiction came the realization of your loss. Your art! Utterly sacrificed! And for what? It all started when Sophie Armstrong fell pregnant with your child. You needed her out of the way, her and her unborn brat. No one could blame you for

358

that. But fate had saved up a savage irony for you. Once you had accomplished your goal, you discovered you were no longer able to create. Your talent had deserted you. Such is the perversity of genius! Tell me, when was all this? Seventeen, eighteen years ago? It's interesting to reflect – is it not? – that if the foetus had been allowed to go to full term and the child had been born – a boy, was it not, or so the quack who aborted him informed you – he would have been about the age of Jimmy Neville the day you bled him. Was it that unborn child you killed then, and killed again, repeatedly, with the three other victims? The child who had drained the life from your art ... now you set yourself to drain the life from him.'

A groan of suffering was Marjoribanks' only answer.

'If art was your great ideal, then Oscar Wilde – the man who had attempted to turn his life into a work of art – was your hero. Somehow in the person of Jimmy Neville, the unborn child who had destroyed your creative impulses was merged with the shabby renters and the upper-class homosexual lover who had destroyed Oscar. And the pain, the pain that you had felt on ending your addiction – suddenly you found relief from it. As the blade went into Jimmy Neville's throat, and his pain began, your pain eased. The techniques you had taught yourself practising on cats came into their own.'

'I have allowed you to spout your slanderous lies,' said Marjoribanks through clenched teeth. 'But I have admitted nothing.'

359

'Lies? Why deny your genius? Remember, whatever is realized is right. You took that as your moral as well as your artistic code. What else was it that Oscar Wilde said? "To deny one's own experiences is to put a lie into the lips of one's own life. It is no less than a denial of the soul." Do not deny your soul, I beg you!'

'What do you want from me?' The question was wrung out from deep within Marjoribanks. It seemed that at that moment he was afraid of Quinn.

Quinn remained silent for the rest of the journey.

They left the main road behind, and with it any street lighting. The moon shivered above, as white as a bone.

The beams of the taxi's headlights severed the darkness, calling into being the desolate landscape of the area, the endless brick fields, dotted with ghostly ruins, like giant bottles half-buried in the ground. The acrid aftertaste of chemical processes hung in the air.

It seemed impossible that any human being could live here. The empty factories and looming chimneys that flashed momentarily into vision were themselves the residents, wraithlike and retiring.

Marjoribanks directed Macadam into a street of grim houses, some with broken windows, others boarded up. The taxi juddered to a stop with a small explosion, behind the looming shape of a parked motor van.

'Is that what you used to transport the bodies?' asked Quinn. 'It was your intention to place them in locations that would mock the foundations of the Empire, was it not?'

'You are wrong about that,' said Marjoribanks quietly. 'Quite wrong. The purpose was to fortify. To strengthen the country's institutions for what is to come.'

The house appeared to be derelict. It no longer had its original front door, but instead was secured by a crude board, roughly hinged and fastened with a massive padlock. Marjoribanks struggled with the key and swung the board open. He gestured for Quinn and Venables to enter first.

They stepped into an impenetrable blackness. It seemed to hold within it invisible fingers that groped their faces and probed their eyes. It held something else too: a foul and pervasive stench.

There was the scrape and flare of a match. Marjoribanks lit a lantern. Then he pulled the board closed, and secured it from inside with the same padlock.

He turned to face Quinn. 'The final mystery is oneself,' he said.

Quinn recognized it as a quote from Wilde.

'Here is where I keep the mystery of myself.'

Quinn looked around, frowning.

'It is here that I keep the blood,' explained Marjoribanks.

'The smell?' enquired Quinn.

'Blood is organic matter. It goes off.' Almost as an afterthought, he added: 'Oh, and I have a boy downstairs, draining.'

'Will you show him to us?'

'Of course.'

Marjoribanks became suddenly self-conscious, almost shy, as he shone the light down into the cellar. His movements seemed constrained by a kind of reticent pride. Quinn realized that this was a momentous occasion for him. He was like an artist about to unveil his masterpiece, half-afraid that it was not the great work he believed it to be, perhaps even more afraid that it was.

'Be careful. Some of the steps are missing.' The solicitude of a murderer is strangely touching, Quinn realized.

Venables descended first, now utterly cowed. There had been no bursts of loutish laughter for some time. Quinn followed, his feet cautiously questing the darkness beneath him, arms out-stretched so that he could feel the clammy, crumbling brickwork on either side.

Each step took him deeper into the stench of rotting blood.

The lantern was little use, its beam blocked out by his own back. Whenever he reached a miss-ing step, he always felt as if he was falling into an infinite abyss, that the next step would never come, and that he would fall forever through the enveloping blackness.

But at last, with a final lurch, he reached the ground, which was gritty and loose under foot.

Venables and Quinn instinctively huddled together as they waited for Marjoribanks to join them. They looked up into the beam of his lantern, not daring to look behind them at what-ever might be lurking in the darkness. The only indication of what that might be was an irregular dripping sound that echoed coldly.

362

Marjoribanks stepped between them and held the lantern high. They could not resist looking in the direction of its beam.

The body was naked, suspended upside down by the ankles above a metal pail.

Quinn confronted the blood-streaked face. 'Petter,' he murmured.

Marjoribanks must have misheard him. 'Yes. It is better! Better that I should have his blood, his energy. That the power that is released by killing him is harnessed in me to bring about the new age of Set, the age of chaos and destruction that will make the world anew.' Marjoribanks moved the lantern and showed them the pails of dark liquid that stood around the edges of the room. 'That is my work now. That is my art. My life.'

'And what of your fiancée?'

'She would approve. When I was in New York I met certain individuals, initiates in the highest order of an esoteric society. Jane was one of their number. Their high priestess, you might say. Some held her to be an avatar of Isis. We talked about many things and undertook magical operations that were preparatory to those I have performed alone.'

'She does not know about this?'

'Not yet. I have performed all this on my own initiative. It was necessary to maintain absolute secrecy, in order not to jeopardize the operation. When she finds out, I have no doubt that she will celebrate my acts.'

Quinn looked back towards the suspended corpse. He saw a red droplet fall from the wound and join the bucket of blood below.

'Sin and suffering,' said Marjoribanks. 'Beautiful, holy things.'

'Modes of perfection,' added Quinn.

'This is the most profound, the most perfect symbol ever created,' remarked Marjoribanks.

'But the smell,' objected Quinn. 'And these foul surroundings. Do they not rather mar the perfection?'

'But the smell is central to what I am seeking to create!' cried Marjoribanks. 'It is the stench of corruption. The body is cleansed and perfected by the draining of the blood, it becomes an object of art, rather than life. And the driving force of life is revealed to be a stinking mess of corruption.'

Quinn nodded slowly, as if in dawning comprehension. And perhaps he had finally understood the extent of Lord Marjoribanks' insanity.

'Do you approve of what I have done?'

'More than that. I am in awe of it.'

'Do you remember what you said? That it is not easy to kill someone. You must understand how hard it has been for me to do this. You must understand what I have suffered to bring about this work.'

'I do.'

'You asked for my help.'

'Yes.'

'I will help you. I will show you how to do it. How to kill.'

There was a bench against one wall. Quinn noticed a stack of bowler hats. He realized now what he had sensed missing from the victims' clothes that day in the Golden Lane mortuary.

Marjoribanks crossed to the bench and put down the lantern. Something metallic glinted in the light.

Quinn looked uneasily towards Venables. 'Him?'

Marjoribanks smiled strangely. He took down a brown bottle and a rag from a high shelf. With the absorption of a creative artist, he unstoppered the bottle and tipped some of its contents into the cloth. A twist of ether worked its way into all the other smells of the cellar. He held the cloth out for Quinn to take.

Venables' eyes flashed alarm; Quinn sought to reassure him with a look of his own that he hoped inspired trust. But by now, Marjoribanks had gripped the young man from behind. Venables' struggles petered out as Quinn held the cloth over his face. Marjoribanks eased his inert body to the ground.

'Shall I undress him?' said Quinn.

'This has nothing to do with him,' answered Marjoribanks. 'This is between you and me. And for what is about to pass between us, there can be no witnesses.'

Marjoribanks began to undress.

His hand enclosed the object that had flashed in the lantern beam. 'A cutthroat razor. Like the one you once tried to wield against your fellow-lodger. Now is the time for you to overcome your fastidious nature and to discover what you are capable of.'

He came towards Quinn as if he would attack him, with the lithe athletic spring of a hunter. But at the final moment, he stopped and held the

365

razor out, the handle towards Quinn. As Quinn took the weapon, Marjoribanks threw back his head, making his throat as large as he could. 'Add my blood to the blood of my victims. Perfect me, as I perfected them.'

'You? But why?'

'The pain always returns. The blade goes in, the pain eases. But it always returns. You will end the pain forever. It is the last act in the operation. Perform this and the new age of Set will begin. Chaos and destruction on a scale not known before.'

'But what of Jane Lennox? What of your plans to marry?'

'She will understand. More than that, she will rejoice.'

Quinn reached out and took the blade to the other man's throat. But the intimacy of the moment, the man's nakedness before him, the startling immediacy of his eyes, the soft, dark pleading of those eyes, robbed him of his courage.

'Must I make you practise on him first?' murmured Marjoribanks, his lips barely moving.

Quinn looked once more at Petter's savagely inverted body. Like a long-lost friend rushing to embrace him, the rage flooded through his veins and fortified his sinews. He felt it enter the tips of his fingers. He tensed the muscles of his whole arm as he tightened his grip on the razor. And then he pushed with all his gathered strength.

The blade must have been exceedingly sharp. It found the soft dip between the thyroid cartilage and the hyoid bone, and burrowed into it. Quinn drove the blade deeper with a slicing motion. Something dark spurted from either side of it, and he felt a sense of immeasurable release.

There was a gurgling cry from the man at whose throat he was working, and then his body buckled and he fell forward. Quinn took the weight of his fall, and the brunt of his blood. He held the man with one arm and lowered him gently to the floor. With his other hand, Quinn kept the blade pushed into Marjoribanks' throat.

The dying man's eyes looked up at him and seemed to hold a smile.

In less than a minute the violent shuddering of deep shock took hold. Seconds after that, he was dead.

There was a groan from the floor behind him. Quinn eased himself away from the dead man and turned his attention to Venables.

The young man's eyes swam as he came round. The moment they settled on Quinn, panic bulged in them. Venables tensed and backed away.

'It's all right,' said Quinn. 'He's dead. He attacked me with the razor, but I managed to overpower him. We got a full confession. The case is closed. You did well.'

'I feel sick,' said Venables.

'That will be the ether. I'm sorry about that. But I felt it best to go along with him for as long as possible. As a precaution, I turned the cloth in my hand, so that you did not inhale the full force of the fumes. I would never have let you come to any real harm, you know.'

Venables seemed to pout, and then vomited over himself, an appropriate response to Quinn's reassurances.

Quinn stood and held the razor up to examine it. He sniffed the fresh blood, which had a sharpness to it that cut through the foul atmosphere of the cellar.

For the first time in a long time, he felt at peace.